KIRKOS: THE RISE OF THE CLOWNS

T BALOGH

KNOWHERE MEDIA

Published by Knowhere Media LLC
Denver, CO
Copyright © 2017 T. Balogh
All rights reserved.
ISBN: 978-1-943990-04-7

I dedicate this book to the memory of Viveka Mason Breitzman, one of my closest friends. It is to me one of the greatest tragedies that I could not share this novel with her, as she passed away only months before it was finished.
Still, her influence on me and my life will always live in the periphery of my tales, for she helped me understand the meaning of friendship, the joy of the adventurous wind, and the importance of holding on to your true self.

For more books in this series and other great titles, go to knowheremedia.com/publishing

C soda stood on the stage using all of his strength to pull the muscles along his spine and neck together so he remained straight and tall. This simple effort to stand was difficult to maintain. His body was skeletal, his muscles weak. His effort made even harder by thick lacerations, both old and new, cut across his back, chest, legs and arms. The act of standing pulled apart the edges of the fresher wounds leaving them open to release slow trickles of blood.

He held back his gaunt features from wincing when his own thick sweat pooled in the open wounds, its salt stinging. He refused to wince, refused to slump over in pain, even though his body begged him to do so. He defied his body's desire to collapse by focusing on the pain that tormented him. He recognized the pain, let its sting travel through his frame and then, eventually, adapted to it so that it dissipated, at least from his attention.

This is how he chose to face his torment, with a straight spine and resolute expression. The starvation had made his eyes look bigger than normal, large globes sunken into the wide sockets of his skull, haloed by dark recessed shadows. Still his eyes had fire as he stared defiantly ahead, their gaze steady and strong despite his emaciation. His sharp edged jaw stayed set. His high cut cheekbones framed a thin lipped mouth and his nostrils flared as they took in deep breaths of the molten desert air.

Before him a crowd of strangers stretched out from the base of the stage to the edges of the stone walled arena. Their forms were both familiar and foreign to him. Their clothing, dyed in rich colors, was in sharp contrast to the raw and nearly naked humanity of Csoda's tortured body. Their voices were a wall of sound that only occasionally released a trickle of words he could hear and understand. Their language was familiar, but it was not his native tongue.

A desert breeze had swept into the open arena as Csoda was forced onto the stage. The breeze's intensity grew steadily as he stood there, but instead of being a blessing from the heat, the wind was a furnace blast against his already sunburnt skin.

Small blisters bubbled up on his shoulders, along the tops of his bare feet, and around the edges of the fiery hot metal cuffs shackled to his wrists and ankles. The metal collar around his neck inflamed the blood pulsing through his jugular so that he felt the heat deeply circulating through his body and brain. His only protection from the midday sun was a dirty, bloodied and thread barren cloth they allowed him to wrap around his waist, its tattered hem stopping right above his bony knees.

With the hot wind came more than physical torture. The heat brought memories of blackening hissing smoke covering the skies and filling Csoda's lungs. This memory tightened in his throat, filled his gut with a rock of anger and shame and, for a moment, Csoda's body slowly swayed, rocking ever so slightly. The vision from his eyes blurred and the hot air burned his tears, unforgivingly drying them into white salt on his cheeks.

His steady gaze wavered with emotion as the memory created shadows before his drying eyes. Shadows of the ashen faces of the dead, his family, his people. His heart pulsed in his ears, drummed in an aching rhythm that he had never heard before, a deadening pulse of soul shattering pain. For a moment the memory held him, and it was the memory, not the torture or his weakness, that almost brought him to collapse.

Yet, before the memory destroyed his will the sounds of the crowd pulled him away from the horror of his past and back to his present hell. Little tendrils of conversations reached him from their ambient rumblings. Voices echoed, gasps and murmurs that he understood, "That is him?"…"My…he doesn't even look afraid…" Their awe reached out on invisible threads and sent strength back into his form. The reasoning for his current efforts was justified by those statements. At least they would know that, despite everything, he still could stand.

With his will newly strengthened he dared to look out into the crowd and saw them as a mass of noisy, dusty color that moved as one shape before him. He could feel their energy. He could push his own energy mentally towards them and when he did he watched the shape react to his efforts. It rippled ever so slightly like a veil of color and noise that had been touched by a slight wind.

To the crowd, Csoda still looked tall and solid. This is what he put his energy into, his straight spine, his refusal to be lessened as a man. He pushed the dark memories aside and focused on all the strength that was left within him. He focused, even in this moment, on the collapse of the evil powers that had bound him and destroyed his people. He focused on righteous anger and with it he imagined the walls of this cursed stage he stood upon ripping to shreds.

For an instant he actually believed he could see the massive crowd surging towards the walls. He could hear the sound of rubble crashing to the floor. The roar of men and beasts reverberated against his chest as they pulled it all down around him in a storm of anger.

He felt the rumble of thunder deep within him and he imagined himself dancing as he used to, his body undulating behind a stretched leather drum that he would hold before him like a shield, his face hidden behind a veil of beaded cowrie shells. He danced to the thunder, to the storm, to the anger, his body new and strong again. He imagined his voice, thick and wet, singing out, over and through the destruction and its sound relieved him from the dehydration and heat.

The crowd shape shifted to his imagined music, its form became more transparent with every hit he played on his unseen drum. The crowd's sounds and colors muted, it whispered and hummed until its entire form became more like a curtain that waved quietly in front of an open window. The illusion gave him a moment of peace–a mirage–making him feel as if a cool breeze caressed his tortured skin.

All but one figure had fallen away into this faceless curtain. A young boy, surprisingly clean, dressed in a strange multicolored checkered tunic. A floppy leather three-pointed hat with the points facing down was cocked loosely at a tilted angle on his head. The boy stood in the front row staring right at Csoda with intense greenish blue eyes. He looked around nervously, as if he was unsure of where he stood and then he glanced worriedly down at something in his hands. When the boy looked up and met Csoda's gaze, he still seemed confused, but compassionate.

"Csoda?" The boy said quietly, but his voice came as clear as if he was standing right next to Csoda's side, as if they existed alone in a private room. "Father? The watch...it is not working..." The boy looked back down at his hands, tapping the object he held. Csoda heard a small dog bark in the distance as the boy's voice began to drift away and he realized that this boy's voice, so comforting, was speaking in his native tongue, "Csoda?....Father?"

The mass crowd shape came flooding back with a wailing roar and a wave of billowing color that overcame the image of the boy. Csoda's thoughts rushed through his confused mind, "Did he say Father?"..."What is a 'watch'?"

Then these questions were cut short from his concern. He felt a shearing pain across his neck as the chain on his collar was yanked backwards. Suddenly, there were hands grasping his wrists and legs. The growling crowd was deafening. His head was being pulled backwards, his mouth pried open, the hot air flooded into his dry throat and across his swollen tongue.

He heard the Emperor's angry voice echoing from somewhere behind him, "HOW DO YOU LIKE THE REVOLUTIONARY POET NOW?!"

A flash of metal glinted in front of his eyes. His mouth filled with hot pain and blood, his scream came but was muted as his own parched throat filled. He was drowning in his own blood. His senses were engulfed with the smell of fire, his own burning flesh, the muscle tearing grip of multiple hands on his arms and legs, the screams of the massive crowd–and then...finally...darkness.

2

The first thing noticed was sound.

Even before it could be identified as a sound it was present, for it ebbed and flowed with each shallow breath, hummed with the struggling functions and mechanics of mortal flesh trying to survive. The wind of breath, the pulse of liquid flowing blood in throbbing temples, the rasp of a gurgling cough, the hollow gulp of a forced swallow. All sounds of his life functioning were loud in his head.

There were distant sounds, too. Murmuring voices, the raking of metal against wood, and a grinding echo of wheels rolling through sand. Over all of the sounds a dominant ambient and endless sob gasped and moaned in the pattern of waves crashing against a hopeless shore.

The second thing noticed was pain.

Every muscle raged with it and when his body willed him to shift, even slightly, it was punished with a chorus of pain that shot through his entire being.

The pain increased the sounds of the sobbing until, slowly, by observing the connection, he realized that the sobbing was his own. This realization caused the sob to turn to a wail. The wailing increased the movement of his heaving chest and therefore increased the pain until, at some point, the process of being conscious became a crescendo of pain and noise that overwhelmed his body and mind until he lost consciousness again...and again. This cycle of consciousness and unconsciousness went on for an unidentifiable amount of time, where he would awake and pass out into a blackened state that neither felt like, nor gave, the comfort of sleep.

At first this was all he experienced, but as time went on he became aware enough when he was conscious to know that he was not alone.

In the layers of sound he began to notice a voice that was consistently present. A deep and growling voice that used words he recognized but did not have the energy to try to understand. Later, he became aware of smells, the pungent smell of his own urine, the stale stench of unwashed straw, his sweat, and the musk of different beasts of burden. He could feel that whatever he laid on was moving. He sensed the rocking of a wagon, heard the rhythmic rumble of wheels on dirt and the clopping of hooves upon the ground.

He could also sense whoever it was that spoke to him in the growling voice. He noticed that at times the air near him was warmer as if another person sat by his side. Not capable of doing anything, he chose to listen to the sound of the voice, and assumed that whomever it belonged to meant him no harm. Surely they would have already harmed him while he lay there incapable of movement. In his current state of no physical comfort that singular thought brought him a sliver of hope, allowing him to fall into unconsciousness with a fragment of peace.

Eventually the moments of consciousness pulled him

out of the haze and he was better able to understand bits and pieces of what happened around him. He would awake to the sound of chains dragging on wood. Recognized when a pain in his arm was due to the fact that it had been pulled into a different position by a force that was not his own. He would feel a strong hand holding his chin and smell an unidentifiable food. Corn? Oats? Salted meat? Water? The smell would pass in front of him and a warm soft gruel would pour into his mouth.

He became aware that he had no tongue, or at least not a complete tongue. What he did have was stunted far in the back of his throat. The food's taste was muted and he struggled to control it when it passed through his mouth. The gruel burned against wounds in the back of his throat, but his body recognized the need for nourishment. His stomach spasmed in hunger as his throat convulsed in desperate, swallowing gulps.

Again, this stage went on for what seemed an endless rhythm of changing time until his strength increased enough for him to try to open his eyes, the lids pulling against a dry crust that had glued them closed.

A blurring image of straw, wooden and iron walls, and chains came in and out of his vision, always masked by a dusty haze and a shallow darkness. Until, one day, he awoke when the rays of the sun filtered through cracks in the planks above him. His eyes strained against the light, but he forced himself to keep them open while he tried to focus and orientate himself to his surroundings.

He determined that he was lying on his back. His left side was propped up a bit more than the right, by what felt like the scratch of straw and sawdust against his itching skin, so that he was ever so slightly tilted at a right angle. His right arm lay heavy against the floor in front of him. His left arm was bent at the elbow and crossed against his naked stomach. The left felt lighter and soon he could see why. His right wrist was locked in a tight metal shackle that was attached to a heavy chain curving away from him on the floor.

He followed the chain with his eyes, slowly, trying to see where it went and found that it raised up through a neighboring hump of straw and ended in another shackle. This shackle was attached to another wrist that was not his own.

He stared at the other wrist for a long time, not wanting to move his head. He saw the hand of another man, a thick and muscled hand, streaked with dirt and sweat. He saw a massive forearm rippled with hard use, the skin a built up layer of scars making it look more like tree bark than human skin. He heard the other breathing and could not tell if this man was sleeping or just laying still.

He lay there, seeing, noticing this other person who was chained to him, this stranger. His mind, more alert than before, remembered images of other bodies lying near him, people who were not strangers. Unlike this stranger, these remembered bodies did not breathe. His memory released a surge of adrenaline that overcame the weakness. A moment of internal panic triggered his heartbeat to speed up, racing painfully in his chest.

He remembered last standing, before the crowd, before the searing blade had taken his tongue. A memory that made his body suddenly and uncontrollably lurch. His mind demanded understanding, "Where am I?!" A thousand uncontrolled thoughts rushed into his newly awakened brain. Shaking violently he jolted upright only to fall back out of exhaustion and pain.

The neighboring shackled arm moved like lightning next to him, and the owner of that arm sprung in front of him, becoming a silhouette of a massive man that blocked the light and invoked more panic in his already peaking fear.

He reached out to strike at the silhouetted man in front of him, but his weakened arms were caught in the air by thick iron hands and the voice, that growling voice, emanated from the silhouette speaking familiar words low and deep, words his panicking brain tried to understand.

The language, familiar, brought more than understanding, it brought the stab of nostalgia, other memories, memories of horses and cattle in pastures, of his brothers riding horseback through rivers and fields, of warm fires and feasts of lamb and bread, of rich flavored olives and the sound of cicadas filling the air...and laughter...he remembered laughter...he heard laughter.

The silhouette in front of him was laughing, a hushed but powerful, deep laugh. The voice spoke to him in the language of his native tongue, a language he thought was wiped out to extinction in his memory of the horrific fire, the language he thought was silenced when they severed his tongue...and the words...the words...they started to make sense.

The man in front of him continued to laugh and then he proudly whispered, "Csoda...you live...that's right...you live. They told me you would die on me...but I told them you would live." And just as Csoda began to feel himself falling back into the dark delirium, the black unconscious, the deep voice growled, this time not out of pride or a simple statement, but in the tone of an order. Speaking in the language of his father and all of his ancestors the man commanded, "Csoda. You will not die on me. You will live."

His head was spinning, the forms blurred in front of him, the pain spiked up his spine and a strong ache of emotion filled his chest. His heart pounding hard, tears streamed down his cheeks and the sobbing and darkness engulfed him even as he remembered his own name. "My name is Csoda," and lingering as his mind slipped into unconsciousness again, "I will live."

3

The fog hovered and drifted only a few feet above the ground of the vast plains. It moved like the back of a mystical blue serpent, shifted and slid, undulated slowly and curled into itself, exposing scale like shimmers of opalescent dew. Occasionally small patches faded or pulled apart revealing the tall thick grass it quietly coated.

Abelardus sat tall upon the back of his horse as he surveyed the land from the top of a small hill. He could see for miles across the immense barren grassland that was covered in clouds. The fog dulled all sounds and grew thicker every moment. There were no birds in flight, no rustle of a spooked hare, no herds of deer or roaming wolves, no hum of insects. Even the sound of the shifting movements of the proud armored horses and the twenty men that accompanied him were muffled.

In all directions he could only see the rolling flat fog along the ground and above rolling gray clouds filled the sky. The world, it seemed, was a cool pocket of misty air sandwiched between two skies. He and his soldiers seemed to float upon the backs of horse shaped boats, their steed's legs hidden by the thickening brume.

Abelardus had signaled his men to stop so that he could contemplate his next move across this surreal ocean of fog. Its emptiness frustrated him. There were no clues, for the misty gauze covered any bending blades of grass and the tracks they had followed there were lost to them.

Not a single sign of the pack of rogues they were pursuing. Not a single whisper or horse whinny in the distance. No sign to help him decide which direction to go. He had never seen such a strange fog and he wondered at the cause of it, which God or spirit was protecting the men he followed?

Perhaps he had misjudged the direction to pursue long ago, at the riverbanks or within the forest, and now his mistake had led them far away from their prey. By now those they pursued could be sitting and laughing around a fire in a distant mountain cave. They could be resting, happily content that they had given the Legionnaires the slip, their bellies full with the supplies they had stolen.

The thought of their escape nauseated Abelardus and he privately rethought each decision he had made while tracking them. He reviewed his choices carefully and still swore to himself that he and his men had tracked the vandals effectively. He could not think of one moment along the trail that they could have been fooled. He had been sure that when he and his men entered the open plains they would see the distant fugitives clearly. He had counted on them being exposed in the vast plains, where he could finally keep them in sight.

Now, however, he questioned everything. He even questioned why they had chased them this far to begin with, over a theft of meat and wine. He and his men hovered in this clouded damp landscape, hungry and tired, far from their Legion's encampment. Their own horses looked lethargic, the hounds paced slowly in exhausted boredom, tongues lolling. It was apparent to Abelardus that this chase had ended. The trail was cold, the weather unfavorable and he did what was rare for him to do, with a heavy shame weighing down his heart, he accepted defeat.

He was about to turn away and order the men to move back in the direction they had come, when he noticed the fog part over what appeared to be a small patch of water down in the fields below. He noted the drying foam of sweat on his own horse's neck and could see the same on the rest of the steeds. He lifted his hand and pointed out the patch of water to his men, then led his troop down towards the pond. They and the horses would at least have a good drink before they started back on their way home.

The fog barely parted as the animals pushed through it. Occasionally, one of the hound's heads would poke up out of the haze in front of them as it leapt into the air, trying to see ahead. Otherwise, the earth bound fog covered the movement of everything below the stirrups of the men's saddles. It thickened around their legs, leaving dew on their boots. All the fields were quiet, the air heavy and still.

At the edge of the pond Abelardus had some of his men dismount and take turns drinking and watering their horses. He heard the hounds splash into the pond and then quiet down shortly after as if they had found a desirable spot to take a quick sleep. He marveled at the quiet. The horses refused to even nicker. He himself felt like he wanted to stay hushed, choosing to signal to his men instead of using speech.

When most of his men were refreshed, Abelardus dismounted and led his horse to the water's edge to let it drink. He dropped to one knee so that he could scoop the cold water up to his mouth. He took one drink and splashed his face. He noticed that upon kneeling he had dropped his head just below the level of the fog. He was surrounded in clouds, only the flat water in front of him open to view.

Across the water, upon the edge of the pond shore, he saw the hounds lying down, fast asleep, their heads resting in front of what appeared to be a rock. He watched as the fog parted slightly around the rock and there, instead of stone, he saw the slight glint of metal, a flash of hammered brass. There, behind the hounds, lay the head of a horse with an armored bridal.

The sight startled him and briefly he thought the creature was dead until its nostrils barely flared with quiet breaths and upon its side something slowly moved. Abelardus stared in shock at what he realized was a man, laying belly flat against the horse's side, bow and arrow on his back, knife held in his teeth.

The entire image moved, slow motion, like an unstoppable nightmare. The man locked eyes with Abelardus as he rose up from the edge of the pond yelling to his Legionnaires to mount up, to draw their swords. But before his men could react, before Abelardus could even lift himself back onto his own horse, the still quiet of the fog filled with the rustling of disturbed grass and he saw the clouded landscape undulate, revealing solid shapes of men and horses as they rose up from the ground, surrounding him and his men.

Hundreds of nomads had lain under the fog upon the sides of their quiet, downed horses. They waited, weapons and reins in hand, and in one instant their cleverly trained horses stood, the riders shifting from their prone positions to sitting straight on their backs with uncanny horsemanship. They rose like underwater creatures from the depths and they filled the air with the hiss of arrows and a terrifying unified cry of war that broke into a chaos of whoops and jackal-like howls.

Abelardus remounted, even though his horse reared in fear, but a handful of his men had been pulled down by their attackers under the edge of the fog. Abelardus did not know if they were captured or dead. The loose horses, free from their captured riders, ran into the hands of their ambushers.

Abelardus and his remaining men instinctually banded together. They formed a tight circle, their large shields held to the outside trying to manage some protection, but they were surrounded and outnumbered. The foggy landscape before them bubbled and erupted with more and more armed ambushers.

Their closest attackers swung wide weighted nets over their heads that they threw towards the Legionnaires. The nets parachuted over and around his men pulling them from the backs of their horses. Before he could maneuver out of the way, one of the nets engulfed him, pinning his arms close to his body as he was pulled to the ground. For a moment, right before he fell from the back of his struggling steed, his eyes glanced ahead of him, across the small pond. There Abelardus saw the five men they had pursued to this place–laughing at them.

4

"That's right my friend...eat...I can tell by your breathing that you're getting stronger."

Csoda had been woken by a spasm of swallowing. He opened his eyes halfway to see the large man still chained to him, hurriedly chewing on a strip of tough meat and glancing occasionally towards a slight opening in the ceiling. Rays of light shone down and across the man's face, creating deep shadows.

For the first time Csoda could actually see this stranger's features and they were well matched to his robust body. His strong bearded chin tapered down from a broad cut jaw, his lips were full and clearly defined his mouth, even through unkempt facial hair. His substantial hooked nose, mimicking the shape of his chin, was both wide and long. His beard and eyebrows were full and thick and his long black hair was pulled back and tied haphazardly into a knotted braid behind his head.

Csoda did not feel fear this time, just an apathetic weakness, his only current strength fed by a slight curiosity. The man spoke his language and his general appearance, though different than Csoda's, was familiar.

The man continued to talk even as he chewed on a piece of meat. He did not seem to be addressing anyone in particular. His conversation changed its focus constantly so that sometimes he seemed to talk to himself, then to Csoda, and then to someone outside of their wagon prison. The man's voice shifted as well and its robust sound was surprisingly varied. Sometimes it was a tenor growl and other times it lilted at higher pitches, especially when he seemed to be mocking something.

"Yes..." the man went on, "We both need our strength. We have time. They want us alive...but...it is up to us to be strong." A shadow passed outside the wagon. The man watched suspiciously, narrowing his intense dark eyes, he spoke under his breath, "Look at you...dirty guard...you think I am caged....huh? You...you in your little costume given to you by your master." He chuckled to himself then turned his attention back to the half eaten piece of meat. He swallowed what was in his mouth and violently tore off a new piece.

The man stopped speaking, his focus shifted to the food. He stared into space chewing and chewing, until the food was completely turned to liquid in his mouth. He cupped his hand, spitting the masticated food into his palm and turned towards Csoda. Their eyes met and the man startled a bit at seeing Csoda awake. Then he smiled wide, his smile as broad and strong as every other aspect of him. "You're awake? Yes...that's right...you are getting stronger. You must eat...or you will die on me...and that will not do."

The man reached over with his free hand, cupping Csoda's chin gently, he tilted Csoda's head back even as he pulled down on his chin, opening his mouth. Csoda was too weak to protest as the man poured the newly masticated food into his mouth with his other cupped hand.

Csoda did not gag. He swallowed the offered food. His throat spasmed, his stomach rolled, he could feel the food feeding his body, feel his blood surge with new life. He closed his eyes but didn't black out. He let himself feel the food, the life returning. He let himself smell the stench of their cage and the occasional fresh smells that came from a slight breeze through the wood panels. He listened to the sound of the man talking next to him and the sounds from outside their wagon. He heard the groans of wood and other men, a distant lion roar, the shuffling and snorting of what must be oxen, camels and horses. He felt the man pat his shoulder kindly and speak to him.

"Yes...you are getting stronger...I will help you...sleep now...we have some time."

Eventually, Csoda did sleep, and this time he dreamed. He dreamed of the shores of the sea covered with the bodies of dead lambs. He dreamed of horses running and the smell of salt water air. He dreamed of his tribe and clouds of thick smoke darkening the sky. He dreamed he was behind the eyes of a soaring hawk, and he dreamed of a child.

He saw a young boy dressed in colorful clothing made from dyed patches of leather. The boy stretched his thin arms up towards Csoda. In his small hands he grasped a strange brass object covered in fine detailed carvings and full of intricate pieces all connected together in a complicated pattern.

The boy looked up at him with greenish blue eyes that sparkled like rare cut gemstones, his ebony hair tussled loosely over part of his face and he spoke in Csoda's native tongue, "Csoda...the watch...it is not working..."

Csoda hovered between two worlds for a while, half

asleep, half awake. In his mind he whispered, "What is a watch?"

Csoda's dreams melded with the world that his weak body occupied. He no longer fell into unconscious blackness when he passed out, but instead drifted between a conscious recognition of the space around him and an elaborate dream space full of dramatic imagery and untouchable meaning. This dream state proved to be both an escape from his physical and mental pain as well as an amplifier of it. He remembered his name and who he was, but he could barely recognize what was real and what was imagined.

When he first heard the rhythm it mixed with his dream seamlessly. First it was the thunder in the distant clouds and then it was the stamping hoof of a moon gray horse standing before him and pawing the ground. Soon the images faded but the rhythm became louder, its beats more precise.

The rhythm pulled him out of dreams and into memories and for a brief moment he thought he was back in his homeland, sleeping upon the back of a strong horse, the movement of the animal inspiring song. The memory was strong enough that he actually opened his mouth, filled his chest with breath and attempted to sing, but only a weak, infertile sound gurgled forth. The pathetic sound was accompanied by pain and sorrow and he was pulled back into the reality that he had no tongue to sing with anymore.

Still the rhythm tapped against the wood floor he laid upon, it blended with the rocking of his body that moved with the shifting motion of their prison wagon. They were being pulled through what appeared to be a dark night. This was not a dream.

His eyes adjusted to the dark and he could see the strong man sitting next to him, tapping the rhythm onto the floor, humming a familiar melody that Csoda remembered singing a long time ago.

"You are from the Nagy Föld?" Csoda thought to himself... wishing he could speak...could ask.

The man turned his head and locked eyes with Csoda, as if he heard his thoughts, and maybe he did. The man's gaze was as steady as steel, his brown eyes were so dark that it was hard to distinguish where his pupils ended and his irises began. Csoda, in response to his wish to communicate, began to tap along with the song's rhythm. This made the man smile, a wide open smile that enlarged his eyes and exposed a set of strong, straight teeth.

Csoda did not know this man, at least they had never truly met, they were not old friends, or from the same tribe. However, he knew now for sure that they were both of the Törzsi Nomádok. They were Children of the Steppe, Brothers of the Stag, Falcon, Wolf, and Horse. They were the nomads, the travelers, the wind runners and the drum singers. They spoke each other's language and they recognized each other's culture. They had learned similar stories as children, ate the same meals, had the same traditions. Their mothers had probably played familiar games, their fathers had taught them similar skills, and they had learned the same songs while sitting with their tribes by the campfires.

They stared at each other as two wolves greeting after they had not seen their own kind in many years. A stare that is terrifying to others but makes the wolves rejoice. This was how it felt to be in the presence of a fellow countryman, a creature of his own ancestral pack. Even in these horrid circumstances, and maybe because of them, it brought the forbidden feeling of hope into Csoda's heart.

He began to tap against the floor in more complicated

rhythms, the rhythms of a stampeding herd. If he could no longer sing, at least he could still drum. They both smiled now as they played against the wooden floor and their efforts built increasingly complicated rolling patterns and beats. The man changed his voice from a rumbling baritone hum and started to sing more of a melody, but with only sounds not words, "hey deya data heaya deaya data."

Each sound punctuated the rolling combination of rhythms and Csoda's heart ached. Even in this horrible place, his countryman, he himself, could smile, could find a way to raise their hopes and he felt strength in that realization. Perhaps his struggle and his recent defeat was not a true failure but a strange shift in destiny.

They finished the song somewhat quietly, letting the rhythms trickle into simpler patterns and the man's deep voice returned to a nostalgic hum. The crickets started chirping around them and they allowed the music to drift into the natural sounds of evening. They sat in silence for a while, each taking in the air and surrounding sounds. Then the man spoke, quietly.

"I know who you are," he murmured, "But I know you don't know me, do you?" He winked, as if the joke was on Csoda for not being informed. "Of course not. You were a leader and, well, I...I...well, I am not worth knowing. Heh." The man chuckled for a bit, his private joke increasing his smile. Then he turned his head to look at Csoda again. His expression became serious and he adopted a steady formal gaze, nodding his head and stating, "My name is Biro. I am of the Észak-Vadászok, from the Turul Mountains."

Csoda nodded, looking Biro in the eyes. This was what he suspected. A fellow tribesman from the Nagy Föld, the great land of the Törzsi Nomádok, the nomadic tribes.

The nomadic tribes were, or at least they used to be,

great in their numbers. Different groups of them had specific territories that they frequented within the Nagy Föld, though all of the nomads considered each other kinsmen and often crisscrossed each other's territories as needed with no problems.

Csoda knew of Biro's group, the Észak-Vadászok, hunters from the north. Biro fit the description of their tribe, a group known for their skills as hunters and warriors who possessed great physical strength, resilience, and fortitude.

"I saw you speak once," Biro continued. "Speak and sing. I was in the crowd, at the meeting of tribes, and you told us that we needed to stay together...to stand as one against them." Biro's eyes were bright now, his smile broadening as he spoke. "I remember your voice, ahhh...it made everyone's heart ache. Old men who barely could walk were pulled up to dance, women wept. They took your tongue for good reason, eh? But now, sitting here, even with you halfway dead, I think they made a mistake. You may be silent but there is something about you that makes me want to rise to action, even now." Biro nodded knowingly, leaned in towards Csoda, "You have 'it'? Yes?" And then with a hushed voice he declared, "You know...the Húzza Művészet...The Art of the Pull."

Csoda, upon having the magic spoken of, hurriedly looked for the shadows of the guards that occasionally passed by their darkened cage, frightened to have more of himself exposed than had already been stripped.

Biro shook his head quickly, dismissing Csoda's fear, "Do not worry...the guards are away, and they don't know what it means...even if they did speak our language. Plus, I speak all the time, when you are passed out and when you are awake. It helps numb them to hearing my voice." Biro smiled and cocked his head, giving Csoda a knowing wink. "They think

I'm crazy after all. I prefer it that way. But…I know what The Pull is." He sat up straight and pounded his chest with his thick fist "That's right my friend. We are brothers in blood… as well as in piss. You will live. I will make sure of it or die in the effort. And…if you can, I want to know…I want to know the magic of my people…I want to reconnect with my ancestors like we used to. Teach me The Pull and I will be loyal to you forever. Will you?"

Csoda paused. He looked Biro over, trying to see something beyond the physical aspects of the man before him.

Biro was obviously strong, even in their horrid conditions he was muscled and athletic. He could also tell that Biro was sharp minded, but what he was trying to see was subtler. While some aspects of the magic they called The Pull came naturally to all of the nomadic people, an individual who wanted to learn it on a more advanced level had to have an extra spark of something special to be worthy.

Csoda found that he wanted to teach Biro. He wanted the art to live past his own life, but he could not tell, he was too weak to truly read Biro's potential. However, he would not say no—not yet. He pursed his lips, looked down at the dirt on the floor and with the fingers of his chained hands scratched the symbols of their written language, "If I can."

Biro nodded happily, content with that response. He took in a deep breath and leaned back against the wall. He was silent for a while, just staring into the air. Then he spoke, as if in prayer, confessing to the space before him, as if his God sat there with them in the filth. "Yes, I have not always lived in a way that would make you proud, but I have survived, and that is worth something." He calmly turned his head, addressing Csoda directly, "Csoda, the Gods have put me here now, in this hell with you, with all of my faults…but I know how to survive in hell and maybe that will be worth something to you. Just as you...being blessed with the magic of our ancestors...is worth everything to me."

Again they sat in silence for a long time, so long that Csoda could not tell if he had drifted in and out of sleep a few times. Their wagon rocked methodically and in the distance he heard men talking and the grunts and growls of different beasts. His curiosity awoke once more and he tapped the floor, getting Biro's attention before scratching in the dirt. "Where?"

Biro read the note, his eyes narrowed as he nodded solemnly and with a deep and grave tone he answered Csoda's inquiry, "We, my brother, are captives in the Grand Kirkos." He smiled sadly, as if the meaning of his own words weighed on his heart. Letting his eyes survey their small cell slowly he continued, "You should sleep now....you will need your strength...we still have time."

5

———

Dust lifted into the air from the churning wagon wheels, marking the departure of the Kirkos caravan as it traveled along the dry dirt roads that led to the outskirts of Critias. The Capital was far behind them. The Grand Kirkos events had come to a close in the Emperor's greatest coliseum only a couple of months before and the Kirkos had shifted into its second manifestation, that of a traveling caravan, which moved throughout the Empire of Critias and sometimes into the fringes of adjacent territories. Its entourage was much smaller than before the Grand Kirkos events had begun. The left over tatters of men and beasts that survived the brutal entertainment had limped away from the last coliseum walls, leaving the echoing arenas to the ghosts of those who had perished there.

This was the aftermath of the intense Grand Kirkos tour, violent spectacles that took place inside the coliseums of twelve of the major cities within Critias, always ending at the Capital. Each event brought weeks of performances to each city, war games and races, many of which led to the death of those who participated.

The Capital events completed, the Kirkos caravan would travel for over a year collecting slaves, captives, performers, and exotic creatures as it moved through the land. At first it would move quietly, with hardly any fanfare, as it entered town after town, city after city. However, after leaving each town its ranks would grow. The empty prison wagons would once again be filled with captured convicts or slaves. One small village after another would hand over their thieves and the Emperor's Legions, marching back towards the Capital, may meet them along the way and hand over some of their captured enemies. Eventually, as the caravan grew in size it would take on the appearance of an exotic parade until it was finally ready to start again with the first Grand Kirkos event held in the city of Phaedon.

At this time, however, the many wagons were mostly empty. The elite performers and lucky captives who had survived were worn, injured, and tired. At this stage of the cycle only the beasts that pulled the wagons seemed the same as they were before the Grand Kirkos events had taken place.

Still, even in this anemic state, the people in the villages that the Kirkos traveled through were curious enough that they would peek out their windows or gather in small groups to watch it pass. Sometimes groups of small children would gather and follow the caravan through the town trying to get a glimpse of the survivors.

The rare performer who had made a name for him or herself and had lived to carry that name into the next season's events could sometimes be seen, stooped over in not so crowded wagons, their eyes closed, their bodies limp with fatigue. Even the most adept acrobats merely walked when they left their wagons to stretch their legs. Only occasionally did they perform a flip or juggle some small balls to entertain the curious onlooker. The brutality of their experiences in the coliseums weighed heavy on their minds, their wounded bodies were still recovering.

The Kirkos was part of the Empire of Critias, but in reality it was a culture in and of itself, one that did not mesh directly with the general society. It existed in more of a parallel relationship with the Empire, one that was used by the Emperor and the ruling class of Critias to their greatest advantage. While the citizens of Critias who flocked to the coliseums en masse to watch the Kirkos events praised the Emperor for the entertainment, the true power behind the Kirkos lay in the hands of the Ringmaster.

To those who lived within the world of the Kirkos it was the Ringmaster who was their King and the controller of their lives. It was he who gave out orders to the guards, owned the slaves, chose the performers, and ruled over their training. It was he who decided their punishment, care, and fate.

A large and muscular man, the Ringmaster stood two feet taller than the average warrior. His face was long and broad with well-defined cheeks and a slightly furrowed brow. His eyes were icy blue and his brows and thick pointed beard a tawny yellow, whose tips were bleached by the days in the sun that also tanned his dark bronzed skin. Throughout every day and every night, his expression was always stern and focused.

The Ringmaster's height was increased by a slight heal in his boots and a headdress made with black and white silk stretched across ribs of stiff leather and bone in the shape of a cylindrical crown. The headdress had a wide brim of rolled up silk with an extra piece that draped down past his shoulders and back, protecting his neck from the sun.

His performance robe was a mixture of black, white, and

maroon silk with gold stitching and embroidery that was patterned after the markings that could be found on the feathers of a rooster. This robe stretched like bat wings over three spines of light bone on each of his shoulders. It hovered ever so slightly over the top of his actual body and extended out to the sides beyond his already broad frame. From there the robe's material dropped and tented to the ground angling in towards his feet, making him look like a divine and slightly fluttering statue, triangular in form.

The robe did more than just increase the Ringmaster's already large size and give him a surreal, otherworldly majesty. Its draping materials and length allowed him to accentuate grand gestures when he desired and it was an effective prop to make these gestures noticeable to crowds who may watch him from far away. The same draping material that could swing open and wide to add drama to his movements could also be used to hide more covert actions. When needed, it hid his body and hands, concealed his armor, and even his weaponry.

Under the Ringmaster's curtained exterior his silken and elegant façade hid brutal potential.

The Ringmaster wore leather armor sewn and plated like scales across his chest, back, belly and sides. Under the tented top hat his head was covered with a short helmet of hard ivory and bone. His shoulders and neck were shielded with light yet strong brass plating, and his stomach and heart were covered with disk-like, brass shields. Around his hips hung a skirt of linked metal armor that protected his thighs, upper legs, knees and groin. His heeled leather boots were those of a warrior, thick and sturdy, his ankles and toes shielded by inserts of brass.

Along with the armored protection the Ringmaster always carried weapons. He had small knives in his belt and boots. The thick leather arm guards that shielded his forearms were strapped on with brass bands that were razor sharp, ready to slice someone with one strong swipe or punish the attack of a biting animal. Even his jewelry, which glinted of gold, copper and brass, disguised violent potential. The rings of his left hand were broad with thick heavy plates. In his right hand, his four fingers were decorated with a band of solid brass and silver that formed an image of two fighting roosters and could easily be gripped and used like brass knuckles if needed.

Yet all of these were only in addition to his true weapons of choice. A long gilded shamshir with sculpted feathers on its hilt and a trident short sword that was shaped and sculpted to look like the clawing foot of a rooster. If anyone, man or beast, made the mistake of thinking the Ringmaster was merely an unskilled brute, or took his gilded costume and weapons for that of a simple showman, they would be sorry. He was a masterful tactician, in life and in battle, and he wielded his weapons with brutal grace and ruthless efficiency.

The Ringmaster's platform towered behind the rest of the wagons in the caravan, high enough that it allowed him to see all and all to see him. It was placed on top of a high profile carriage made of polished black wood with brass fixtures, decorations and wheels. It was a long and impressive size, taking eight wheels to hold its weight and pulled by two elephants, each controlled by a rider that perched on their necks right behind their massive fanning gray ears.

Attendants, ready to serve him in whatever fashion they could, walked alongside or rode horses nearby. Behind his carriage a small herd of riderless camels, horses and more elephants moved in a group, encircled by a troupe of handlers. The handlers kept the animals in line with long sticks that they used to direct them and the help of a few keen-eyed, swift herding dogs.

While the inside of the carriage provided him with elaborate private quarters, the majority of the time the Kirkos traveled the Ringmaster preferred to ride aloft on his platform. There he would comfortably sit on a suede-cushioned throne, legs wide as he relaxed into its slightly angled back.

A maroon canopy kept him shaded from the sun and slave girls sat next to him, cautiously rubbing his arms and shoulders, careful to avoid the hidden sharp blades of his decorative armbands, as well as his wrath. His favorite concubine, wearing only a thin, translucent short dress, would languidly lounge on display at his feet, her heavily made up eyes averted and her head ducked down so that her hair and the strands of gold from her beaded headdress slightly hid her face.

Less noticeable than the rest of his entourage were his elite guards who rode standing in shallow alcoves built into the sides of the carriage. Their black hooded cloaks hid their bodies against the black wagon, blending them into its surface. Even their white expressionless face masks looked like decorative ornamentation until one of them moved. The Ringmaster's elite guards were always hovering near him or guarding his private quarters. They never took off their cloaks or masks in public and their identities, even to the other Kirkos guards, were completely unknown.

The elite guards were the only men, other than himself, allowed into the Ringmaster's private chamber. When the Ringmaster was away there was always at least one of them posted at the heavily locked door. Even his concubines never entered his chamber, instead entertaining his needs from their own quarters, needs that he kept purely physical, void of emotional attachment.

The wagon held the Kirkos treasure, which was more important to him than the affections of women. It also held the decrees and papers signed by the Emperor permitting the passage of the caravan through all parts of the kingdom. All the trappings of his business dealings, the scrolls and lists of assets, logs of slaves bought and sold, and records of events and travels. Upon its anchored counters sat an abacus, ink and pens as well as the brands and seals of the Kirkos emblem. Its closets and cabinets held his weapons and armor, gowns of silk and linen, all dripping with golden details and embroidery.

There were also more curious items whose purposes were less obvious. Upon the inside of the door were nailed two large dried rooster feet, the talons equipped with sharp metal spurs. On a nightstand next to his bed sat a small gold censor that emitted a continual thin stream of incense smoke, an undecorated bone athame, a clay dish filled with a handful of rich black earth, and a small silver chalice filled half way with salt water.

For there was more to the Ringmaster, both in costume and character, than most men would ever understand. Further removal of his costumed shell of clothing and weaponry would reveal a hardened and muscular body coated in tattoos. Intricate and symbolic black designs that had been inked into his skin over the years for different reasons. Some of the tattoos were given by the Emperor in remembrance and as honors to celebrate his dedication and violent service. Others he had given to himself for his own reasons, both nostalgic and ritualistic.

He was a curtained force capable of swift, brutal disciplinary action and he directed all aspects of the Kirkos with a capable and merciless grip along with a cruel, intelligent mind. This alone may have been enough to keep the Kirkos under control, the guards loyal, the slaves passive, the performers obedient, and the events profitable, but this was not all the Ringmaster had in his favor.

Within his soul was a darker resource, a shadow behind his eyes that he had cultivated through years of merciless existence and the remorseless study of savage and darker arts. An ominous nature that loomed deep within him had allowed him to tap into more sinister powers, which helped him create a spiritual bond with all who were trapped in the Kirkos. A shackling chain of energy radiated from his gestures and voiced commands, creating a faint electrical charge in the air that wove and integrated itself into the everyday functions of the caravan and the overall world of the Kirkos. It knitted itself into the hearts of the performers, guards and slaves, holding its inhabitants in the clutch of unseen irons.

So effective were these enchanted manacles that even the most talented, those with the seemingly freest minds and greatest physical abilities, even they rarely considered escape or revolt. Instead they conceded to their fate as imprisoned souls locked to the Kirkos and to the Ring-master himself. Slaves to the brutality who were only given permission to use their talents for the benefit of the Kirkos, the Ringmaster, and ultimately the profit he craved. For them, their only sense of release was while performing before the adoring crowds, a brief moment of time in which their souls could feel free. For them, their only true escape was in death.

6

In the halls and gardens of Coracis Dominicus Thrax there was always the sound of music floating through the air, though the musicians themselves were hidden. They played behind meshed fences and gates made of painted twisted iron shaped like abstract vines, flowers and the long legged wetland birds common in the fertile lands of the Empire of Critias. The musicians were never allowed to see or be seen by the Emperor, whom they played for all day, every day.

It was not only the musicians who the Emperor barred from direct access to his private rooms and personal self. Limits were set for everyone who he had direct relations with and those that served him on all levels. For this reason, despite their grand size and elegant décor, their high arching ceilings and vast spacious interiors, the halls of Emperor Coracis' estates and chambers were eerily empty of people, with only the ghostly music to fill their echoing rooms. This afforded him the desired isolation he required to feel safe from the physical and spiritual daggers of his enemies.

Coracis did not trust anyone, but he did enjoy the delicate lilting melody of the flute, the rain drop like notes played expertly on the lyre and the accompanied energy from the rhythm of the tympanum. Most of all he counted on the occasional low clarinet like vibrational sounds of the aulos to wash through the corridors. It was a common belief in his culture that the bending notes and atonal depth of the aulos helped to clean the air both without and within the body, keeping illness at bay and purifying the body and mind. He, after all, as Emperor, worried not only about attacks upon his kingdom and his physical self, but also the attacks that could be executed through the realm of the lemures, the restless spirits of the malevolent dead.

It was easy to see why such cleansing melodies might be necessary in the vast empty chambers of Coracis. For here he often rested and walked alone amongst the plaster and bronze death masks of the Emperors who had come before him, as well as the people that had been closest to him.

The older masks were more abstract than those made during Coracis' life which were skillfully carved in a more realistic style. However, each one, even those from long ago, contained delicate details that identified the man or woman it represented, a hint at a unique scar or a touch of paint or stain to represent their eye color. All of them were kept free from dust and occasionally they were coated with a thin layer of transparent wax that gave their surfaces a delicate sheen, an illusion of sweat, moisture and life.

In the Atrium the candles were always lit around the pale settled features of the mask of Argustus Thrax, Coracis' step-father, who had died five years before, setting Coracis up to ultimately take the crown. Across from the mask of Argustus rested those of Coracis' mother, positioned next to the infant features of Coracis' nameless stepbrother, Argustus' full blooded son.

Coracis walked between these masks, often pausing, his head ducked ever so slightly, his hands unconsciously tugging at the sleeves of his robe or wrapping it tighter around himself as if he felt a chill. Here he would sometimes whisper comments and occasionally he would speak out loud as if addressing his family in life. In either case the dialogue was often the same.

He would greet his stepfather curtly, "Father," and then turn to the unresponsive features of his mother and in a scolding tone, state, "You did not have to accuse me so publicly." He would then pause and solemnly glance over the features of the baby that had never reached a full year of age. Here his voice softened and his right eye would begin to twitch. His shoulders would slightly drop as he sighed, defeated, "Tell her brother. Tell her how foolish she behaved."

Coracis' right to succeed Argustus had been questioned by the Senators because of Argustus' full blooded male child, the same one remembered by the hallow death mask which he spoke to. It had been Coracis' persuasive Uncle Tiberius who had strongly supported him to be the rightful successor, tipping the scales in Coracis' favor. With Tiberius as a supporter, and Argustus' full son only a babe, the Senate and the people eventually agreed that Coracis should be crowned Emperor.

Soon after Coracis' accession to power, the full blooded infant child of Argustus mysteriously died in his sleep. His distraught mother openly blamed Coracis and was therefore charged and found guilty of treason. Her punishment, death. From this moment forward Coracis' personality was blanketed with a tendency towards suspicion and what he considered practical paranoia.

To the surprise of many, after his mother's execution, Coracis exiled his great uncle Tiberius, the very man who had helped him gain power, to a villa in the distant islands to wait out his "retirement" far from Coracis' side. He also established rigid rules that managed his palace and villa estates, as well as his social and political interactions with everyone, including family and friends. To break the strict rules and formalities he put into place was seen by Coracis as a direct attempt to weaken measures he had erected to protect his very life. Therefore, any rule breaker was considered a traitor to the Empire, and traitors were often sentenced to death.

Noone was immune to his suspicions.

In five years Coracis had executed cousins and even his first wife with the title of traitor stamped to their records.

Perhaps it was the constant silent gaze of the death masks that watched over Coracis as he wandered the empty halls that began to influence his state of mind and darken his mood. The hallow gazes of those who had held his title long ago were a quiet warning of all that could be, and had been, taken away from powerful men.

Within his self imposed isolation the Emperor allowed his mistrust to grow. What was perceived as a perfect place for peaceful contemplation actually became the perfect place for his mind to turn on him, allowing him to develop elaborate theories and internal stories about the people in power around him and those in neighboring kingdoms. He took actual events and actions and embellished them with extra fears so that his concerns, while based partly in reality, were inflated in his mind into direct insults and attacks upon the Empire and himself, the Emperor.

If it wasn't enough that he was prone to flights of suspicious imagination, Coracis, while a broad man standing six feet tall with an aquiline nose and a strong jaw who could hardly be considered weak, was prone to occasional unprovoked seizures. He often took these incidents to be supernatural signs that supported his fears.

Woe be to the individual whose name the Emperor contemplated as he paced alone in the vast marble halls when, suddenly, his broad frame would sway then collapse forcefully to the cold floor. His teeth gnashing violently against a plug of thick leather he kept tucked in the back of his mouth like a horses bit that was always in place when he was alone, kept there to protect his tongue and teeth from the effects of the harsh convulsions. His massive figure would shake uncontrollably, the sheathed sword at his side would rattle, the royal purple toga tangling in his flailing arms for the duration of the episode.

When it was over he would often lay staring at the decorative tiles of the domed ceilings, or the open sky above his garden courtyard, alone, his mind dazed, his heart palpitating in irregular rhythms, his head aching, tremors sporadically crossing his face–left over spasms. Sometimes his body would bleed from cuts or his skin would turn blue with bruises he acquired from the uncontrolled thrashing.

Occasionally he would jolt upwards and begin pacing frantically with a surge of adrenaline filling his veins with manic energy. He would then remember the person he had thought of before the seizure dropped him to his knees rendering him helpless, and he linked that unfortunate name with the episode.

At best the individual would simply be mistrusted more than before. At worst, the Emperor found a reason to destroy him or her in whatever way seemed most fitting. For surely, he thought, the Gods gave him such tremors of body and soul as a warning against the true motivations of his enemies.

When he did leave his isolated private spaces to interact with the Senate, his generals, his family, and the public, his thoughts about the intentions of each individual or the events of the day, no matter how mundane, were tainted with the perceptions that he had manifested in private. It was not long before the Senators and generals, family, and servants learned to dance a fine line between what was happening and what the Emperor believed was happening. They understood that a misstep in actions or words, even those motivated by kindness or loyalty, could lead to execution if the Emperor interpreted them as malicious.

The servants and guards were the quickest to adapt, many of which had learned to form their ways to the individual natures of the Emperors who ruled before Coracis. They became efficient and effective in all essential duties, but they also learned that it was best to be available only when needed, remaining otherwise unseen and, if possible, nameless to the Emperor. Keeping a low profile meant that one's name would not get mixed up with his imagined fears.

The generals, too, adapted quickly. Their own station allowed them a bit of protection, for they had the armies behind them and they could consistently prove their loyalty through acts of war. If the Emperor did focus negatively on a general then that general could usually win back favor, or at least delay the Emperor's wrath, with a successful military campaign.

The Senators and ambassadors were in less of a position to defend themselves against the Emperor's moods. Quick witted politicians, they could usually work their way around negative circumstances with well thought out words and diplomacy. However, this tactic was not effective against the Emperor's illusion since it was impossible to fully understand what the exact illusions were and when they might change. Plus, the Senators' diplomacy and elegant speeches only made the Emperor mistrust them more.

So the politicians took to hiding behind their social status and the rights afforded them by their family lineages. The most skilled of them kept themselves humble and made sure they did not become too popular, or too brash in their protests, ensuring that their names would be less likely to invade his thoughts. All of them quickly took note of the tactics of the generals and were quick to focus on external campaigns or rumors of adversaries outside of the Empire. This provided them a way to redirect the Emperor's unpredictable disfavor, pointing it away from them and aiming it at their common enemies.

After all, even if the Emperor's heightened mistrust set him into a pattern of unpredictable behavior, he was always a believer in expanding the Empire. Conquering the neighboring lands and imposing his rule, his Gods, and his beliefs upon populations as far and wide as his armies could reach was his natural purpose, one that he was born into. He saw war campaigns as his gifts to the Gods who had held him in favor throughout his life, ultimately handing him the throne.

He also knew that such successful campaigns not only brought him wealth, they also brought him favor with the people of his kingdom. His people reaped the rewards of his conquests through cheaper trade, exotic imports, abundance of food, and the readily available slaves and captives that fed the violent entertainment they craved– most notably, the blood games of the Kirkos. If his brutal and paranoid nature could not win the heart of the populace, his conquests would win their pride and violent lusts and, Coracis believed, would ensure their dedication to the Empire.

Two cultures had proven to be the most upsetting to the Emperor and were becoming an easy mark for his wrath. One was the nomadic tribes of the vast lands called the Nagy Föld. The nomad's very way of living proved hard to control and, therefore, easily disturbed the Emperor's mood.

If a culture never settled in an exact spot it was hard to find them, hard to impose rules, and hard to attack. While the tribes tended to keep to the plains and hills of the Nagy Föld, they did not let that limit their movement if they felt the need to leave their familiar territories. They had proven capable of adapting to harsh environments when needed. More than their way of living however, it was their tendency to outright defy anyone who tried to control them that upset the Emperor the most–that and the rumors of their abilities both in war and in matters of what could only be considered supernatural arts.

The other culture was one more familiar to the Empire and to Coracis personally, the neighboring Kingdom of Zenobia, the Queen of the hidden desert canyon lands. The Kingdom of Zenobia bordered the western shores of the Sea of AyRuh, the same Sea that met his own kingdom's ports on the eastern side.

Coracis had met Zenobia when he was young, they had played as children. Her father had been allies with his step-father, the Emperor Argustus Thrax, and the two kingdom's ships were known to regularly cross the Sea of AyRuh carrying traded goods and passengers.

Yet, at the death of Zenobia's father, Coracis noted that

the Queen took to commanding her kingdom with an amazing and unexpected grace and skill, easily defending her lands against her enemies. Even the Emperor Argustus who was still in power when Zenobia ascended to the throne shook his head in disbelief upon hearing of her army's success in battle, exclaiming, "A man that does not fear this queen because she is a woman, is a man who has never faced a lioness."

This alone was a reason for Zenobia and her kingdom to spark Emperor Coracis' envy and fear, but more recently it was matched with new rumors and concerns. Zenobia, it was said, spoke the language of the nomads and stayed in contact with the tribes. She was known to encourage art, philosophy and theatre within her land. It was said that these artists, philosophers and actors would openly discuss and even criticize the Empire of Critias, and the Emperor himself.

Ambassadors took note of such insulting practices by everyday citizens and, it was said, when these issues were brought to the Queen's attention, she would politely dismiss them. One report even stated that she joked about the subject saying, "Why would a strong ruler, supported by millions, be threatened by the poetry and songs of individual men?"

In that one rumored comment reported to him by the ambassadors upon returning to his land, Coracis had decided, despite the feigned treaty between their lands, that he would ensure the Queen's presumptuous nature to be restrained, her kingdom made his own, and her ridiculing poets, artists and musicians to be silenced.

He had already begun to move against her, though their treaty was officially still in place. He had spent years waging wars on the barbarian tribes who lived in the Nagy Föld, a territory that bordered his kingdom to the far south, spanned around the southern edge of the Sea of AyRuh and continued into the Turul Mountains to meet up with Zenobia's territory on its South Eastern edge.

His attack on the tribes accomplished three things. First, it rid his world of the nomad culture, one that proved threatening to his personal views of order, society, and control. Second, it opened up the Nagy Föld to be settled by the citizens of Critias, thus expanding the Empire into lands that were known to possess good water, fertile soil and plentiful wild game to hunt. Finally, and less noticeably, it gave Coracis direct access to the Queen's southern border so that he, if desired, could march troops through the Nagy Föld to enter her land, troops that could either support, or be supported by, his navy fleets, which could reach her Western border by traveling across the Sea of AyRuh.

Even the generals of the Legion troops, who he asked to push further and further into the territory of the Nomads waging destructive wars against the tribes, did not know his full intentions. The Senate did not know that his attacks on the tribes were more than police actions against barbarians. No one questioned his desire to wipe out the culture of the Törzsi Nomádok, or at least they kept those questions to themselves. Many of the Senators had already been able to increase their own land holdings by fencing in pieces of the Nagy Föld. Coracis would be hailed by all those who benefited from the destruction as a great expander of the Empire's wealth and territory.

Then, after the land was open, after his access to Zenobia's kingdom was secured...well...then he would find justification for a direct war with her. It was a covert plan that he had put into place, but told noone.

Noone, except for the mask of his stepfather whom

Coracis addressed in a hushed voice to reveal a piece of the strategy. "Do you see Father..." he would explain. "It will be a great prize for Critias. Our kingdom would double."

Somehow, the mask of Argustus seemed to approve, with his solemn empty glare and inevitable silence.

7

———

As the days passed by in the confined monotony of their moving prison, Csoda became physically stronger. Biro was determined to fulfill his promise to make sure Csoda survived and the strong man became a focused, and somewhat ruthless, physical coach. He started with bending and stretching Csoda's legs and arms back and forth manually so they did not fail him from disuse. Then he was determined to get Csoda to stand and move about on his own.

Depression weighed heavily on Csoda and while he was heartened from meeting Biro, he was not overly eager to participate in his own physical rehabilitation. He felt pain in ways he could never have imagined possible and every waking moment plagued him with a yearning to give up. It was as if a weighted smoky fog had settled in his heart and in his mind. It pulled him physically and spiritually down, made his breath shallow and dulled his vision. On many days this sadness lulled him into apathy and a desire to struggle no more.

However, Biro was not about to allow defeat to creep

into his new found friend's head for very long, and being chained together left Csoda no choice but to comply with the northern hunter's crude but effective daily physical regimen.

They spent hours using the chain that bound them as a tool for tug of war or standing in the middle of the cell jumping up and down, dropping to the floor and then raising back up, over and over. Sometimes they faced each and, with the palms of their hands matched together, pushed against each other for resistance. Biro, being a bull of a man, always had more power than Csoda. However, over time, Csoda felt some strength return, and every now and then he could brace his legs and hold back some of Biro's force.

With his physical strength returning Csoda also began to recover a glimmer of the unstoppable revolutionary he had once been.

Deep in his heart he did not believe he would ever fully recover. Still, he started to take more initiative, meagerly at first, to wake on his own accord and stretch or perform pushups without Biro's prodding. He worked around the stiffness of the deepest scars and began to feel his blood circulating again. He meditated when he was still, but only as a way to relieve anxiety. He avoided any attempts at magic, telling himself that he should avoid deep trances when his sleep was so full of nightmares. Yet his real fear, one that he was not ready to face, was that he had lost his abilities. For now, he would focus on physical recovery.

It was at this time, when Csoda was showing greater strength, that Biro decided to further reveal what he knew about their fate and the Grand Kirkos.

"Did you hear the roars the other day? Most likely lions," Biro began as he stood by one of the walls, peeking through a small slit in the wood that allowed them to occasionally glimpse a piece of the world. "We are traveling now through the last few towns before we reach the first coliseum. They have been gathering others like us this entire time. Slaves, prisoners, and rare animals."

He paused for a moment and took in a deep breath continuing with a grave tone, "Listen, Csoda, when they get close to finishing this slave parade they will start to train some of the stronger, more talented captives to perform in the Kirkos as acrobats and fighters. The rest they will save to be killed in some massive show. I think we, you and I, are meant to be butchered."

Biro moved away from the wall and sat down near his friend. "You are a known revolutionary and our people have been marked for destruction. I think they would like to have both of us destroyed in the first Kirkos, in the coliseum of Phaedon. It would help them show the masses that our people are finished, if they notice us at all."

Again he paused then sighed heavily before he continued, "We have little hope my friend, but what little hope we have will count on us surviving whatever they make us face." He leaned back, his head nodding, agreeing with himself, "The Kirkos arena is brutal but it is possible to survive. Before you came I survived the arena in the Final Grand Kirkos held in the Capital's coliseum. I faced off some of the lions they thought would get the better of me. If I had not been of the Törzsi Nomádok they would have raised my status above a captive and had me participate in other acts. That did not happen. The Emperor does not want us to survive."

Biro looked at Csoda and smiled knowingly, "The war of your tribe had just been fought, you had just been captured, so instead of killing me they chained me to you..." he sat up now, raised his eyebrows and made a comical face that mimicked the Kirkos guards as he mocked their voices, "Ok, proud fool. Let's see how well you perform with your dead revolutionary leader chained to you." He returned to his own voice and pointed to the chain on the ground, "They made bets that I would tear your arm off to free myself, but..." He stopped and turned, winking with a slightly manic grin. "You were stronger than they imagined. I felt that you were not dead yet. We will prove them wrong. Yes?" His teeth glinted in a vengeful sneer and Csoda, while he trusted Biro, saw that this man would do whatever he had to do to survive.

Csoda was impressed with Biro's knowledge. He proved to be more than a simple strong man, showing the intensity of a quick thinking warrior. Csoda felt pride at this realization. His people, all the tribes, always proved to be clever. Biro's insight into the Kirkos explained some of the sounds Csoda had noticed increasing and changing over time. What used to be the methodical drone of a few wagon wheels and the sound of a handful of marching feet had grown in number and now included more exotic cries. Bellows of water buffalo and bulls, roars of large cats, and the howls of different canines filled the evening air.

Other changes became apparent as well. The guards started to post up regularly by their wagon in the morning and checked on them throughout the night. They delivered more food and water through a sliding slot in one of the walls than they had before. Occasionally, when the slave caravan came close to a large body of water they threw buckets of gathered water, salt or fresh, down upon them from an opened hatch in the roof.

These rough showers usually were accompanied by the guard's crude remarks about how the two prisoners smelled. Biro would remark back to them, his deep growling voice sometimes shifting to a high pitched mocking whine as he threw his own insults towards the guards. He insulted them in their language as well as his own. For the most part they ignored him, but occasionally they opened the ceiling hatch a bit wider and threatened him angrily. However, none of them ever came into their wooden cage. This amused Biro, who used it as proof to himself that they were cowards. While Biro often paraded his strength, wit, and a dramatic act of insanity towards the guards he made a point to tell Csoda to act weak. He would often stop him from physical activity when he saw the guards coming.

"They expect me to bite," He explained, "But they think you are nearly dead, merely a symbolic token of blood to be spilled in the arena. Let's not give away that you may be a fighter. It could help us in this mess, for them to think of you as easy prey."

This strategy sat well with Csoda, and so he complied and made sure that only Biro knew the full extent of his recovery–and recover he did. Each day the pain became less, his mouth healed and the old lacerations closed into thick roping scars that wove themselves over his entire body. Some of them were thick enough that they pulled the skin taunt, making it hard to bend a knee or a finger, but bend them he did, pushing and pulling against the scar tissue, stretching and forcing, coaxing and working the muscles and skin until his limbs and joints regained a decent range of motion.

Days continued to pass, and then one evening, at dusk, Csoda was surprised at how peaceful he felt. He had just finished stretching his legs and sat leaning against the wall of their wagon cage. He was observing how skinny his limbs remained, but at least he could see the muscles returning. He was gaining strength.

Hours earlier the guards had doused them both with water and thrown them each a bowl of food. The food included grains and meat as well as some limp but edible vegetables and olives. It was, for them, a feast.

Csoda had to smile to himself, how strange it was that their captor's efforts seemed aimed at ensuring that, at the very least, they were not just half dead sacks of bones when they threw them into the arena to die. Biro ensured him that if they survived past half of the Kirkos parade's traveling circuit then at a certain stage, right before the first Kirkos shows, the Ringmaster would see to it that the captors who were still alive were fattened up for the crowds. Still, having a minimal amount of flesh on one's bones seemed a far cry from what Csoda considered "being fattened up".

They were not safe, if anything, the better treatment was a sign that they were closer to facing death. Yet, at this moment, dropping all of his thoughts of the past as well as his anxiety over the future, Csoda felt at peace.

He shifted his legs to sit with bent knees, careful to avoid dragging the chain loudly against the floor or pull against Biro who slept heavily. He had noticed how Biro could fall asleep as soon as he closed his eyes, and yet, at the first sign of a problem or an unidentified sound those same eyes instantly opened and Biro was ready for action. He was a skilled and alert man who accepted his circumstances for exactly what they were. He didn't let the oppression of it weigh on his mind any more than he had to in order to survive. Csoda admired this quality and took to emanate it as best as he could. He had to recognize that his revolution, his people, were gone. The very weight of that pain burdened his heart and seared his sleep with nightmares, but, for whatever reason, he still lived. This was something he would have to accept, at least for now.

The light around him was changing to a dusty amber glow as the day turned to dusk and for once everything seemed quiet. Their wagon had stopped earlier in the day, the horse that pulled it had been released to graze. The guards walked methodically around the wagon cages, occasionally checking locks or giving each other a polite greeting but they didn't speak in depth. Even the rustling sounds of the captured animals, the lions and tigers, the groans of the camels and bulls, were minimal, as if the entire entourage had agreed to take a well needed nap.

Csoda fell into the calm, letting the call of the cicadas in nearby trees sing to him, letting the peace of the moment refresh him. He gazed out towards the space in the wall. Somewhere along the journey the boards had cracked and moved away from each other slightly. The space was just big enough for him to put his flattened hand through, but not his wrist. The guards had repaired it by bracing its edges with brass plates on the outside, but Csoda could still see out of it. It did not provide him with much of a view, but he could at least imagine that the shimmer of blue he saw in the top half of it was a lucky glimpse of the ocean or sky.

As he stared there was a flutter of movement, a slight hum in the air, and what he thought was just a passing leaf caught in a small spiral of wind suddenly proved to be something more intelligent. "A bird perhaps?" He thought, until the fluttering creature suddenly flew through the crack and Csoda was faced with a large hovering hawk moth that began inspecting their prison. The moth was the size of, and moved like, a small hummingbird. Its striped body darted around their cell, a rusted red brown color flashed with its fast beating wings. It hovered close to the ceiling for a moment and then instantly dropped to just over an inch above the barren floor, only to change course again and zig zag back up towards the ceiling. Its flight was fluid, but chaotic, as if it was desperately searching for flowers that didn't exist, or maybe a resting place to sleep.

"He is beautiful... isn't he?" Biro spoke and Csoda startled slightly at hearing his friend's voice. Biro sat up, staring at the moth that now hovered in the corner opposite him. For a few minutes they both simply watched. Then Biro spoke again, "They are good luck you know. We used to see them at dusk in the hills, right before an evening hunt. When we did we always had a good catch. They help you move through darkness."

Csoda nodded, he had seen these creatures, knew their meaning, but he had never seen one of them up close in such an isolated, confined space. In the fields they blended with the grass, flew with the wind, were part of an expanding landscape. But here, against the dark walls of their dimly lit cage, the moth was an intricately detailed splash of unexpected colors, patterns and movement. Then something occurred to Csoda. Biro's familiarity and admiration of the creature sparked an idea, and Csoda decided to try something.

Tapping Biro on the arm he got his attention. He wrote quickly in the sand next to him and pointed to the moth. "Remember how you felt before a hunt." Biro raised a curious eyebrow, but the look on Csoda's face was one of obvious excitement and so he tried to comply. Biro believed that Csoda wanted him to talk about his home in the Turul Mountains, so he began to explain out loud. However, Csoda quickly shook his head, signaled him to be quiet, and reached over and patted on Biro's chest above his heart. Then he wrote in the sand again, "Feel. Remember."

Biro nodded, though he did not fully understand. He leaned his large back against the wall and concentrated on the moth. He tried to remember the days that seemed so far away they hardly felt real anymore.

Dusk in the hills where Biro's people frequently hunted often included fog. Not always thick fog, but snake like shifting fog that slid through the tall grass and through the brush. The fog picked up the subtle shades and colors of the setting sun, and the sky was often a display of gold and purple. The dramatic results were entire hillsides that shifted with the color and light of the sky. Everything seemed to glow, the horses coat's shimmered, the air thick with an opalescent golden light. Even the hunter's dusted skin looked like rich amber sap, their beards and hair rimmed with the sunset. Their smiles were wide and heartfelt, their voices deep and resonating with laughter. On evenings like this they could see the hawk moths hovering over the brush at the lip of the forest they were about to enter. The quick flying omens would dart from flower to flower as their horses pushed through the tall grass. The moths seemed to rejoice with the hunters, their fast beating wings matched the tremor of the men's own excited hearts. Whether boar or stag, rabbit or pheasant, abundance was sure to be theirs, their families would be well fed.

Biro remembered. He remembered the feel of the brisk wind. He remembered the powerful movement of his horse. He remembered hearing his brothers laugh as he laughed with them. He remembered the joy, the beat of his excited heart, the race through the woods, the sighting of the stag, and the hunt. The joy and love of the hunt. He remembered the gratitude for his well fed tribe, the comfort of seeing their women preparing warm clothing with the skins of his catch, clothing that would keep them safe and warm through the winter. He remembered, and the love he felt for his life seemed to explode beyond him. The love reached from his simple humble form and united with the sky, the forest, and the earth. He remembered joy...pure, exalted, unfettered joy.

The feeling of joy washed over him now. It came from the depths of his memory and hovered within him even as he pulled himself back to his current dark reality. Then he realized that Csoda was excitedly pounding the floor, laughing as best as he could without his tongue, making a strange coughing sound. Biro felt a slight tickle on his hand and, still mesmerized, he looked down to see the Hawk Moth sitting quietly in his palm. For the first time since he could remember, Biro began to cry. A releasing cry of a thousand wounds gently began to flow from his eyes. It was not a sob but a quiet steady movement of thick streaming tears. Csoda, on the other hand, was ecstatic, and reached over, slapping Biro's shoulder as if in congratulations. He excitedly wrote in the sand, "You can learn The Pull," and then he went back to tapping the floor and clapping, unable to contain himself.

Despite Csoda's ruckus, the moth rested in Biro's cupped hands. Biro sat quietly, the tears still flowing. He dared not move to wipe them for fear of scaring the delicate creature he held. So he simply let the tears stream down his face unimpeded as he stared at the moth in fascination. Inside, his heart felt as if it was bursting and his mind had gone quiet. He sat for the rest of the evening, guarding the resting moth, long after Csoda fell asleep. When the break of dawn came the small creature lifted up out of his hands, hovered briefly before his eyes and darted out through the crack in the wall. Biro, who had stared in awe of it for the entire night, didn't even feel tired.

8

Húzza Művészet- translated as The Art of the Pull or Pulling Art. The secret of the magic was masked by its name, for The Art of the Pull was not, as it may be assumed, about taking or even pulling anything at all.

Instead, its power came from the ability to intensely connect with others–both human and animal–to connect and give strength to the living world as the living world returned that strength. This was a magical art, but one that could not be controlled by mere sorcery.

Truly evil human beings, while they could feel and recognize the power, could never really understand it nor master its technique. Individuals of not such noble character who began to learn the techniques would be transformed by practicing the art and could not hold on to both a corrupt nature and the knowledge of The Pull at the same time.

Csoda and Biro's people had once been a considerable force, living in tribes that numbered in the thousands. Split into multiple clans, their population was spread out and each tribe moved independently across the Nagy Föld and beyond on horseback.

Some traveled as herdsman, some as shepherds, and others as hunters. What they all had in common was a bond of strength and a powerful connection to nature, as well as an unbreakable relationship to the spirited horses that carried them. It was this connection with nature and each other where they had learned what they called the Húzza Művészet.

The Húzza Művészet was a type of psychic connection that terrified those of other cultures who did not understand it. It was a magic that grew as the nomadic tribal numbers increased. The more people that knew the art, or simply had a natural ability to accidentally tap into its power, the more the affects of the Húzza Művészet were amplified. This meant that when war did come into their lives, and they pulled together, they created an intense energy that could be felt by both their enemies and their allies. Those who witnessed their tribes in battle would tell miraculous stories afterwards.

"On the clearest of days... no rain for weeks... we met them in the open fields, and as their army approached and their horses lined across the horizon, a storm built up in the sky behind them. By the time our swords clashed the blue sky had turned black and the rain poured down mercilessly, blinding us as with sheets of water. Yet they, the Törzsi Nomádok, fought as if their eyes were clear, as if the mud did not pull on and anchor the legs of their steeds."

"They can speak to the animals...it must be true...for my most loyal and brave hound refused to attack them. Our war hardened and best trained horses acted wild and untamed..."

"It was like nothing I had ever experienced, and I dare say I hardly think I can explain it. They sing in battle and their voices

engulf you. The air around me crackled with energy, like light-ning had struck nearby. The hairs on my arms rose up and my heart was filled with a sudden sadness and regret. How could I fight such men?"

"We clashed in a great battle, like none I have been in before or since. I have never seen such warriors. They could easily jump from the backs of their horses to the ground and then back onto the horses again. They ran along the backs of the running herd as if it was a strategic hilltop. Their arrows came down on us like rain. I have never seen such speed, such strength. I was lucky to survive, but...and this feels strange to say...I have felt grateful to have witnessed such...art in movement."

"Their horses can climb cliff sides...or fly... I do not know how else to explain it..."

"They can see in the dark..."

"They have no fear..."

Story after story from different armies would confirm the tales told by others. Many said that the nomadic tribes were known to sing through battle, that their music was the pounding rhythm and gaits of the horse's hooves, their songs the boom of thunder and their voices the wail of the wind of a powerful storm.

It was said that if the enemy retreated they would find no relief in running, for the tribes were known to pursue their enemies day and night. They raced at top speeds with a herd of loose horses, some that they brought with and some that they gathered from the fallen. Leaping from one steed to the other as they moved, or even standing on the backs of two at once, they ensured that their animals were never as burdened with weight as those that they chased. They carried dried meat and bladders filled with water on their belts and it was even said they were so adept at riding they took turns, some leading and some sleeping on moving horses. This meant that they rarely stopped, rarely fell behind, and, with the addition of what could only be described as magic, they were able to stay strong and unified for days on end. It did not take them long to chase down anyone they pursued and it was impossible for the armor-laden enemies to catch them if the tides were turned.

They were called *wind runners* in the fields and *cliff jumpers* in the steep hills. They rode through different terrains as freely as a wild herd, their horses never balking at obstacles, leaping and racing, climbing the muddy banks and swimming through deep rivers.

If a nomad's horse struggled on an unstable or rocky ground they would leap off their backs, running beside them, helping the horse progress if needed. Then, once past the obstacle, they ran seamlessly beside the horses and leapt back onto the moving creature.

Even the women with babies and young children would arrive and disappear with unimaginable speed on what appeared to be at first glance, a band of wild horses. They were never daunted by rough terrain or distance and it seemed that they were shielded from the weather, natural elements and animals of all kinds.

If they had to escape into the desert in the midday heat, the sky would uncharacteristically cloud over, shading their path. If they ran from an enemy into the mountain ranges, the snow would hold back until they passed and then turn into a merciless blizzard when their enemies tried to follow. If they traveled in lands known for vicious predators, they and their horses were left alone. Bold wolves, bears and even lions ran from their camps–the same animals that chose to attack the camps of their enemies.

For many years it seemed they were unstoppable. At best the Emperor's campaigns merely kept them from traveling closer to the edges of his territory. However, the Emperor's resources were strong, the population of Critias massive, and though many battles were lost, Coracis kept sending in more troops year after year.

He made sure that along with direct battle his troops hunted extensively in the Nagy Fold whenever possible, depleting it of its once abundant game. The Legions were even ordered to kill off the nomadic herds of sheep and horses in great number if they could find them. Coracis also gave favors and wealth to other kingdoms that bordered the nomad's territory for doing the same.

Though the nomads had once been a massive force to be reckoned with, over time they suffered from the endless wave of wars and oppression that were imposed upon them through the years. They were forced to move more often, through all seasons, and this affected their ability to recoup resources and their strength.

The Empire's Legions became more adept at resisting the empathy that The Art of the Pull imposed on their men. In stories, the nomads were given titles of demons or described as lazy and stupid. The Legionnaires, as a result, grew colder and more brutal, and the Emperor ordered that when found and conquered the tribe's people, their horses, and all of their supplies should be completely destroyed.

Their tribes became drastically smaller and their people, mourning the deaths of those they loved, fell into dark depression and fear. With these changes the magic, the Húzza Művészet, became weaker, until even those who were well versed in the magic found themselves occasionally lost and disconnected from its power. Some families and individuals, seeing the coming destruction as inevitable, left the tribal lands, hiding their culture if they could as they attempted to blend in with the peoples of neighboring kingdoms.

The tribes became more and more distant from each other. Their family groups grew smaller in numbers. People in other cultures feared them. They were labeled as sorcerers, witches, con men and thieves.

Even in these weakened states, disconnected from their tribes and the knowledge of The Pull, it was said that the magic still worked through them. However, despite the dark rumors that followed their culture, the tales told about them still held a tinge of respect, a hint of awe at the nomad's very nature and connection with the world around them. It was rumored that even the most untrained of their people could change the course of events for others nearby simply by walking through a room. Their connecting and empowering nature was so unintentionally strong that before anyone knew what had happened, weakened men would stand, silent men would sing, confused men would find meaning and–in times of oppression–revolutions would begin.

9
___

belardus, stripped of his armor and weapons, sat with his ankles and wrists bound, tied to a wooden wagon wheel and facing the campfires of his captors. His men had survived, though some of them were injured. All of them were stripped of their armor and weapons and spread throughout the nomad's camp, bound and tied to trees and wagons, far enough away from each other so that they could not speak. The two he could still see were positioned so their backs faced him, robbing them of the ability to signal to each other or read each other's expressions.

Their horses were stripped of saddles, bridals and supply packs before being led to join the herd of grazing horses that freely roamed at the edge of the camp. The supply packs had been rummaged through and all of the contents taken somewhere out of his view.

His shame was overwhelming.

A deep lump in his gut rolled within him as he recognized that he and his men had been plucked out of the fog like a covey of dull witted quail. He hated that he was a captive and would have preferred to die in the attack. They had fought hard, but the massive tribe had overwhelmed them. He was appalled at himself and unforgiving of his actions as he recognized that he was the one who led them directly into the trap, straight into the surprise attack in the thick fog.

He could not blame his men, they all fought bravely. The nomads that first attacked them, grabbing at their legs and reins, had paid for their eagerness with decent wounds. In the end the Legionnaires were done in by the heavy rope nets thrown over their heads and the sheer number of nomads that they faced. They had struggled against what had felt like a hundred strong hands as they were dragged from their horses and rolled in the nets until they lay bound in cocoons of rope, like flies tied up by an efficient nest of spiders.

Now Abelardus wondered why they had captured him and his men at all? If they simply wanted to rid themselves of being followed after stealing from the Legion encampment then surely they would just kill them. Instead they went to great efforts to avoid that result. The nomads had even taken to doctoring and healing the wounds of their captives after the skirmish. They bound him, but they placed leather strips and wool between the rope to make his bonds more comfortable. They offered him water and food, and they made sure he was escorted politely away from where he sat and given a modicum of privacy in some taller brush when he needed to relieve himself.

However, none of them tried to directly communicate with him aside from these basic offerings. He was not brought to a leader or chief. He could not recognize exactly who their leaders were, as it was hard for him to identify the hierarchy structure that they lived by. There did not seem to be a formality to any of their interactions together. They laughed and spoke with each other as if they were a giant family, a massive band of close brothers.

He had thought for a moment that a burly man who wore a thick fur pelt on his shoulders that draped down his back stood out as a leader, but as the late afternoon air grew colder, more of the men wore similar furs or pelts of wool. All of their clothing had decorative stitching and their leather tunics, vests, hats and boots were covered in ornate and uniquely tooled designs. The designs might be meaningful, but were too foreign for Abelardus to understand. Nowhere did he see any symbols or particular ornaments that he could recognize as symbols of social or military ranking.

To his dismay and disbelief, his two traitorous hounds lounged contentedly at the feet of his enemies. Their tongues lolled as they happily stretched across the ground near the fires. Not only had the dogs failed to warn him of the massive ambush, they now fed happily on the leftover bones handed to them by men cooking at the fires. One would have thought they were raised within this tribe and not in the kennels of the Emperor's military. Abelardus could not make sense of this, as these were the same dogs he had taken into many battles, the same dogs who had thrown themselves in front of oncoming enemies without hesitation in the past. Usually these hounds were eager to bare their fangs at strangers or alert the troops with deep rumbling barks that sprung from the base of their bellies. These were war dogs that took it upon themselves to attack when his men were threatened. Yet here they were, rolling over and acting like friendly puppies with the nomads. The sight of it was perplexing.

While he contemplated this strange change in his hounds, he noticed the usual sounds and social manners of the camp changing. The rustle of men and animals, the raucous laughter and animated conversations peppered with the occasional bellow of a hearty yell were quieting. As the sun set the camp became more and more calm and as each man grabbed a share of the cooked food they retired to the edge of the campfires to sit and eat in silence, one by one. As each man settled, the noise in the camp reduced until with the last red glow of dusk the camp became ghostly quiet. Only the occasional sounds of humble human movement, the crackle of fires and the distant rustle of grazing horses could be heard. The entire camp ate in complete silence.

What Abelardus had expected was to be surrounded by a loud and riotous camp of barbarians who would, with the cover of a darkened night, fall into drunken and boastful song, stories or fighting. What he witnessed confused him, and while watching this silent camaraderie amongst these men Abelardus grew surprisingly relaxed. His energy and heart felt a tug of admiration and a deep awe for his captors. The manners of these nomads seemed otherworldly to him, for in their common silence they remained linked together in an indescribable way.

The quiet allowed him to attend to his thoughts. Despite his anger and shame at being tricked and held captive, he marveled at how this tribal army, easily over a hundred men strong, had set up such an effective ambush. He was impressed with their ability to train their horses to lie so quietly in the thick fog. Whatever skill this was, or perhaps magic, Abelardus decided it was this same ability that must be responsible for taming the teeth of the Legion's war hounds.

Easily an hour passed in the silent camp. The dusky light turned to black sky filled with a canopy of stars and shining with rich celestial light. The full moon peeked out from the east, leaving a halo of navy and indigo on the horizon. The fires crackled and sparked as wood was occasionally added to the flames. The wind sung an ambient melody, the herds settled into a still sleep, and the men still sat quietly. Finished with their food, they leaned back against their bedrolls or saddles propped up on the ground. They drank warmed mare's milk mixed with blood, spices and liquor from hand tooled leather cups.

In the distance, the sound of howling wolves drifted across the night sky but noone seemed to fear the calling predators. One of the nomads stood up from the fire in front of Abelardus, turned toward him and, to his surprise, brought him a cup of the warmed milk, placing it in front of his mouth. The nomad looked down at the ropes that bound Abelardus' hands and, as if in apology, he smiled and motioned for him to drink. Abelardus drank what proved to be a sour and spicy concoction that instantly warmed the back of his throat. The man nodded and then returned to his place at the campfire, leaving Abelardus alone again with his curious thoughts.

The cries of the distant wolves disappeared into the night, the wind replacing them with a chorus of rustling grass. A vibrating hum started softly, a rhythmic sanding sound that seemed to float out of the blackened night. So subtly did the sound enter his head that Abelardus first questioned if he heard it at all. Then he wondered if it had always been present and he just did not notice it before.

The drink had warmed his body, his muscles relaxed and the ambient light of the entire world seemed to change. The men at the fires were dark silhouettes with golden outlines that danced with the flicker of the flames. The stars had halos of gold and Abelardus could see that the moon was the gleaming silver wheel of Luna's chariot, spinning with the vibrating hum.

It wasn't until the first trickle of a more punctuated rhythm reminiscent of falling rain penetrated the night that Abelardus realized the sounds came from a lone figure standing at the farthest edge of the camp. Upon seeing the figure he first felt fear, not knowing what form of creature he was looking upon. Briefly he wondered if he was witnessing a vision of the hunter Actaeon being changed into a stag by the goddess Diana. The figure he observed had the body of a man draped in fur, ropes and bells, but his head was crowned with branched antlers. He held a round shield like drum in one hand while his other quickly tapped the drum surface with dancing fingertips, producing the trickling rain of sound.

The antlered figure danced around the fires, ever so slowly getting closer to where Abelardus sat. The complicated sound of the rhythm increased in speed, as did the figure's prancing movements. Eventually, a deep rumbling hum vibrated from his belly and throat until it almost seemed impossible to believe that so many sounds could come from one instrument and one man.

In this strange music one could hear the echo of the Steppe in the building song, storms of rain, running horses, the leaping stags and howling wolves. His fingers tapped the edges of the leather drum, his palms drummed the vibrating center, his hand slid across the tight leather to create the sanding sound, his voice vibrated over it all. It was at once a rhythm and a melody with no true distinction over which was more prominent, for each existed equally together.

Abelardus felt physically drawn towards this figure, the sounds reaching deep into his being. He felt a pressure in his chest as if the drum was inside of him, vibrating out through his heart, echoing in his rib cage and traveling up his spine. He could not escape the sound, or the feelings it pulled out from the depths of him. By the time the antlered man came close enough for Abelardus to see him in detail, the sound was fully embedded inside of his vibrating core.

He could see that the antlers were a part of the man's headdress, fitted tightly onto his head with a band of leather. Behind the antlers was a fan of owl feathers. A beaded curtain fell down from the rim of the headdress hiding the man's face and head. His hair was a dreadlocked mane of deep black and brown that arched up behind his head and dropped down in massive ropes against his back.

His clothes were pieced together patches of different colored leather and fur sewn into a long tunic that nearly touched the ground. His drum was covered with intricate designs and symbols shaped into the forms of stags and flying hawks. He wore brass bells that dangled from his hair, wrists, and ankles and around his neck and waist there were necklaces and belts made of animal bones, feathers, teeth and swatches of fur. This, Abelardus assumed, was a shaman, for he was unlike any of the other nomads in appearance and the song he sang was more powerful than that of a simple bard.

Abelardus watched as the shaman danced in jerky steps around the nomads and their campfires, weaving his way towards him. Then, suddenly, the antlered shaman was directly in front of him, smelling of campfires, incense, burning flesh and hair. Swaying, jerking and dancing like an otherworldly bird of prey, he hovered in front of and above Abelardus. The drumming slowed, the shaman's hand slid, sanding against the surface of the leather. He crouched in front of Abelardus, cocking his head to one side. The beaded curtain opened slightly, exposing two ice blue eyes framed by blackened halos of smudged ashes.

Those eyes held Abelardus' gaze like iron braces and pierced his mind. A sensation of warm gel filled his head and moved down his spine into his heart and stomach, mixing with the knot of feelings the drum had awoken in him earlier.

The shaman spoke in growling bursts of sound that came from deep in his chest. His words entered Abelardus' mind, into the feeling of flowing liquid that now filled his entire being, rendering him helpless to respond. He was a mere witness to his own thoughts and as the words of the shaman entered his body he realized that he could understand them. He did not know the language but their essence mixed with his, and his mind spoke them back to him in a translation.

The words the Shaman pressed into him with his focused gaze and growling voice were, "Who Are You?"

The question was repeated insistently, but Abelardus did not feel like the question was aimed at him. Instead it was aimed at the flood of feelings that swirled in his gut and heart. It was aimed at his shame, at his failure, at his desire to die for being weakened and caught. It was aimed at his pride, at his worry and at his anger. His anger.

The question grabbed hold of his anger, yanked it up through his chest and pulled from the anger his fear...his fear...his fear...it held onto his fear. All of the flowing liquid flooded to and surrounded his fear, moving it up through his spine and neck. For a moment it seemed to get caught in his throat, making him feel like he was choking. The shaman moved closer, his unblinking eyes looked into Abelardus who shook uncontrollably, gasping for air. Those eyes searched beyond the soldier's gaze. They focused on the ball of liquid fear and, with a hushed whisper, the shaman sent the words once again into Abelardus, "Who are you?"

Abelardus' body convulsed, his mouth dropped opened and out of the fear caught in his throat came a black, swirling, oily smoke.

Upon seeing the smoke the shaman backed up, his spine undulating like a serpent. His focus left Abelardus and aimed instead at the wisp of smoke that moved in front of him. The shaman's hand continued to move in a circle on the drum and as the sanding shifting sound emanated from the drum, the smoke moved with the speed of the sound. The smoke grew in size and took on a ghostly form, one moment a snarling face in profile, the next a wispy black skeleton of a spiraling tower. Again the shaman asked in a guttural hum, "Who are you?"

The smoke's snarling profile answered, hissing, "I aaaaammmmm Uuuuraaalom...I aaaammm Empiiiire." The Shaman moved like a hawk on the ground who faced a serpent. He drummed with a determined and precise rhythm. The smoke responded by snarling and hissing in front of him, and then the profile came again...this time it sneered, "Iiiii ammm moooore than onnnne....Iiiii ammm maaannny...I am Uraaalom...Iiii aaammm Empiiiire...yooou caaannn do nothing against meeee."

The shaman cocked his head again, staring at the smoke, his drumming stopped, the quiet of the camp returned, the smoke creature hissed in front of him and then–then the shaman began to laugh.

A true and full laugh came from the core of his belly. He put his drum down on the ground and sat cross-legged in front of the demon and he laughed. From his laughter, a song began to form, a full and hearty song, a joy filled song.

Clapping in front of himself he laughed and sang and the smoke began to quiver, becoming more and more transparent even as it shook in agitation. For a moment the wispy creature seemed to strike out towards the shaman like a snake, but instead of reaching him it dissipated into the air, hissing, "Iiiii ammmm Uuuuraaalom...yoouu caannn do nothing against meee..." The hiss gurgled into the subtle sound of a drowning scream right before it evaporated into the air. The shaman kept clapping, kept singing, and now the rest of the tribe joined in, humming quietly and clapping along.

Abelardus had fallen back in shock when the smoke was pulled from his throat, but he watched the surreal event from a strange state of calm. His body felt lighter, his emotions cleared. He was empty. That was the only way he could have described his current lifted thoughts and the lightness in his body.

Nothing he had witnessed made sense to him, he did not understand these people, or their magic, or the smoke creature that had come from his own body. He did not even feel like trying to understand. He simply observed that the light of the campfires seemed brighter, the stars clearer and the entire tribe was now singing a melodic and sedated tune.

The shaman slowly stood and walked away until the black night hid him from sight. Abelardus tried to stay awake, tried to see where the shaman went, but the cool air of the night and his exhaustion overtook him. The last thing he remembered was relaxing just slightly against the wheel. He drifted into a hazy sleep and right before his eyes shut, his hounds, the dogs who had failed him against this strange army, walked up to him and laid against his legs and side, keeping him warm.

10

———

In the days following Biro's encounter with the hawk
moth, the personalities of the two trapped men seemed
to switch. Biro's usual brash, bold and aggressive manner
quieted, his booming voice hushed. At the same time Csoda
became more energetic, prone to bursts of comical movements and spasmodic dances. He even took to occasionally
entertaining himself by laying against the open slit in the
wall and peeking with his boney bearded face through the
crack at weird angles, making faces or laughing manically
with a gurgling sound as he exposed his tongueless mouth
to the guards standing outside.

The change in behavior was noticeable enough that the
guards wondered if both men were ill. In response, they
stood further away from the wagon and eventually made
reports to the Ringmaster. The Ringmaster, hardly personally concerned with the weakening of captives, was more
interested than normal in these two men for they were
different than the others.

Biro had caught the attention of the Ringmaster once
before. In one of the last performances in the Capital's

Grand Kirkos, in which Biro was sent into the ring with a group of convicts. This specific show was meant to show the convicts getting picked off by a dozen lions that were released into the ring with the men. Biro had stood for a while with the trembling group, but at some point he stepped away from the others and walked boldly up to one of the beasts. The Ringmaster watched as Biro approached one of the starved lions and the crowd responded to the man's courage with raucous laughter and cheers that eventually built into a unison stomping throughout the coliseum. Perhaps it was Biro's confident stride that frightened, or at least confused, the mangy lion. Perhaps it was the sound of the stomping crowd. In either case the lion retreated. Biro then continued herding the first lion towards the other beasts, the entire time using his deep voice to chant a rhythmic song. In the end the lions proved to be more afraid of the roaring crowds and the aggressive chanting man than they were hungry for human flesh.

Even the Ringmaster had to smile when, to the delight and amazement of the crowd, Biro skillfully herded the lions towards the stands that held the royalty. There, with the beasts huddled before him, he let loose an eerie wail of triumph while staring directly at the Emperor himself. The crowd went wild. The large cats scattered and retreated to the darkened coves around the arena. The Ringmaster signaled to his guards to open the gates and let the big cats leave as well as the uneaten slaves.

If Biro had been another man from a different culture the Ringmaster may have pardoned him for his brave act and skill, but the Emperor was noticeably insulted and shaken by Biro's defiant wail. Before the Ringmaster could interfere, the Emperor sent a dozen guards to swarm in on Biro. The Emperor's decision infuriated the crowd, who expected Biro to gain favor, and they grew angry and restless. The Ringmaster, recognizing the danger of an angry mob, acted quickly, placating them with a speech that implied Biro would be favored. Then he quickly distracted them by feeding their insatiable blood lust with the public killing of the Beast Master, the man responsible for the lion's training.

The Emperor had insisted that Biro must be killed. The Ringmaster uncharacteristically, yet politely, countered the Emperor's desires, suggesting that Biro be thrown into the next Kirkos event to die. By then, he reasoned convincingly, the people would have forgotten him and would not blame the Emperor for being unfair. The Emperor had agreed, hesitant to make a martyr out of a slave. Pleased, the Ringmaster set Biro aside, away from the other slaves. A part of him enjoyed the hunter's obvious showmanship and believed that putting him in future events would prove entertaining for the crowd and, ultimately, beneficial to his pocket.

Biro was marched with the other left over captives back into the caravan wagons. A few months later, Csoda, half dead, was handed over to the Kirkos by the Emperor's guards along with a message. The Ringmaster's earlier conversation with the Emperor about Biro had obviously made an impression. The Emperor did not want Csoda to be a martyr figure, and he feared a simple execution would do just that. The Emperor's message was clear, the Ringmaster should rid him of this nomad revolutionary by having him die in a mass spectacle, one where he was just another man among many.

Yes, these captives were different. They represented the enemies of the Empire of Critias and to destroy them would support the Emperor's power. So, upon hearing of their potential sickness the Ringmaster considered letting them die of disease. However, there was no profit in slaves dying unseen. Their life was worth at least one Kirkos event. The Ringmaster was not on a mission of simple execution of the Emperor's enemies. His life was devoted to profit, above all else, and so he ordered increased care and medical attention.

Csoda and Biro were both surprised when the guards began sending them full meals, two, sometimes even three times a day, and regular fresh water. Twice a week they were given leather buckets full of hot water scented with the intense sweet smell of medicinal herbs and oils so that they could wash themselves. A doctor was even appointed to check on them, and the guards removed a couple of the wooden slates to be replaced with metal bars so that the doctor could peek in and occasionally observe them.

Sometimes, the doctor handed them thick dollops of healing salves and the occasional cup of medicinal tinctures. Csoda would take these medicines and, cackling with his choppy tongueless laugh, distribute half to Biro and half to himself. Biro, who had taken to sitting in the opposite corner of the open barred window, took the medicines from Csoda, but otherwise he simply sat, staring blankly ahead.

The doctor reported "An Infection In The Head or Spirit" and stated that physically they would most likely survive the rest of the travel, given decent care, but mentally they had gone insane. This was acceptable to the Ringmaster, as their sanity was of no concern to him. So the regular care continued, but the doctor visits became less and less.

More than anything, the greatest gift of this change for Csoda was the open barred window. The wind came through that window and Csoda leaned against the wall, pressing his face against the bars. His eyes rolled up into his head as his eyelids fluttered shut, and he took in long full breaths of the wind. The sun came through that window, and Csoda lay in its beams, letting it darken his skin. The stars came through that window, and Csoda stared at them for hours in the black night, reading their familiar tales and trying to interpret their current meaning.

The world came through that window, and Csoda could see the camels, oxen and horses that carried riders, pulled wagons, or moved in herds alongside them. He could see the train of wagons that snaked along behind and in front of their cage. Some of them were boarded up as theirs had been, their contents unknown. Others were built as barred cages, their contents exposed for all to see. Csoda could finally see what was contained within them, tawny thin lions, pacing cheetahs and snarling black wolves.

Biro, too, looked out the new window from his corner seat. The experience with his memories and the magic that had attracted the hawk moth to his hands opened up a portal of sorts in Biro's being. While Csoda insisted that the experience with the moth was evidence that Biro could learn The Art of the Pull, the memory of joy made Biro even more aware of the confines of his current existence in the boxed cage. The open window only mocked him, emphasizing the blocked out expanse of sky he had lived without. It made him fully comprehend his loss, his people's loss, Csoda's loss. All they had lost was painfully apparent to him now.

Csoda was sympathetic to Biro's mood, he knew that the new form of sanity that his friend was experiencing was mind altering but also could be devastatingly sad. Still, having experienced a similar awakening himself in the past he was not overly concerned with Biro's change in personality. He called Biro's malaise "the pain of being reborn to truth" and went about focusing on his own physical rebirth by exercising and stretching his still weakened muscles when the guards or the doctor were not around.

When the guards or other people were close enough to observe him, Csoda continued to act weak. At these times he would lay with his eyes shut, secretly refocusing his mind in a hidden state of meditation. Sometimes he entertained himself by cackling madly and carrying on in front of the guards as if he was seeing things.

Biro participated with Csoda in the physical exercises, though he no longer performed them with intensity. He ate the newly provided food, drank the water, and washed, but he did these activities more mechanically. The intense anger that had kept him alive in this current hell was weakened. The adrenaline he had survived on for years loosened its grip. He felt an exposed, raw and swollen heart expanding in his chest, making it hard for him to breath or move. He escaped mentally again and again, into his memories, sitting in a borderline catatonic state as he did so, only to groan in angry disappointment when he allowed his focus to come back to the moment in front of him. He preferred the world in his sleep and his imagination to the waking hell of his reality.

In the past his dreams were simple, or non-existent. But now–now he walked through the pastures of his homeland. He rode through the forest. He wept with his brothers. He saw her–again and again–he saw her in his dreams. He saw the flashing glint of light dance in her black almond eyes. He saw the occasional hint of dark auburn highlight her thick plated black hair. He heard her quietly breathing as she slept. He heard her laughter as she stood in the forest. He heard her ask him with a voice of dark silk, "Biro... what is to become of us?"

11

———

In times before, when the Emperor's rule and conquest was merely a rumor in the forests, mountains and fields of the nomadic lands, Biro's clan, the Észak- Vadászok, lived as hunters. They traded their furs, meat, and horses with their tribal clans and tradesmen from other kingdoms. Their skill in hunting allowed them to prosper and they lived well. They could always feed and clothe themselves and their families. They could even afford the luxuries of oil, cheese, spices and quality metal to make tools, weapons and jewelry. Their pastoral cousins in the southern lands of the Nagy Föld provided them with goat and sheep milk, fresh roots and wool, which helped them face the harsh winters. They had good relations with the distant traders who brought them exotic spices, teas, dried fruits, oils, dyes, fish and exotic shells from distant oceans. Sometimes the traders would have special requests, skins of special animals, or live animals for them to sell to the far away cities.

This was how Biro's people lived and Biro, as a young man, was very comfortable in this abundant life. While some of his fellow clansmen became enamored with hunting exotic game in exchange for gold and expensive tools or weapons, Biro preferred to hunt in solitary for more traditional game. He was often content to catch a deer or a good sized hare to cook with salt over the fire, feeding himself and his brothers, sisters, and tribe as the leaders and shamans told the tales of truth in hypnotic verse or songs under the stars.

It was on one of these solitary hunts that Biro followed a stag into a distant forest on the edge of his clan's familiar territory. Upon entering the forest he strongly sensed that he was not alone. How he knew this is hard to say, he may have noticed the way his horse perked his ears. Perhaps he caught the scent of leather and fire on a slight wisp of air. Or maybe it was the way the stag he had followed changed course dramatically, as if it was being pursued on two sides.

However it was he knew, Biro felt sure that he was right, and instead of pursuing the fleeing stag he chose to slow his horse and tuck into the deeper brush between the trees. He gingerly navigated his horse onto some softer moss and soil to reduce the sound of their movement. He still faced in the general direction of his quarry, hating to lose a good chance at a prize stag, but his concern now shifted from the hunt to the presence of an unknown human nearby.

His intuition soon proved correct as the sound of a cantering horse echoed through the woods, becoming louder as it grew nearer. Biro backed himself and his horse behind tall brush and forest ferns. He signaled his horse, which obediently lowered itself, front legs first to the ground and quickly laid down on its side. This allowed Biro to maneuver his own body and lay with his belly flat on the broad side of the massive animal. He pulled some of the fern fronds to arch over both of them and ensure they were effectively hidden. Biro reached out calmly to rub the horse's ears, helping the animal remain calm and quiet his breathing, thanking him for his obedience.

The oncoming rider galloped into view. Biro wasn't surprised by the rider's presence, but he was surprised by something else. The figure moving through the forest was a woman–a woman of broad stature, amber skin and dark auburn hair that was plaited in braids crowning her fore-head and falling down her back. She rode astride a tall, lean, golden horse that looked more like a statue than a living creature. Its fur glimmered with a metallic sheen, its eyes were a mirrored jade, and its graceful light-footed movement seemed more like the leaping of a deer than a horse.

The woman wore flowing pants made of bone white linen and a purple silk sash wrapped generously around her waist, its ends fluttering behind her. A leather armor plated vest protected her torso. Woven into her hair was a purple metal band encrusted with green jewels attached to a small cap of a brass helmet, slightly pointed at the top. Her pants were tucked into tall leather boots that fitted tight against her legs and a six inch knife sheath was attached to her right boot at her calf. A light bow and sheaf of arrows were strapped across her back and a short sword hung at her waist. She wore long leather gloves, but the rest of her arms were bare and the taut definition of muscles that could be seen in them emphasized that she likely knew how to use the weapons she carried.

A falcon cried from above the tops of the trees and the woman glanced up to look at the soaring bird, quickly adjusting the direction of her horse to match the direction it flew. Upon seeing this Biro also noticed the leather ties that hung from the falcon's legs and he nodded his head as he began to understand. She was hunting the same stag he chased, but the falcon allowed her to do so without tracking the ground.

As quickly as she appeared she rode out of sight through the thick woods, leaving Biro quietly lying in his hiding place. He watched the silhouette of the falcon above the trees grow smaller as they left him behind. He waited for a while, petting his calm horse and gently rubbing its ears, laying low and making sure that no other unknowns came thundering through the woods, or that the woman was not circling back towards his hiding spot. Then, when he was confident he was alone, he signaled his horse to stand, expertly shifting his body with the animal so that he sat on his back by the time he was fully upright.

He did not want to interfere with the hunt of the woman. Her appearance, make of weapons, horse, and flying falcon did not match any tribes or trading cultures he recognized. He would have to find new prey to hunt for the rest of the evening. He started looking for signs of rabbit warrens or other promising tracks. Soon his luck improved and he caught a good sized hare, lashed it across his saddle and made his way back to camp in the darkening evening. However, his mind remained on the strange huntress following her falcon through the woods.

It was this curiosity that brought him back to the same forest edge a few days later. He explored some rock outcroppings up in the higher hills of the forest and found a decent perch on top of a cliff ledge that looked out over the nearby forest and grasslands. He came to this perch regularly, letting his horse loose to graze as he sat on the cliff ledge and waited. He waited, sometimes for hours, sometimes for full days. He returned, again and again, at different times of the day to see if he could catch a glimpse of the falcon and the huntress on the golden horse.

One afternoon, as he watched over the forest, two horsemen appeared. Biro's first reaction was a feeling of disappointment, this was not the huntress. Then he noticed their horses. These two men, tall in stature, rode lean graceful horses that were the color of polished black stones, their manes and tales and even their eyes reflected the midday sunlight as if they were made of dark silver. They were similar to the golden horse of the huntress and they moved through the forest with the same gazelle like grace.

Biro leaned back against a rock outcropping and for the first time since he had started to watch for the huntress, he wondered why. Why had he spent hours, weeks and months riding up to and perching himself on the cliff edge scanning the forest? What was his reason for such determined curiosity? Unable to answer his own questions, he shook his head in bewilderment at his actions. Then, not wanting to be easily seen from below, he stretched out on his belly so that he could look over the edge more covertly.

From the ledge, Biro observed a small herd of deer right as a falcon flew above them. The falcon cried out in a screeching call as it turned and shot back towards the horsemen. The deer, unaware that the bird was a sign of pursuing predators, grazed unconcerned as it flew to report to the hunters what it had found. Biro's eyes followed the bird and when it passed above the two horsemen he saw a third golden horse emerge from the forest to join them. The huntress.

The huntress and the two horsemen followed the falcon towards its discovery. The bird circled above the deer, marking their position. At first the hunters moved slowly and quietly. When they had closed the gap by over three quarters of the distance, the huntress placed the reins of her horse down hooking them to a clip on her saddle and, proving to be adept at directing the animal by other means, used her free hands to remove her bow from her back and smoothly position an arrow into place. The horse moved up to the edge of the thicket where the deer grazed, then began to run. The horsemen held themselves slightly back, allowing the huntress to take the lead.

The deer were not concerned with the falcon, but they reacted to the sound and site of the oncoming horses charging out of the woods. They raised their heads sharply towards the direction of the sound, then leaped into the air and bolted in the opposite direction. Fanning out, the herd separated from each other just as the huntress was upon them. The huntress ignored the does with small fawns that shot into the thicker ferns, attempting to give cover to their young. Instead, she charged right behind a larger buck that had dashed into more open ground. The buck was fast, but the huntress already had an arrow in place and shot it skill-fully, aiming it in front of the darting stag, anticipating the direction of his flight. The stag leaped into the path of the flying arrow and it pierced through him, firmly embedding into his arching neck.

The stag stumbled, but he did not fall. While weakened, he continued to run and leap, zigzagging before the oncoming horses. The huntress had another arrow ready, again she shot at the fleeing buck, but this time he swerved and the arrow missed. Before the huntress or her compan-ions could react, the buck spun around in the air. Surpris-ingly, he ran straight towards them and then dashed like lightening past the charging horses back into the thick brush and ferns behind them. Quickly he disappeared into the depths of the forest.

The hunters could not spin so fast. Their horses had to slow down and turn, losing much needed ground. By the time they entered the forest they could no longer see their prey. The huntress whistled and looked to the sky for the falcon. The bird responded by returning to her position and then sweeping through the air above the trees, looking for the lost, injured buck.

Biro was caught in the action, his heart racing with the adrenaline of the pursuit. He was impressed with the huntress' skill both in riding and in shooting. He was also surprised by the bold stag's deft maneuver and uncharacteristic charge towards its pursuers. Biro felt admiration for both sides and, on one hand, wanted the skilled huntress to find her prey, while on the other hand, felt sad for the destruction of the bold stag. Yet, he had seen the first arrow hit the stag squarely in the neck. He was sure the animal would not survive such a lethal hit. Knowing this he found himself scanning the forest determinedly, not wanting the stag to die unfound.

The falcon flew back and forth over the last place the buck was seen. The huntress, with a watchful eye on the falcon, pushed her horse through the thick ferns. The two accompanying horsemen fanned out on either side of her, searching. All of them called back and forth to each other. Occasionally they made loud whooping sounds in hopes of spooking the animal from its hiding place. They searched for a long time, but the buck did not appear, his trail eluding them.

After many tense minutes passed, Biro noticed, far to the south of where the hunters searched, at the edge of the forest by the shore of a deep river, the silhouette of a buck appeared. At first, because of its distance from the hunters, Biro assumed it was a different animal. Then he saw the distant buck standing at the waters edge, swaying as if in a daze. Biro held his hands up to block the sun and squinted so that he could better see and there, in the side of the neck of the swaying animal, was the impaled arrow. How the stag had made it so far away from the hunters without being seen shocked Biro. He had to hold himself back from yelling down to the hunting party to alert them to the location of their dying prey. He had to remind himself that the hunters were of a different culture, unknown to him, strangers.

He reassured himself with the knowledge that surely the falcon would see their elusive prey soon and signal to the searching hunters which way to go. Yet, before the bird turned in the air in a direction that would have allowed it to see the deer, the buck, dying from the blood loss and exhaustion, stumbled forward, tipped at the edge of the river and fell into the water's depths. The slow but strong current pulled his body under and carried it downstream, hidden from the view of the falcon.

Biro gasped and pulled himself up back into a sitting position, frustrated by the futile loss of a decent hunt. Annoyed that the strong stag's death would not be honored or useful. He stood up, unconcerned with staying hidden, and called down to the hunters below, waving his arms to try to get their attention. However, the wind carried his voice away and they could not hear him and never looked up to see him on the rock ledge. He watched helplessly, as they pushed through the forest, going in the opposite direction of the southern river that now carried away the body of the fallen deer.

Biro may have attempted to ride down to their location and lead them to the stag himself but before he considered doing so the weather began to turn. The clouds above darkened the sky and carried the rumbles of an oncoming storm.

The hunting party regrouped and headed north. Seeing this overwhelmed Biro with the need to take action. Quickly, he walked back to where he had left his horse grazing, full of determined energy he swiftly gathered his supplies, mounted his horse and rode down to the bank of the distant river.

One trait Biro possessed, even at a young age, was a determined will. It was this will that kicked in when he grieved what he saw as a waste of a decent hunt. It was not just the loss of the deer, or the thought that the meat would be unused, the skins untanned, the antlers un-carved. It was the thought that the stag itself would be dishonored, ignored, its soul unsung and left to wander in between worlds. He believed such neglected deaths created haunted hunting grounds, that the disgraced animal would never be given the chance to pass into the fields of its ancestors. This thought disturbed Biro deeply. He had witnessed the miracle of this stags bravery and strength, witnessed it courageously charge the hunters that pursued it. He had witnessed it deftly escape the searching eyes of the falcon, even as it must have been delirious and confused from the loss of blood. These thoughts invoked Biro to find the body of the slain deer, even as the storm brewed up above, the same oncoming storm that had convinced the hunting party to reluctantly give up their search. It was his strong determination that had him riding along the riverbank as lightning crackled through the sky. The rain turned the bank into thick, slip-pery mud that his horse must maneuver through and around. He found the body of the stag in a downstream bend of the river. Its antlers were caught tightly in the low branches of a twisted tree that swept the surface of the flowing water. The buck was now clearly dead, its body firmly anchored under the water by a pile of snagging branches and logs.

Biro dismounted, unsheathed a long knife from his belt, and cut through the thickened entangled brush and trees that blocked him from the shore closest to the deer's body. Once there he was able to cut at the snare of branches that held the stag to finally release it and let it float out of the deadly current of the river bend and move downstream. There, in less turbulent waters, he swam out to grab the body of the deer and floated with it partway downstream until he was able to pull it up onto the nearest clear bank of sand.

Exhausted, wet, tired and cold Biro held the head of the dead stag in his hands and quietly sang the song of the hunter. He thanked the stag for his brave death and for the gift of abundance and food. He promised the stag that the body his soul had left would not be wasted, would provide food, clothing and tools. He asked the stag to forgive the hunters who where unable to find him and praised him at the same time for his cunning and skill at evading them. Then, with tears in his eyes, Biro asked the stag's soul to pass safely into the fields of the his noble ancestors, the forest of those who came before, the world beyond what we now see. Then, and only then, did Biro stop and rest, gathering the deer's body and his tired horse under the shelter of some old forest trees, he waited for the storm to pass.

If it was his concern for the stag's soul that urged his will to help him find the slain deer, it was another motivation that made him decide to search for the hunters who had lost their kill. The decision to do so barely even registered in his thoughts. Instead it came to him like an instinctual action. The next morning, after strapping the deer on the back of his horse, behind where he sat, he started riding towards the north. He crossed back through the thicket where the hunt had started and onward, beyond the forest he was familiar with and into unknown territory.

At first the hunting party tracks were hard to find, washed away by the force of the strong rain. Yet, the same wet ground that had hidden the shallow older tracks had become mud. Soon he was following the noticeable impressions of three horses, heavy with riders, pressed deep into the softened earth. He followed them north, out of the thicker forest and into a dryer landscape of sparse brush and smaller twisted trees. Hours later the hills began to flatten, the ground became dryer with patches of sand and flat slate rocks. He came across a thin creek, which had carved a crevice in the rocky ground over the years. The hot afternoon was upon him and he was hungry and tired. His horse held its head low in a slow walk. The trail of horse hooves were still noticeable to him, though their occurrence was now only visible in patches of softer earth, divided by the shifting sand beds and impenetrable sections of rock.

As long as he had their trail in sight he was unconcerned about traveling in the foreign land. While the tribes of his people preferred to frequent the open and more lush plains where their valuable horses had ample grass, they were a nomadic people. They occasionally crossed over into the desert or to the shores of the sea to trade with other cultures, pursue exotic game, avoid uncommonly harsh weather, or to simply explore. For this reason Biro was not concerned with his environment, and the landscape was open enough to his view that he was not worried about being ambushed. Plus, he had no reason to fear these hunters he pursued, at least not yet.

He wanted to continue, guessing that he could not be far from where the huntress and the horsemen had come from.

However, his own hunger and his weary horse would need to be addressed. So he followed the thin creek, which eventually led him to a place where it collected into a small pool of clean water at the edge of a patch of lush grass, big enough to supply his horse with a good meal. He dismounted and let his horse go to drink and graze. He drank of the clean water himself, splashed his face and considered building a fire and eating some of the venison he carried. He decided against that idea, feeling a need to save the deer for the pursued hunting party ahead. Instead he contented himself with eating the dried meat he always carried at his belt and, after placing the deer in some high branches of a nearby tree, he found a small shaded patch of sand close to the waters edge where he could rest through the hotter part of the day. Eager to continue, he slept only briefly. When the hot sun lowered in the sky and the air began to barely cool, he decided to keep going, at least until the night made it too difficult to follow the tracks. He filled his leather canteen with water, retrieved the deer from the tree, packed his horse and continued on his way.

He followed the tracks for over an hour and, despite the lowering sun, the waves of hot desert air could still be seen radiating off the sands and rocks ahead of him. The dry heat wicked away all moisture, so that even the sweat on his skin could not use the wind to cool him. Ahead was nothing but a large expanse of desert, with no shelter or water for him or his horse. Even when the sun set and the air cooled, his horse would need water. He considered going back to the creek to rest into the cooler evening and start again fresh when the moon provided him with decent light. Then, suddenly, before he could turn his horse around, he saw a falcon rise up above the ground only a short distance in front of him. The bird seemed to come out of nowhere, circled briefly, and then dove down and disappeared as if it flew straight into the sand.

Biro urged his horse forward faster and gently loped to the place he had seen the bird dive, but as he rode up a slight incline he was forced to quickly pull his horse to a stop. Ahead of him, the illusion of what seemed an endless flat desert was broken. Only twenty feet from where he stopped his horse, the ledge of a barren cliff that overlooked a vast canyon fell before him. The shocking change amazed Biro and he turned his horse, backtracked forty feet and then looked again towards the cliff. The illusion of the endless desert was in front of him once more as the barren flat land in the foreground matched the cliff edge on the distant side, hiding the canyon from view.

Riding back, he laughed in amazement as the canyon opened up before his eyes. He jumped off of his horse and carefully walked up to the edge, smiling widely at the rush of warm fragrant air that met him as he viewed the green fields below.

A winding river dotted with occasional clusters of gracefully tall elegant palm trees led his eyes further down the canyon. There he could see the landscape cut into sections of agriculture with small farmhouses placed throughout the fields. Far in the distance, the valley widened and he could see the edge of steep white and tan walls that connected to the more elaborate buildings of a town. On top of a small hill the pillars of a white stone palace overlooked the fertile valley.

Biro laughed at the wonder of this hidden valley and, as he scanned the side of the cliffs for a trail or way to descend into it, he could see the nests of falcons hugging the cliff walls, the birds themselves crisscrossing the sky below him.

He walked along the edge of the canyon until he saw a

place ahead where the cliff transformed into a slightly less harsh drop off. There appeared to be what looked like the zigzagging marks of a hillside trail. Upon finding the entrance he also noticed a small group of lightly armored men on shimmering horses who appeared on the horizon of the cliff. They rode right above the zigzagging trailhead, looking and moving directly towards him.

If Biro had not yet considered that his presence in this foreign land would put him in danger, he started to consider it now. Seven horsemen came quickly towards him, their horse's nostrils flaring, their strange mirrored eyes wide with fresh energy. He did not remount, his own horse was hot and in need of water. He had no choice but to attempt a conversation with them, show them the deer and the arrow of the huntress, and hope that they would be hospitable. He stood with his arms held wide, showing that he had no weapon in hand.

The riders slowed and stopped twenty feet away, their elegant horses prancing and snorting in place. The rider in the middle moved forward a few feet, placing himself ahead of the others. His right hand rested on a small black spear that lay against his leg. His left hand held the reins of his fiery black horse whose fur shimmered like polished iron as it snorted and pawed at the ground. He yelled out words in a language foreign to Biro, but Biro guessed that they wanted him to explain his presence.

Biro bowed his head and in his own tongue he politely answered. "I am Biro of the Észak- Vadászok, one of the clans of the Törzsi Nomádok. I am returning a lost kill to one of your hunting parties." He motioned to the deer on the horses back. When he looked back at the man it was obvious that he did not know Biro's language. The man shook his head, confirming his misunderstanding.

Biro switched languages. There was a trading language that the tribes used when working with other cultures. It was a language the nomads and traders had pieced together over hundreds of years of business transactions. Biro was not an expert with this language, but he could speak a few rough sentences. He stated crudely "I am of the Nagy Föld. I found what is yours. Return it to you."

This time one of the horsemen on the sides called out to the man on the black horse and quickly spoke to him in their own tongue. The man on the black horse nodded and the new man, his hair dark and long, his horse an effervescent opal gray, moved forward. He nodded at Biro in quick greeting and then spoke to him in the trader's tongue.

"You came from the south, the Nagy Föld?"

Biro nodded.

"The deer? Is this what you found?"

Biro nodded again.

"You say the deer is ours?"

Biro hesitated. The deer was shot by the huntress. The woman who rode the golden horse, who had similar looks, clothing, and rode a similar type of horse as these men. She had been accompanied by men who looked like these men, which made Biro assume she was from this land, but the deer was hers, not this group of men in front of him. He didn't want to mistakenly give it away to the wrong people. He shook his head and held up his hand, giving himself a moment to determine how to tell them whose deer he had found. His knowledge of the trader language was limited.

Then he remembered something. He held his hand up and pointed at the supplies that his horse carried. He moved slowly back towards his horse's side and said, "Have more. Show you." The man with the long dark hair nodded and Biro reached below a flap of leather, unhooking the bronze arrow he had retrieved from the slain deer. He held it out to the man as he spoke. Upon seeing the unique arrow all of the men took in their breath. The horseman he spoke to quickly dismounted, walked up to Biro, bowed to him slightly as he held out his hands to receive the arrow. Biro placed the arrow in his hand and stated, "Who owns this, owns deer."

The man nodded then raised his head looking Biro in the eye. With a wide smile he replied, "We know this arrow. We are thankful. Ride with us." Biro nodded in agreement and the man turned to face the rest, speaking in their tongue as he held the arrow up for them to see. The horsemen all cheered, laughed and smiled, nodding to Biro happily as they signaled him to mount his horse and follow them into the valley.

12

———

Long ago Zenobia had learned the language of the Törzsi Nomádok, the nomadic tribes of the Nagy Föld, and she still found herself amazed at how useful that knowledge had proven to be. When the messenger arrived at her palace she was in the company of diplomats and court ambassadors from neighboring lands. The Emperor's Senators from the West of the Sea of AyRuh and the ambassadors from the Great Eastern nations were all present. They were eating and drinking while discussing the events of their lands when the leather clad horseman walked into her court.

Upon seeing him she couldn't help but smile at his humble confidence, it was a mark of his culture, a trait that allowed him to be composed and calm in the presence of nobility. She knew that to him these nobles were just other men and women. In the nomad's world all men and women were considered noble at birth, and he was raised knowing that he was as worthy as any other individual. He was born a Child of the Steppe and nothing could take away the confidence of a man born knowing that he was a meant to be in this world.

He showed respect, of course, went through the normal social greetings, nodding and bowing when appropriate, but his posture was relaxed. He waited to speak out of respect, but his eyes met hers unwavering, slightly tilted at the edges so that even with his composed demeanor he seemed to be smiling at her in secret.

The nobility looked on curiously. Zenobia sensed their eyes glancing towards her when they lifted the gilded goblets to their lips to sip at spiced wine. They continued to talk quietly amongst themselves, but their conversations became more hushed. The message was meant for Zenobia alone, but she also knew that the messenger would speak in his own tongue and that this was a language no one in the royal world had bothered to learn. For this reason, she felt no need to leave the event to hear what the nomad had to say. Leaving, after all, would start more dangerous rumors than staying.

She nodded her head and, in his native tongue, she told him he was free to speak.

So the messenger bowed again and then released a flood of information to her in a lyrical and complicated tongue. The nomad language was amazing, its versatile structure allowed the messenger to arrange the sentences in multiple different orders, even to form new words at a moments notice by meshing known words together. An entire sentence could actually be created out of one newly minted word by a creative speaker. This made speaking to a native in their tongue extremely complicated, even with knowledge of some of their more common phrases and words. It also made the sound of their speech almost hypnotizing as their natural tendency towards wordsmithing and poetry often turned the simplest of conversations into musical compositions.

Zenobia leaned in to focus on his message. While she had intimate knowledge of his language it was one she had learned later in life, not one she was born into, and she had not used it in a very long time. She always found it thrilling to hear, but she also had to focus intently to follow it completely.

She held the steady gaze of the messenger, and in doing so allowed the other mystery of his culture to reveal itself to her. With his steady gaze, the words seemed to come into her head through his eyes, even as she listened to the sounds through her ears. Soon, she felt as if the words and sentence structure no longer mattered. The sounds entered her mind and somehow she simply began to understand them, as if he spoke to her in a form of telepathy or hypnosis.

Her joyful fascination with the seemingly magical abilities of his culture and language was quickly muted as the meaning of his message became clearer to her. He was telling her about the movements of armies on the fringes of the Nagy Föld, the great expanse of territory occupied by the nomadic tribes that bordered the southern fringes of her country. His elaborate descriptions of the armor and flags, the methods and languages of the described armies were revealed. It soon became apparent that these armies were the Legions of Critias, the Legions of Emperor Coracis, whose many Senators stood only feet away from her seemingly engaged in peaceful conversations.

Zenobia was well aware that Emperor Coracis had been instigating wars and violent actions for years against the multiple nomadic tribes that lived within the Nagy Föld. He branded them as thieves and barbarians and his systematic attacks had resulted in the expansion of his own Empire into their lands. In truth, while Zenobia did stay at peace with the tribes, she was unsure of how many of them were left since the Emperor had imposed his aggressive campaign against them. The messenger revealed that his own tribal elders believed that the Emperor had more covert intentions to move his armies further and further into the territory of the nomads. This messenger was sent by the remnants of the Törzsi Nomádok. It was sent to warn her of the danger she and her kingdom now faced.

Then he told her that one of the nomadic hunting parties had successfully tricked and ultimately captured a small group of Legion soldiers. They now held those men for her to interrogate, if she wished. These captives were in an encampment on the Great Plains just south of the Turul Mountains, a territory that was considered neutral hunting grounds for her and the nomadic tribes. It was a place that she could reach in a long days ride.

The message was a dangerous one, revealing the deceit and warlike activities of the Emperor, and it was directly related to some of the people who stood in her immediate presence. If the beliefs of the tribal leaders were correct and she was in danger of attack by Emperor Coracis, then the people that now ate as her guests were lying to her about their intentions of unification and peace. Yet, Zenobia had mastered the talents of diplomacy and she never allowed her facial expression to break from the first calm smile she had given the messenger upon his arrival. His message confirmed her initial intuitive mistrust of the Emperor, as well as the Senators she currently entertained. However, she would never reveal to her potential enemies, especially through an un-calculated reaction, that she was suspicious of them. Just as they kept their intentions secret from her, she easily masked her knowledge of some of their military secrets as well as the fact that she had just been offered captured soldiers from the intruding army's ranks.

For those observing, she was seen as greeting the nomad's message with a gracious smile. She nodded in a delighted and carefree manner as if he was merely telling her that the tribes had been overwhelmed with successful hunting and now brought to her palace a gift of fresh venison for a courtly feast. At the end of his speech she hid the weight of his information by reaching forward to grasp his hand warmly and thanking him brightly.

Then, turning to her curious guests, she looked directly at the offending Senators with a naive twinkle in her eyes and a light laugh before her words as she exclaimed, "Absolutely delightful. We will have an extra treat at our feast tonight."

And the noblemen and women smiled wide as they now believed they comprehended the message of the tribal hunters speech to the gracious Queen.

Zenobia turned back to the messenger, smiled and said in his native tongue, "I understand and I will come to the camp when our guests have left our kingdom."

Then, thanking him in her own language, she held his hand up in the air and the crowd of nobility cheered in response. The messenger smiled and bowed, then turned and left the court.

Zenobia moved casually back to her throne taking only a brief moment to pause and whisper to her most loyal guard, Erastos, "Have the kitchen put twice as much meat into the dinner tonight, include the wild pheasant, eggs and a side of wild boar."

Erastos nodded, waited for his queen to take her seat at the throne and then swiftly, but quietly, exited to execute her orders.

13

———

The slave parade wound its way through the narrow twists and turns of a desert canyon trail, its dust covered wagons and beasts creating a sinuous line up one side of the red canyon wall. Csoda could see the full length of the train of performers, cages and slaves that zig-zagged behind and below their own wagon as he looked down a shear drop off of rock that they precariously moved alongside. The trail itself consisted of loose rock, sand and patches of solid slate. The pitted and sometimes unstable surface made their wagon jerk and bounce uncomfortably. At times the wheels lifted and bashed back to the ground, dangerously close to the unforgiving ledge, causing the driver to curse loud, forceful commands to the struggling ox that pulled them.

Csoda imagined for a moment their wagon slipping off the ledge. He imagined the oxen pulled off of its feet, and how they would fall like a rock slide, crashing and shattering down the mountain, smashing into the wagons, men, and creatures below. Surprisingly, imagining it did not make him feel fear, instead the thought made him quietly laugh to himself as he recognized the absolute hopelessness of such a crash, as well as the fact that he had no control over his fate in this situation. So he contented himself with observing in awe the surreal view. The struggling line of exotic beasts and humanity, the bright painted wagons and Kirkos flags suffocated with red and grey dust, the vast openness of the endless sky, and the subtle blend of tan, beige, pink and gold that accented the desert landscape below.

As the parade made its laborious climb upwards, a larger wagon pulled by two mawing oxen behind them loosened a patch of gravel, causing a brief rockslide with their front wheels. The loss of gravel in the trail opened up a jagged hole in the ground that the wagon's back wheels immediately jammed into, locking the heavy load deep in a rut. The oxen bellowed as they were pulled to a solid stop. The two beasts heaved forward, their legs bracing against the road, their necks bulging against the strain, but they were unable to budge the grounded wheels out of the pit.

The stuck wagon blocked the rest of the train behind it from continuing up the narrow road and the front of the parade pulled away, leaving a noticeable gap before it was decided that the wagon was going to require assistance to move forward. Guards on horses quickly and nimbly maneuvered around the wagons and up the trail to report the incident to the Ringmaster. Eventually the leading wagons settled and paused and the parade came to a standstill. Men and working slaves were rushed to the stuck wagons side to work on freeing its back wheels from the earth's grip.

Csoda's cage window gave him a good view of the proceedings and he relaxed against the bars, smiling slightly at the chaos of it all. The guards and wagon drivers barked orders and snapped whips. Slaves with shovels attempted to dig and fill behind and beneath the back wheels to give them traction and space to move. The oxen bellowed in frustrated protest as they pushed their weight forward into their harnesses. Yet the wagon remained firmly stuck, barely even swaying with the activity, entrenched in the hard mountain.

Recognizing the weight of the stuck wagon was going against them, the surveying guards ordered its contents and passengers to offload and soon a small group of well muscled but lean men wearing short beige tunics stepped out of the doors and began helping unload trunks and supplies from its interior. As they did, Csoda saw piles of fantastically colored costumes being pulled out and stacked to the side. There were gold leafed masks with twisted faces, many with sharp cheekbones, large ears or pronounced hawk like noses. There were elaborate tricorne hats and leather pointed toe boots dyed in multiple bright colors, all decorated with shells, sparkling beads, and bells that jangled as they moved.

He noticed a specific pile of distinct costumes. Multicolored checkered tunics created with leather and cloth patchwork patterns were haphazardly bunched together with a few floppy leather three-pointed hats.

The sight of them startled Csoda and he stepped away from the bars. His heart beat quickly, his hand reaching up to his throat as he felt a memory of the burning pain of having his tongue cut out. The flash made him shake and for a moment he thought he would be sick. For in his mind he replayed the vision and the voice of the child that had called his name from the crowd on that horrific day, the child that called him Father.

Biro, who had been sitting back in his usual corner, lost

in his own thoughts, noticed Csoda's sudden distress. He moved himself to the window to look out on the activity in the caravan, trying to see what had brought on this panic in his friend. The men who unloaded the costumes now helped guards and slaves alike to lift and push the wagon, but Biro could not identify the cause of his companion's anxiety.

Csoda, with his hand still holding onto his throat, pointed at the pile of checkered tunics and looked at Biro. He was not able to tell Biro of his memory, or of his confusion at seeing this specific costume design that the boy in his memory had worn. All he could do was point and wish for an explanation that would mean something. Biro followed Csoda's frantically pointing finger and shrugged his shoulders, confused by his concern.

"They are acrobats, Csoda, clowns, fools, entertainers. Those are some of their costumes, that is all." Biro explained, his voice calm. Csoda moved back to the window, frustrated he could not explain more. He stared at the checkered tunics and tried to discern for himself if what he was seeing truly matched the image in his memory. Biro, still puzzled by Csoda's distress, tried to comfort him. He patted him on the shoulder and stated, "Look, they've gotten the wagon out of its rut." And sure as he said it the oxen heaved forward, the wheels turned on the wagon, and the men gave a slight cheer. Horsemen ran ahead to inform the Ringmaster, the supplies and costumes were reloaded. Then the entire parade continued, slowly coming back together in its tedious journey along the cliff side pass.

The caravan soon fell back into a steady and even pace, the sounds of the beasts of burden falling into a more predictable rhythm, the guards switching seamlessly in and out of their shifts. The evening breeze came with the setting sun, cooling the hot air to a more bearable temperature. Csoda and Biro both settled quietly into the individual corners of their rocking cage, their bodies left swaying to the motion as their minds traveled into their individual memories and thoughts.

Csoda's mind was not calm. The sight of the costumes had not only sparked a horrific memory, but they made him consider that his vision of the boy was something more than a pain induced hallucination. He had not risked entering a full trance state since his capture. He was not sure if he still could find his way through a vision. His fear of failure to connect with the otherworld had kept him from any attempts at deep meditation.

He sat in fear while the dusk turned to black night. Rocking with the rhythm of the cage, clutching his hands together as he hugged his knees. However, his desire to better understand his fate became overwhelming, more powerful than fear.

He pulled himself up into a straight sitting position. He placed his hands in his lap and let the rhythm of movement comfort him. He listened for the sound of the caravans of many horses and oxen, letting their sounds pull him into memories of his youth. Silently, his mouth began to move as he chanted without words, asking for understanding, calling to his ancestors with his thoughts. By the time the light of the stars peeked through the window he had fallen into a deep trance.

The darkness of his mind engulfed him, and though nothing could be seen in the space surrounding Csoda's thoughts, he could feel that there was something beyond. He sensed that he was in a circular tunnel, no wind, no flow of air or variation in temperature against his skin, only a slight pressure of energy that echoed his own. It was as if his skin and the enclosing walls were one and the same, divided only by an illusion of space.

He stood in this shrouded tunnel surrounded by the dulled ambient sound of a muffled hum and the pulse of a distant heartbeat. If he turned to face the curved walls on either side of him the tunnel shifted with his movement, so there was always the sense of an opening in front or behind him and the feeling of a curved wall on either side. He could not see and he could not be seen, but his mouth was moving, chanting without sound. For a moment he stood, opening and closing his eyelids trying to determine if the motion changed his ability to see, but it did not. The same impermeable darkness existed whether his eyes were open or closed.

Finally, he took a step forward, despite his blindness. Then another. With each slow and cautious step he could hear his movements echo around him, reverberating off of the walls. The vibration made the ambient hum louder, as it seemed to travel down the tunnel in front of him, building in volume with each step. He could feel the vibration of the sound through his feet. The surface he walked on bent as he stepped down and sprang back into place as he moved his weight off again. It was as if he was walking on a giant piece of tightly stretched leather.

When he first saw the flicker of light in front of him it was a dim fleeting flash. Yet, as he continued to walk, as the vibrating hum grew around his movement, the dim flash took shape. First it was a small wave of light, but it grew in size until he finally made out the distant image of a flickering fire that pulsed with each vibration of sound. He startled when his foot stepped down on a surface that did not bend underneath his weight. The change in the ground made him pause, and he slid his foot curiously across the new terrain that he still could not see. It proved to be hard and compacted with a thin layer of something like gravel that shifted and crunched against his movement. When he was confident the new ground was stable, he readjusted his balance and continued towards the fire with the same small, cautious steps.

With the new ground, the energy around him changed as well and what before had been a circular tunnel now fell away to a more open voluminous space. The vibrating hum shifted and spread out before him, transforming eventually into the sound of a light breeze, though he could not feel any air current against his skin. He remained blind to everything but the flickering fire and he confirmed it was there again and again by holding his hand up in front of his eyes to block it from view and then dropping his hand to check if it still was in front of him. It was, and as he moved it came closer to him, faster and faster, as if his slow cautious steps were actually covering a great distance quickly.

By the time the fire was about one hundred feet away, the environment changed again, this time dramatically, and Csoda found the blackness pierced with a wave of stars that suddenly lit up the sky above with a blue glow, revealing the rest of the landscape. He could now see the open fields surrounding him, the blue tinted tall grass bending in the breeze that he could only hear before, a breeze that now grew into a real gust of cooling wind. Upon feeling the wind he stopped walking and opened up his arms, allowing it to envelop him fully. He took in a deep breath and let the scent of the clean grasslands fill his lungs. Tears welled up in his eyes and he let himself stand in a pure state of relief and awe, taking in the feeling of the wind, the cleansing aromas of the grass and gently perfumed wild flowers mixed with the crisp moisture of the evening. Around his bare and battered skin the wind began to flutter in a strange frenzy, until it suddenly took the shape of a long white tunic with a stiff short collar and golden embroidery that traveled in two decorative patterns down the straight seam from his collar to right above his feet. The tunic was the same style he wore on his last day as a free man, the last day he had raised his clear voice to the heavens and ignited the hearts of those that heard it. He opened his eyes wide and gazed into the stars, reading in their blanketing light the familiar constellations and the stories of his childhood.

He was home.

Home, the undulating and expanding fields of the grasslands, the caress of the welcoming wind, the comfort of the guiding stars. He felt as if he was floating in this familiar space. This place he had left so long ago shocked him with how quickly he identified with it, how deeply it could move him. His heart stretched within his chest as a feeling of intense longing was replaced with love. He was home, and a sense of peace washed over him.

How long he stood engulfed by this landscape he did not know, but eventually the wind brought with it the spiced sent of the burning campfire smoke and Csoda's attention returned to the flickering light that had drawn him to these familiar fields. He could see the shadowy figure of a man hunched over the campfire and behind him, the silhouette of a single horse grazed on the outskirts of the flickering light. Csoda knew, as keenly as he knew he was home, that he was meant to speak with whoever, or whatever, now waited for him at the fire.

14

Zenobia entered the royal stable alone, earlier than her two faithful guards expected her. She waved off the attendants and watchmen who ran to her aid as she approached the opened doors. She wanted to be alone.

The stable itself was cool and breezy, insulated by thick walls. Large stone pillars placed in rows down either side of the main aisle raised up to the tall arched blue tiled ceilings above, marking the sides of each stall entrance. The large, heavy wooden doors on either side of the long building were often left open during the day and multiple arched windows were placed high above each stall on the outer walls. These doors and windows, along with the tall ceiling, allowed a breeze to flow through freely, keeping the air fresh and the building cool.

The desert oasis valley that was the keystone of Zenobia's kingdom was rarely cold, never freezing. The stone stables throughout her land were there to protect the rare breed of horses that her kingdom was known for from the heat of the sun and from theft. For this reason, even the smallest stables in her land were made with thick stone walls that were impossible to break and insulated against the heat.

She walked slowly past each stall, talking to the horses that she knew so well. Even in the shade of the stable their coats glittered with a metallic sheen, unique to their breed. They came in multiple colors, but each one was instantly recognized by their shimmering coats.

The black looked like marble or dark silver and iron, the white and grays looked like opal or the shimmering foam on ocean waves, the chestnuts gleamed like dark rubies, and then there were the goldens that matched their description perfectly, glittering within a range of polished gold or coppered bronze.

The breed had additional admirable traits other than their exotic coats. They were exceptionally fast and full of endurance even when pushed through the heat of the brutal desert lands. They were smart and often grew attached to their rider, developing an almost psychic ability to adapt to the rider's needs if they were well cared for by the same person for their entire lives. They were ethereal in their body structure, their graceful arching necks and thin legs were longer than other breeds. Their muscles, stretched thin and long, were still surprisingly strong. Their powerful and graceful movements sometimes seemed more like the movement of gazelles than horses. Their manes and tails were not quite as metallic as the fur on their body, but they were long and thick and often the same color as their coats with the addition of thick streaks of black, white or grey.

Most of all, upon coming close to them, after one looked past the dazzle of their shimmering coats and their graceful forms, it was easy to be mesmerized by their large reflective eyes. Their eyes could be jade green, indigo blue, golden amber or ebony black, and they were so clear that they reflected your own image back to you almost perfectly as if you looked into a colored mirror.

Those outside of her kingdom called the breed Jeweled Horses or Silken Horses, but in Zenobia's language they were referred to as Gifts of the Sun.

Her personal horse was named Inanna, a brilliant, shining golden mare with jade mirrored eyes and an ebony black and copper streaked mane and tale. Zenobia's father had given her the exquisite mare as a filly when Zenobia was a young girl, barely 11 years old. Zenobia was raised with the young horse, working with the stable trainers and attendants to care for it. When Inanna was old enough to ride, she became Zenobia's key to the outside world, much to her father's distress, allowing her to escape again and again beyond the borders of her land and the pressures of royal etiquette and responsibilities. Inanna took Zenobia to where she could hunt or race, free.

True to the nature of the Gifts of the Sun, Inanna psychically bonded with Zenobia over time. Eventually Innana knew Zenobia's thoughts so well that she rarely needed to direct her with reins or commands. Instead the horse became a part of her natural movement when she rode, an extension of herself. Inanna even seemed to agree with Zenobia's rebellious streak and sometimes would leave the stable on her own to meet her at the edge of the connecting paddock gate where Zenobia could sneak her out for a secret ride.

So when Zenobia saw Inanna's long and delicate head peaking out of her stall at the center of the stable, staring at her with her bright jade eyes as if she had anticipated the Queen's arrival, Her Majesty was not surprised. Instead she smiled gladly, and warmly greeted her long time companion with soft crooning words and clicks of her tongue.

Zenobia had come to the stables alone because she preferred the solitude she felt in this airy and comforting space, full of the sweet smell of fresh hay and the humbling musk of clean earth. While she was no longer a girl, and her title of Queen now made it unnecessary for her to worry about being reprimanded for her actions, she still felt a need to act outside of other's expectations. She often wished to spend time away from her servant's attendance to her every need. She needed time to think. Time to consider the information that the messenger from the tribes had brought to her.

She needed time to consider the devious motives of the Ambassadors and noble guests whom she had finished entertaining only a few hours ago. The same men and women she graciously escorted to the Sea of AyRuh, where she waved and smiled as they boarded the many ships docked there, where she watched the ship's sails, fluttering in the building winds, fill proudly as they set firm on their course, moving back towards the west, towards the shores of the Empire of Critias–back to what was soon to be the kingdom of her undeniable enemy. She knew they lied, even before the message from the tribes had arrived. She could see their lies in their smiles and in the way they moved. She could sense the shadow of a sneer on their lips as they praised the wealth and the bounty of her lands. She knew well that deep in their beings they were bothered that such wealth was not their own and, even worse, that it was controlled by a woman.

Ever since the passing of her father Zenobia stood solid in her position as queen. She was not a woman to be trifled with and proved her ability to lead not only in hard fought battles but in the devotion she inspired in the people of her land. Her father had left her with a strong kingdom, but

Zenobia took that kingdom and refined it, increasing both its cultural and financial wealth. She encouraged wisdom, philosophy and art for every citizen in her kingdom and ensured that even the poorest were fed and healthy, and would have their needs and concerns addressed. In doing so, her people thrived and they were devoted to her not out of fear, but out of deep love, respect, and admiration.

In contrast, the neighboring noble families either admired and loved her, or feared and despised her success. Her military prowess and ability to lead was showcased early on in her reign, when some of the kingdoms to the east of her lands had coveted her kingdom and attempted to make it their own. She proved her ability to defend her lands against direct attacks, and now the challenge was to battle more covert operations. It was difficult to determine which nobles were sincerely on her side and which were smiling, power thirsty wolves.

Yet the kingdom and the shifting politics were not all that weighed on her mind. The messenger from the tribal lands had sparked old memories in her heart, and she felt herself wondering, yet again, about Biro. What had become of the young man that years ago stood proudly smiling at the steps of her palace with the deer that she shot slung over his shoulder? What had become of the man who had taught her his language and learned hers in exchange? The young man who had inspired her to sneak away from the palace late into the evening so that she could ride out and find him on the fringes of the canyon lands, the young man whose presence had so worried her father.

She knew about the conflicts in the Turul Mountains, the battles the Emperor Coracis had brought to the Törzsi Nomádok. The last time she saw Biro they stood at the edge of a small pool hidden in the forest where he had first watched her hunt. There he had told her of the wars that his people were facing.

"The Legions of Critias are now deep in the Nagy Föld, we are being pushed from all sides of our territory. If it is not the Legions of Critias then it is his allies that mean us harm." Biro had informed her while holding her gaze, his face steady and stern. He was silent for a moment after that statement, and then, breaking the gaze, he turned to stare over the water of the pond, gazing, it seemed, into the future. His hands clasped behind his back, his broad shoulders blocking a bit of the morning light so that it made a slight glowing halo on the edge of his strong frame.

Zenobia's own heart had always felt pain when Biro felt pain. An expansion in her chest had made it hard for her to breath. Even the memory of the conversation made everything within her body feel stretched thin and tired. She had wished with every inch of her soul that she could have reached out and somehow removed the pain from the man she loved, touched his shoulders and lifted off the dark shadows that haunted his thoughts, but somehow she knew, then and now, that she was not capable of such a thing. She had waited in silence until he chose to continue speaking. When he did he had not faced her but continued to gaze over the pond, his voice the steady tone of a fortune teller with grave news.

"The Törzsi Nomádok, all of us, have declared war... revolution against the Emperor Coracis who has invaded our territory..." he had paused to take in a deep breath, then continued, "He is filling our land with armies...decimating the tribes...murdering and enslaving my people...." He had paused again but his intake of breath was sharp before he stated, "We are not winning...my people. The Törzsi Nomádok will be destroyed."

This last statement had surprised her. She had known about the fighting, the wars, the invasion that had faced Biro's people. Yet, their resilience through the years had always seemed so strong, their natures so adaptable, that she, in her limited knowledge of the conflict, had assumed that while they might lose some territory, the Törzsi Nomádok as a people would survive. She had been about to ask Biro, to inquire into what he had seen or knew that made him so sure of his own people's inevitable destruction. However, before she asked, Biro broke out of his trance-like solemn state.

He had quickly spun around to face her, his intense eyes wide as they met her gaze again. He had moved forward and grabbed both of her shoulders with a strong but gentle grip as he pulled her closer to him. The sternness from his expression lifted, his broad features were animated and in them one could see the youthful light of hope, love...and fear.

"Leave with me," he stated, his eyes darting, searching hers. She had been shocked by the intensity of the request, so much so that she could not respond. "We can go beyond all of this. These wars, these lands. There are worlds beyond these territories, far from this destruction. We can find a way to live, we are young and strong, we can build a good life, together, far away."

The request had surprised Zenobia. That and the way that Biro's searching eyes penetrated into her mind, as if he could find her answer without her speaking. A piece of her was being pulled to him, she felt her body sway forward.

"Yes," her body said, but it was a fleeting 'yes' and soon it had been overwhelmed by the image of her father waiting for her at home, the expectations of her lineage. She was expected to be queen, her father was ill, who would rule her people if he passed on and she ran away.

The moment she hesitated, Biro's grip on her shoulders became lighter, his intense eyes softened. He leaned forward and kissed her softly on her forehead, let go of her shoulders, stepped back away from her and with a deep breath he nodded and respectfully saluted her. Then, before she could speak, before she could even process what had just happened, Biro had backed away and disappeared into the forest.

Zenobia had sat down next to the pond when he left. Her head reeling, her heart aching. She sat somewhat dazed for hours at the edge of the pond. She had half expected Biro to return, half wished she had run after him. She had sat confused and in shock, not knowing what to do, as her young broken heart came to the sudden realization that she may never see him again, that this young man she loved, was gone. She had not left with him, but hesitated instead.

She returned to her kingdom, to her ailing father's bedside, where her heart was broken again, this time slowly, as she watched the strong man weaken, his breath grow shallow, his mind become feeble to the point where he no longer knew her name. When her father finally passed on, he left her a young queen with tremendous power but little guidance. At first she wanted to run again, to hide, until she realized that the surrounding kingdoms were waiting for her to be weak. They coveted her wealth and power and wanted to treat her like a little girl that they could brush away while they drained her kingdom and conquered her people. This realization did not frighten her, instead it made her angry, and so she took up her crown with a bold and determined force that surprised everyone.

Now older, she fully recognized her duties as queen. She

even embraced certain aspects of her position and surprised everyone when she proved to be adept at not only leadership, diplomacy and negotiation, but also war. She could fight, she could strategize, and in the conflicts she was forced into, she was smart, brutal, and surprisingly vicious–only when needed. Ultimately, she was victorious again and again, so that now, the circling wolves of nobility were hesitant to attack and she was hesitant to trust.

Her fluency in the nomadic language, the language Biro had taught her, allowed her to benefit through regular trade with many different tribes throughout the years. To their credit, the Törzsi Nomádok still were standing as a people, despite Biro's grim prediction of their fate. However, she knew their numbers were still dwindling. Along with attacking them with his own Legions through the years, the Emperor labeled them as thieves and evil magicians, he identified their free thinking as a threat to his kingdom. In doing so, he continued to gain support from the apathetic kingdoms whose land bordered the nomad's Nagy Föld.

Zenobia continually refused to impose the restrictions and prejudices that the Emperor pressured her to take. She allowed the nomads to trade and travel in her lands without harm as her father had done before her. The current leftover tribes were now often found in lands close to her own. She realized that their presence may have been a greater buffer than she'd fully understood. A buffer that was weakening.

To her benefit, an unintentional spy network had been created by the nomads. This last messenger had proven that they were at least grateful to her, if not attempting to build a more direct alliance. She recognized the significance and her agreement to investigate these captured soldiers had multiple motives. She might glean information from the soldiers themselves. She might gather more important information from the tribes. She might secure a bond and alliance with the tribes more directly, which could help fortify her border. Or, and this last motivation betrayed her heart, she might find out what had happened to Biro.

For in this quiet moment, alone in the stables, she was allowed to drop the mask of diplomacy, the concerns of politics, the weapons of war, her crown as queen, and she could let her mind linger back to her youth, to the open fields and that clear pond in the forest where she had known love. In that space she could still hear his voice, feel his gaze searching hers. Here she could silently wonder, "What became of Biro? Where had the young man, who was so bold and brave, gone? What happened to him as his people were persecuted and enslaved?" The thought pained her, made her ache, and yet somehow she was sure he was still alive.

Her contemplation was interrupted as Erastos and Alexius, her most loyal guards, arrived. They approached quickly, jogging in rhythmic union, two stable attendants followed close behind, one of which balanced a hooded white and dusty red falcon on his gloved forearm. They stopped ten feet from her, each dropping to one knee, their heads bowed.

Erastos spoke, "Apologies my Queen. We are late."

Zenobia smiled and slowly shook her head, "No dear Erastos, do not worry." She signaled them to stand then explained, "I am early and have been in good company..." She reached up to pet Inanna's soft muzzle and, gazed tenderly into the horse's kind eyes. She continued.,"...but now that you're here, I believe we should get ready. We have a long ride ahead."

15

———

A deep, guttural murmur penetrated the darkness beyond the ring of firelight that exposed the lone, strangely dressed figure. A man hunched near the campfire flames. He was balanced in a low squat making it appear at first that he sat, but in reality he was positioned like a bird resting, his knees fully bent but only his feet touching the ground. The position allowed him to shuffle across the ground for a few feet without truly standing. Sometimes he moved to pick up a stick from a nearby pile of wood that he then fed to the fire. Sometimes he moved out of the way of drifting smoke. The majority of the time, however, he stayed in a fixed position, holding a long stick with a charred tip and using it to push and poke at the logs deeply engulfed in the campfire he tended. Occasionally, a dancing spark would free itself from the embers, bouncing and sputtering across the ground, before it turned black and disappeared.

The man wore a leather band around his head with long strings of beaded cowrie shells and small bones that hung in a circular curtain, dropping and swaying in front of his face, over his ears, and down his back. This curtain headdress made it difficult to know which way his head was turned and which direction he was looking. The curtain parted where his broad but skeletal thin shoulders defined his frame. A thick mass of matted long hair identified the back of his head. His clothes were patched together pieces of leather, fur and cloth chaotically embroidered with different types of thread and sinew. The seemingly rough clothing showed hints of expert craftsmanship in the detailed embroidered symbols that pulled all of the material together into a full length tunic, similar in style to the one that Csoda now wore.

Behind the man grazed a bony, swaybacked horse. Huge patches of his seemingly ancient body were completely hairless and the rest of him was covered with flea bitten patches of dull grey fur. The horse's eyes were solid white and he blindly nuzzled the ground with a sickly pink muzzle. He barely nibbled on the grass, and instead, occasionally took to licking the bare patches of dirt and ash with a pale, dry tongue.

When Csoda was close enough to raise his hand in the sign of a formal greeting he was also able to take in the full appearance of the man. When he did he gasped and instinctually dropped to his knees, bowed his head, and turned his gaze down at the ground in reverence.

Before him could be none other than the figure of a Taltos, the highest form of mystic that his people knew. The man did not move, did not seem to change position for an eternity as the fire popped hungrily at the wood in front of him. When he did finally speak, it was in the same murmured tone that had come from his lips earlier, but this time they formed words. His voice was hushed, but Csoda could hear the words clearly within his head, as if they were spoken from inside his skull.

"*Csoda....*" The voice whispered, "*...Csoda must tend the Taltos fire... God's arrow will land to you....Csoda.*"

Csoda bowed his head further down, his body shaking. If he had any remaining doubt about the figure before him, he was now sure that he was in the presence of a Taltos. Where he had been trained in the ancient ways of his tribe as a Shaman, the Taltos were born with the deep knowledge and, unlike the Shamans, did not require training to obtain a direct connection to the spiritual world.

Identified when they were still children, the Taltos stayed with their clan and family until they were nearly grown, then they left. From then on they were known to travel between the tribes, appearing when needed to help identify and teach future Shamans or, occasionally, they appeared when called. Csoda had met Taltos when he was young, he was called out of a group of children by one and identified as a candidate for learning the ancient traditions. Another appeared later in his life when he was being trained in the Húzza Művészet, The Art of the Pull. That second Taltos helped him pass into his first trance state. However, he had never had a Taltos come to him within the trance itself. He struggled to keep his emotions from over-whelming him, fearing that they would knock him out of the trance altogether.

Csoda stayed with his head bowed down and, breathing deeply, he nodded in thanks for the message he had been given, even if its meaning was still unclear to him. He tried to come up with a question to ask, but instead his mind betrayed him. His focus could only hold onto the rhythm of his breath, his consciousness seemed content to simply be in the presence of the Taltos. His concerns and thoughts no longer existed. It was the voice of the Taltos that ended up posing his questions back to him, as if aware that Csoda could not find or express the concern that had brought him to the vision of this strange mystic's camp.

"The vision of the child that calls you father...You want to know what it means? Your enslavement? You want to know where it leads? Your people?...." The voice paused then continued, slowly, *"... you want to know what has become of them?"*

Csoda nodded at his questions on the Taltos' tongue. Knowing these answers would bring him greater understanding. Such understanding would help him stay sane in his current captivity.

The Taltos shifted slightly, laid the long stick down, its tip tucked in the flaming embers. He positioned himself to face Csoda, crossing his long leather tanned arms before himself, his lean hands folding on top of his knees so that each bony finger was equally splayed apart, like the talons of a bird of prey. His shoulders were parallel to Csoda's, the curtain in front of his hidden face swayed back and forth with the movement, the bones and shells gently tapping against each other created a waterfall of delicate sounds. A few moments passed and all became still again, except for the crackling fire and the occasional rustle of the horse behind the Taltos.

Then his voice came again into Csoda's head, its sound taking on a distinct rhythm as it changed pitch and tone in random patterns, punctuating key words with heavy emphasis on their consonants, then dragging out and drifting into a dreamy vocal as it lingered on certain vowels. The words became musical. Their sounds pulled on Csoda like gentle hands lifting his chin, so that as the Taltos spoke he was compelled to raise his head and look directly at the mystic before him.

*"The child will be Taltos born... must live to tend
    the fire.
Born a slave, will be hidden well beneath the
    empire's spires.
Your enslavement leads you on your path to
    become the child's keeper.
The shaman disguised as the fool will become his
    greatest teacher.
Your people, Csoda, our tribal clans, in bloody
    war they fall.
The scattered ashes of revolutions will darken
    and burn no more.
In time unseen, beyond your eyes, the winds of
    fate will blow, and in scattered ashes of
    broken men, the embers again will glow."*

The Taltos did not move after saying these words and neither did Csoda. The two sat in place, facing each other as if comfortably locked together. Yet, the Taltos' words echoed faintly over and over in Csoda's mind. The words physically settled into his brain, as if their truth now became a part of the fibers of his flesh and soul. Neither man moved.

It was the old blind horse's movement that broke the silence as it shifted its position, feeling its way across the ground with its nuzzling muzzle, moving closer to the campfire. The fire was now a solid glowing pile of orange and red embers, the flames had dwindled down to delicate blue ribbons that occasionally reached up and caressed the blackened logs. Csoda still faced the Taltos, but he could see the horse in his peripheral vision.

The creature reached the edge of the fire pit, its nose snuffling deeper into the smoking ash, the pinkish muzzle delicately reaching for, and touching the edges of, the smoking black logs. Its hairless nostrils flared slightly as it pulled the smoke into its lungs. The smell of burning hair and skin mingled with the wood and Csoda watched the creature open its mouth, reach out to the glowing embers and take one between its cracked and blackened teeth, as if it was plucking a sweet flower from the meadow. The ember glowed brighter, enflamed by the breath of the horse, releasing small flames that crawled along the surface of the animal's lips who, in response, hungrily pulled the hot coal into its mouth. Csoda swore that he saw wafts of smoke trailing up from the patches of grey fur on the horses back just as his white eyes took on a reddish hue.

Screams.

Csoda's head suddenly echoed with screams.

The Taltos was gone and Csoda raced through the burning fields leading and pushing a small group of survivors to the forest edge. The black smoke filled the sky, and he yelled to his tribe, yelled to the children who dove into the thick cover of the dark forest ahead, "Run! Run!..." His voice was lost in the screams that surrounded him, his lungs filled with the suffocating smoke and then, viciously, his tongue was ripped from his mouth.

Csoda broke out of his trance abruptly with a sudden gasp of air. His body was trembling, his skin feverish and covered in sweat. He took in deep breaths trying to stave off a panic that was over taking his mind. His heart was pounding, swelling in his chest.

It took all of his will to adjust himself back to reality. The aches in his muscles, the air and smells of his cell, the shock of the sudden change overwhelmed his senses.

He opened his eyes and the darkness helped him recognize that it was evening. He could not see well in the dark and the deep fear stayed with him. His heart still pounded.

He could still hear screaming deep in his mind, the darkness of night was the same black as the deadening smoke that had filled his lungs. He took deep breaths, trying to calm himself, trying to rid his mind of the memory.

His eyes adjusted and he saw Biro sleeping on the other side of the wagon. He heard the big man breathing and the presence of his friend calmed him. Csoda intentionally matched his breathing to his friends and in so doing his heart began to slow, his racing fear dissipated. A few stars peeked out behind the haze of drifting clouds through the window.

When he had settled enough to think straight, he pushed the dark memory out of his head and focused instead on the vision of the Taltos. He gave a brief prayer of thanks in his mind and allowed his thoughts to linger on the message the Taltos had given him. When the entire memory of the trance experience started to become hazy he gave in to his exhaustion. He repositioned himself to lie down. Staring for a brief moment at the drifting clouds in front of the stars, Csoda took in a long breath of air and fell immediately into the relief of a deep and dreamless sleep.

16

———

The morning sun had just begun to lighten the sky. A dark purple glow replaced the black of night. The two hounds, after sleeping soundly for the full evening, snapped their eyes open, their ears raised up and aimed straight ahead as they looked towards the sunrise. They both growled quietly in unison.

Abelardus woke quickly. His first instinct was to grab for a sword, but his motion was cut short by the bonds that held him. The full realization of where he was, as well as a hazy memory of the strange events of the evening, came back to him. His eyes darted around the camp trying to see what the dogs growled at, but he saw no immediate danger. He sighed heavily in frustration and then looked at the dogs who still growled low as they stared at the sunrise. The sight of the attentive hounds suddenly made him laugh to himself.

"Why couldn't you have been this alert a few days ago?" He asked, shaking his head.

Surprisingly, he didn't feel anger at them when he remembered how they had failed to warn him of the nomads hiding in the fog. Instead, on this morning, even though he was still bound to the wagon, a prisoner in the nomad camp, he felt lighter than he had in years. He couldn't explain his good mood and, in truth, he couldn't explain anything that had happened to him since he had wandered into the fog filled meadow of his capture. Still, the dog's attentive stare sparked his curiosity and he shifted his body so he could look into the direction of the rising sun.

The sun's rays were strong enough to blind him to the farthest horizon, but he could still make out two thin flags held high on tall poles, their flickering tails wispy like blue smoke. For a brief moment he considered that his own army had found him, but as the distant flags moved closer, three figures on horses became highlighted by the morning light. Their uniforms and purple and gold flags were foreign to him.

His hopes of an oncoming savior were fully put to rest by the activity of the men in the camp. Some of the nomads had been standing awake, drinking from their water skins and talking quietly over small fires. They, too, noticed the oncoming horsemen and, upon seeing them, they nudged a few of their fellow companions awake. They did not rush to arms. Eventually, five nomads, two of which he had pursued as thieves, moved together as a group to face the oncoming party as if they were expecting them.

The sun was now half way above the horizon, creating an arch of light that blurred into the clear sky above in deep shades of blue, auburn and gold. The three horseman, riding in a unified lope, were now a dark, but well defined image against the morning light. Abelardus could see that the two on the outside wore pointed helmets, each carrying a dancing flag on a tall lance as well as round copper and brass shields. The central figure rode slightly ahead of the other two and seemed to be dressed more elaborately, with billowing flowing material below a wide, armored belt at the waist and a short layered skirt of plated armor. Abelardus could see that the upper torso of this central rider was covered in a flexible vest of armor, the arms were bare except for long gloves. Upon the head, the central horseman wore a headdress of what he guessed by its movement was made of fur and metal. An occasional glint of light suggesting a band of decoration on the helmet that he could not quite make out.

The rest of the men in the camp began to wake up. The rustle of the morning preparations mingled with the sounds of nickering horses who called to the oncoming riders. The smell of rabbit meat cooking on the fires soon drifted through the air. The hounds that had sat alert at his feet recognized that the rest of the camp was not concerned with the oncoming horsemen, and so they lost interest and moved on to investigate the smells that came from the cook fires.

The same man who had brought Abelardus a drink of milk the night before approached him now. This time he offered him a leather skin container full of water. Abelardus nodded, expecting the man to hold the drink up to his mouth. To his surprise the man reached forward to his bound hands and, pulling a sharp knife from his belt, swiftly cut away the bindings of leather and rope. The man handed him the leather container, allowing Abelardus to take it in his free hands and drink comfortably in his own time.

When he had finished with the water, the man unhooked him from the wheel he was attached to at his waist and legs. He had him stand and, surprising Abelardus even more, he freed him of all of his bonds. Abelardus was confused at first, then acutely aware that he was not a threat to these men. It was not that he was incapable or weak, but because something deep within him was changed. He knew it and they, by the way they freed him, seemed to know it as well. While he could not understand what he had experienced, nor did he see anyone around the camp that resembled the strange shaman, he did know that he had no desire or intention to fight these men. He felt free of anger and shame. His only concern was to ensure the rest of his Legion men were safe and learn more about why they had captured him in the first place.

His curiosity must wait. The man who freed him signaled for him to look towards the oncoming horsemen. He turned to face them and wondered who these new arrivals were, and what role they had to play in his sidetracked fate.

The newly risen sun behind the figures turned them into abstract blackened silhouettes, making it impossible to see their personal features or the details on their armor and flags. No, these riders were not the brass armored equestrians of the Empire moving in military precision, but neither were they moving like the wild herds of the nomads across the open plains. These riders approached in a precise yet natural rhythm. Their horses, in an orderly yet relaxed formation, leaped forward in graceful and elegant strides, their positions shifting ever so slightly like the patterns of birds migrating. It was apparent that their horses were taller and leaner than the nomad's breeds, and not as broad and thick as the war horses of the Empire. They sprung forward in elegant cantors on long graceful legs with well curved necks and flowing tails.

Above the riders circled a falcon whose wings occasionally caught the glint of the golden sun. Abelardus at first thought the bird was wild, but noted that it stayed with the group. Occasionally, the bird of prey dipped down close to the central rider making it clear that it was actually part of the entourage.

The sun seemed to rise in unison with their approach. The heat of its rays evaporated the dew on the grasslands producing a light mist on the horizon. The dust of the prancing horses rose between the silhouettes, creating wisps of glittering haze the color of the pinking hues of the emboldened sunrise. The horse's forms sparkled ever so slightly, like glinting jewels, and the sunlight pierced between their forms, blinding Abelardus' ability to see.

By the time the riders were close enough to see clearer, Abelardus had become mesmerized by the image of their forms. He could not determine what was a trick of light played by the rising sun and what was the reality of the shimmering horses. The central one gleamed like the golden statues at the Senator's Hall, its eyes were the color of polished jade stones. The two horses flanking either side seemed to be made of pure black obsidian with silver manes and eyes. All three horse's hooves, the color of polished hematite, barely seemed to touch the ground before their nimble forms lifted them back up into the air. He had never seen steeds like these and they captured his full attention, leaving him unfocused upon the riders that they carried.

It was the diving falcon that brought his attention back to the riders just as they pulled their horses to a prancing stop merely twenty feet from where he stood. The bird of prey dove from above his head, its shrill cry taking him by surprise. It swooped down between him and the riders, close to the ground and then arching up to gracefully land on the central rider's leather sheathed forearm. The forearm was held up as a perch, anticipating the birds approach. As the arm lowered, Abelardus was yet again taken aback, for it revealed the face of a woman and not a man as he had expected. She stared at him with solid discernment from flashing, intelligent, almond black eyes. Her broad exotic features were haloed by ringlets of thick auburn hair that was pulled back into a heavy braid, which fell to the middle of her back. On top of her head she wore a band of purple metal encrusted with green jewels and a small fur ringed helmet of pointed brass. Upon seeing her, the falcon, and the exotic steeds they rode, Abelardus began to wonder if the very realm of the Gods had opened so that now one of the ancients walked in front of him. Then he saw the emblems fluttering on the narrow flags that snaked high in the air, the jade falcon crest of the hidden canyons. Upon seeing it, he instantly dropped to his knee, his head down. The nomads moved forward to speak to her in friendly informal greetings even as Abelardus stuttered out loud in a surprised gasp, "Queen Zenobia!"

Abelardus stayed in this bowed position, his eyes focused on the ground in front of him. He could see the leather boots of the nomads walking past him towards the Queen. He could hear the shifting commotion of the riders dismounting. Then he heard the Queen's silken voice speaking to his captors in their native tongue, only occasionally switching to her own language to speak briefly to the riders that had come with her. Still he stayed bowing, shocked and unsure of what he should do.

He was a soldier of the Empire of Critias, but had never been so close to even his own Emperor, or anyone of such high station. He knew of Queen Zenobia from his country's history of trade with her nation. He would never expect to be within such close proximity to the legendary Queen, especially in such an unlikely location, and in what appeared to be a somewhat informal situation. So he stayed bowing, almost frightened to shift, even as he sensed the crowd moving, even when he realized that she was directly in front of him.

"Soldier of Critias," She said, her voice calm and gentle but solid in tone, "Stand up please."

Abelardus stood but he kept his head down, eyes averted.

"You can look at me soldier."

Abelardus raised his head and met the eyes of the Queen. She was his same height, their eyes were level and she smiled slightly as she spoke, "Give me your name soldier."

"Abelardus," he answered, his gaze fixed on hers, his heart beating so quickly that he could feel it in his throat, making it hard to speak. She nodded and Abelardus quickly bowed his head, relieved at the break of eye contact, content to keep his head lowered.

He did not know why the Queen was here, if she was retrieving him and his men as a favor to his own country, or if she had another purpose. All he knew is that this was a perilous position to be in. The expedition he had led was a failure, he and his men were captured, but upon the Queen's approach he was not bound by ropes or chains. Did he look like a traitor? If she was not here for the benefit of his kingdom, were he and his men to be tricked? Tortured? Could he hold secrets he may not even know he had? These thoughts raced through his head, alerting him that he could be in a perilous position. Yet the anxiety he felt was tempered by the strange peace that lingered from what should have been a traumatic event from the night before. While his logical mind raced through the potential results of this strange encounter, he personally felt no immediate threat.

The Queen did not ask any more questions. She simply stood and observed him for a brief moment. Then she turned to the nomadic men who had greeted her, she spoke warmly in their tongue, her voice expertly emanating the strange lyrical tones and rhythms of their language. The men nodded and smiled as she spoke and then she, returning her attention back to Abelardus, addressed him in his language.

"There is hot tea on the campfire. I could use some food after my long ride. Abelardus, please join us."

She moved past him towards the nearest fire. The scents of tea and spices gave hints of flavor to the fresh prairie breeze. One of her guards folded a thick blanket for her to sit on. Queen Zenobia settled onto the blanket cross-legged with regal grace and straight posture, as if it was the most elegant of thrones. Abelardus followed, pausing at the fire ring, unsure of what to do. Zenobia gestured for him to sit slightly across from her. Her guard politely following her lead by offering him a blanket of his own. He accepted and sat, using the moment before sitting to turn and take note of all that surrounded him.

He could see across to the other fires past some of the wagons and he noted that his men were in a group at the far end. They were still bound by ropes at their legs, but were sitting upright and drank from cups they held in their hands. Seeing them alive and well gave Abelardus a sense of relief, as well as a new found determination to do what he could to get them back to the Legion camp safely.

"My Queen," he stated, surprised at himself that he was taking the risk of initiating a conversation, "Queen Zenobia. I do not mean to be too brash, but I have not spoken to my men since my capture and I do not know the intentions of those that captured us. Can I have your assurance that my men will be cared for and returned to the Legion we came from, unharmed?"

The Queen raised an eyebrow at his sudden request. The corners of her mouth turned up in a slight smile, her dark almond eyes locked onto his and suddenly the light in them seemed to dance, as if she secretly laughed. She nodded slowly, holding his gaze and then replied, "Yes Abelardus, your men will be safe and they will be returned."

Abelardus released a sigh of relief.

The Queen smiled and added, "I admire a leader who puts the needs of his men before his own. Now please, have some tea. My guards will check on the well being of your men."

Abelardus nodded and settled into a comfortable sitting position, taking a cup of warm tea from the hands of one of his captors. After a night of strange magic, he now sat across from one of the most legendary queens of his time. He did not understand why this was happening, but Abelardus felt amazingly alive. It was as if the axis of the world had shifted and the Gods themselves were placing him on a new path towards a new destiny.

17

———

Almost a full year had passed since Csoda awoke in the prison wagon, and it was impossible for him to know how long he had been unconscious before he awoke. Biro was also unsure of how much time had passed. He did not count the days. Instead he recognized that they were close to the end of the parade circuit by the activities, the landscape around them, and a slight change of weather hinting at the change of seasons.

"Soon..." he would say, as if to himself, as he stared out onto the landscape they crossed, "Soon we will be in Phaedon. Soon the Grand Kirkos will begin. Twelve cities, twelve coliseums we will need to survive."

True to Biro's prediction, the traveling Kirkos caravan had grown over the months. The wagons, performers and slaves were joined by cages of exotic animals, lines of chained walking captives, herds of horses, bulls, camels and a handful of elephants. The mounted and marching guards tripled in number and they guarded the entourage with a new determined focus. Sounds of bells, small and large, rung occasionally throughout the day, released by a trickle of random movement or intentionally rung to announce to the guards the changing of their shifts. Flashes of color in newly sewn flags or tested costumes splashed against the barren landscape, and workers could be seen washing and coating the dusty wagons with fresh coats of brightly colored paint.

Occasionally, the voices of women, lilting voices speaking in unknown tongues, floated from certain wagons, lifting the heavy air from the gruff commands of angry guards. For brief moments Csoda saw them pass by in a flurry of colorful, flowing, translucent silk, pearls and chimes. They moved in groups that left the lingering scent of perfume hovering in the air.

Now, the caravan often came to a stop before the evening sun had set, and at times they would stay in place for a series of days. These layovers proved to be set aside for the acrobats, jesters and other performers to practice and perfect their acts. Through his limited slotted cage view, Csoda studied the individual performers, their costume details, masks, props and, sometimes, the trained animals that accompanied them.

These layover days became something that Csoda looked forward to, for while his own situation was still one of dull confinement, the glimpses of the Kirkos performers brought him a sense of hope, or at least the general relief that entertainment can bring to an entrapped soul. On one of these layovers, when the caravan had stopped for the evening, Csoda witnessed multiple men dressing an elephant in a jeweled blanket and gold tasseled headdress.

They wrapped the creature's tail in long beaded fabric with a tasseled end that flicked in the air when the tail moved. Then a woman appeared, wearing a bodice of gold over a short, flowing white skirt that was weighed down around her by an apron like belt with rows of gold coins falling in strips from her waist to right above her knees. Upon her head was a golden jeweled headdress that rose up to a point at the top where a fan of tall white pluming feathers rose high into the air.

Csoda watched as this beautiful woman stepped up to the elephant and, on cue, the immense creature offered her his lowered head. Then the elephant lifted her up into the air in the crook of his bent trunk so that she could gracefully climb over his massive head and seat herself on his neck, her well shaped legs tucked behind the creature's fanning ears. There she perched as they went through a series of drills with the elephant. Csoda watched in awe as this delicate woman stayed steady upon the elephant's neck even as it raised its front legs into the air and sat back on its heavy haunches. He could not remember ever seeing such beauty and grace matched with such force. The act mesmerized him so that the image stayed in his mind for days.

These training layovers increased as time went on until one day they set up camp on a small sandy hill. The wagons parked closely, side-by-side, their wheels locked into place. From their caged position Csoda and Biro could see slaves dig out a shallow trench to form a flat makeshift arena for the performers to practice.

Far in the distance on the desert's shimmering horizon, where the sunlight shifted and the air cooled, a series of squared lines appeared as the edge of a city was revealed. The light of the day fell away into dusk and the lines of the buildings became more defined in long shadows created by the falling sun.

On the edge of the city a large structure dominated, rising twice as high as the tallest buildings and spanning across one third of the total breadth of the city. The shadows on the structure called out large arches that dominated three levels of its design and silhouetted flags snapped forcefully in the wind above the high walls.

Csoda recognized the structure as a coliseum, similar to, but larger than, the one he was pulled into when they cut out his tongue. Its presence in the city before them matched with the performer's extra training and daily practice could only mean one thing. The days of travel were coming to an end and Biro's insight had been correct. Soon they would be put into the ring to face whatever waited for them there.

Biro noticed the city as well and pulled himself out of his tendency to escape into his memories. He paced the short distance of their cage and put all of his attention into his physical care. He took to a military like regimen of pushups, jogging in place and whatever physical trials he could do to prepare himself within their confinement.

"The coliseum you see is in the city of Phaedon," He explained to Csoda, "The first of many before the Final Grand Kirkos in the Capital of Critias."

Csoda understood Biro's new focus. They were close to being released from their cage, but that release would pit them against a deadly unknown. The distant city of Phaedon, its shadow dim in the darkening night horizon, could very easily be the place of their final breath. Csoda looked out towards that city until the darkness of night took it from his view.

In the deepening darkness the newly created practice arena within the camp was lit with multiple torches. This makeshift stage seemed to float, alone in the nighttime landscape. Within it acrobats stretched and went through a series of routines under the dancing firelight that defined the arena circle. Their lithe bodies leapt and jumped, twisted and turned, cartwheeled and flipped, walked on their hands and ran on all fours. Some balanced on and jumped over tightened ropes that were stretched a few feet above the ground. Others juggled multiple balls or other objects with expert precision. The thinnest contorted into seemingly impossible forms and the strongest often lifted or threw the others high into the air where they could flip and cartwheel far above the ground, quickly snapping back into upright standing positions just before they came back to the ground to land, bouncing on weightless feet.

Csoda watched and studied their movements, listened to the sounds of the surrounding guards and the occasional barked orders coming from the troop leaders. In his peripheral vision, lingering on the very edge of the light that filled the arena, he could see the tall, silhouetted figure of the Ringmaster seated on a raised platform, surveying everything.

Below the platform his elite guards circled the Ringmaster's position, their long capes floating around them. It was impossible to tell one of the elite guards from another. Each stared coldly from their white expressionless masks as they scanned the landscape. Csoda felt chills when he watched them and when he looked towards the Ringmaster he felt a deep vibration that lingered in the space between his cage and the distant platform. His senses told him that there was more to the tall figure than met the eye, a mystery that surrounded the man and his special guards.

The rising moon eventually called the camp to sleep, but by the first light of the morning sun it was alive with commotion again. Wagons were opened and from them men pulled large tent canvasses and supplies. By the time the sun rose behind the city of Phaedon, the camp had turned into a more permanent settlement, complete with shading tents where the performers could practice and horses could be groomed out of the brutal heat of the direct sun.

The platform the Ringmaster occupied the night before was now covered with a stretched maroon and gold canvas with side flaps that could be opened or closed and tied into place with golden ropes to whatever configuration suited him. The flaps up allowed the drifting breeze in and opened up his view of the surrounding camp, specific flaps down could help shade and protect him from the moving sun or a brisk wind, and, when needed, all of the walls could be dropped down enclosing him in an instant shield of privacy.

As the day progressed, groups of well attired emissaries, fattened merchants, regal politicians and burly slave traders traveled from the city of Phaedon towards the Kirkos tents. Csoda could see their tiny figures grow as they came from the edge of the buildings on the horizon in wagons or on horseback, and crossed the long expanse of empty desert space. All of them, upon reaching the camp, went straight to the Ringmaster's platform where he either dictated or entertained their needs. So many came that there was soon a line waiting for an audience with the Ringmaster. Those of wealth and higher political rank were given permission to skip ahead of the lower class merchants and traders. However, all of them, no matter their station in life, waited for the Ringmaster to call for them. They stood, in patient respect for their turn, despite the growing heat.

To add to the commotion of the bustling camp, a larger herd of elephants was brought in to join the smaller herd that had been traveling with the parade. Their large forms swayed gracefully around the perimeter of the arena like a moving sculptural wall. Each one was accompanied by a lean, bronze skinned handler, wearing rope sandals and a loincloth. Each handler carried a thin, four foot long stick that was used to easily command the massive creatures.

Csoda still felt awe at watching them. Even when they were not covered in the decorative blankets and performing balancing acts with beautiful women perched on their shoulders, they were fascinating. Despite their size and power they were gentle and smart. They lifted their feet quickly if they even got close to stepping on one of their handler's feet, conscious of their crushing strength, but choosing gentleness. They reached out to each other as they stood swaying, their long trunks wrapping gently around each other's tails as if they were holding hands. It was beautiful and yet painful for Csoda to observe for their kind nature was a rare sign of empathy in the harsh world they shared.

In contrast he could hear the guards shouting at slaves in other wagons nearby. Somewhere a woman was crying, her muffled sobs drifting through the wind like a floating feather of sound, making it impossible to tell where she was located. Csoda's empathy for her made his heart ache. He wished he were one of the noble Elephants, able to reach out and comfort a neighboring soul. He wished, at the very least, that he could send out a comforting thought to her, through a song, or a kind word. His wish was unfulfilled, he had no voice and there was no comfort in this place for himself, much less any that he could spare for another.

The aching time drifted past and some of the morning visitors from Phaedon finished their negotiations with the Ringmaster and took to entertaining themselves by sitting under large umbrellas around the arena to watch the training. Small groups eventually broke away from the larger crowds and began to explore the camp itself. They peered in on the helpless prisoners and wild animals with morbid curiosity. Csoda retreated to a far corner away from the window, sitting cross-legged he avoided looking at the visitors. Biro sat in his usual place, and though he was half hidden by the shadows of the cage, his eyes could still be seen staring coldly at the onlookers.

One after another the wealthy Phaedons sneered, noses pinched. They waved the wood of scented fans in front of their faces and held small pieces of perfumed cloth up to cover their mouths and noses. Some complained out loud with flabby jowls about the stench. Their comments implied that they believed the prisoners were responsible for their unsanitary conditions and that their unkempt cages were a sign of the captive's lower nature. The guards and attendants responded to the complaints by filling buckets with water and scented oils and throwing them onto the prisoners, much to the delight of the Phaedons.

Some of these visitors stopped and stood in front of their cage window, examining Biro and Csoda in stoic silence, hands clasped behind their backs. Some pointed and chatted with each other or the nearby guards, inquiring or guessing at the two captive's physical well being, or from which war they had been captured. Others passed by in groups accompanied with newly acquired slave girls dressed in bells and silk, pretending to hold elaborate conversations even while groping their purchases.

Biro contained himself like a cold statue with glaring eyes, but the affect of the crowd began to wear on Csoda's mind. With each passing onlooker he felt himself falling into fear. Anxiety crept through his body making him shake with the slightest tremor. The closeness of them, the sound of their voices, the scent of their sickly sweet perfumes, the gleam off their small teeth glinting in snarling smiles. The distant coliseum was a dark shadow on the horizon behind them and all of these things reminded him of his last encounter with a similar crowd–the day they took his tongue.

As his body shivered in fear he had a thought. What if the day they took his voice, they had also taken his bravery? Faced with the reality of what was to come, he felt unable to focus, unable to calm his nerves and his racing heart.

He tried to ignore them, stared at the wall, focused all of his usual meditative skills at steadying his breath, but the fear still penetrated his racing heart. It slid into his stomach making it clench and throb until he eventually found himself curled on the cage floor, his back to the crowd.

The voices of the Phaedons echoed behind him, commenting on how sickly he looked. For a moment it seemed that their toxic voices turned into a strange smoky haze and all of his Shamanic training was useless to fend it off.

"Come back, Csoda," Biro's deep voice growled under his breath in their common tongue, "Don't leave me now, my brother."

The statement broke through the haze of fear and cracked the tight rock that was his stomach. The words softened his heart so that its harsh beating felt cushioned. Csoda remembered the Taltos, remembered that he was part of a greater purpose, a purpose that would allow him to survive. Then he realized that he did not know Biro's fate and suddenly felt protective over his only friend and fellow countryman. The circling haze of fear dissipated as he regained control of his breath and, pulling in deep long intakes of air, he began to feel centered again. Still, this long battle within his body tired him and he remained motionless, exhausted, desperate for sleep.

Csoda tapped a musical rhythm on the wooden floor,

trying to say with his limited strength, "I'm here Biro." And Biro, in response, reached over and laid his large hand on Csoda's shoulder, giving it a couple of solid pats.

"That's right Csoda, hold on. We have a long way to go."

Then Biro, guarding his ailing friend from the curious eyes and sneering comments, placed himself between Csoda and the wagon window. He sat cross-legged with folded arms and glared deep into the eyes of each individual as they approached. He snarled at the crowd with a strange angry grin, and the intensity of this solid man, the vibration of his low tuned growl, made the onlookers uneasy. The Phaedons suddenly felt that the cage walls that held this wild man might be a bit flimsy, or they imagined his brutish hand striking through the window and clenching their throats. Soon the visitors became so unsure of their own delicate safety that they gave a wide berth to this prisoner, moving on to peer at other exotic, but less disturbing, captives.

The aggressive intensity of Biro did not go unnoticed. From his platform, the Ringmaster observed the change in the Phaedons who were all taking wide detours around one of the prison wagons. His guards reported to him that this was the cage of the nomads, his two captives from the distant tribes. These were the two prisoners he kept separated from the other captives for fear that the rumors of their people's infectious nature might be true.

Watching the fat merchants and Phaedon's other elite nervously avoiding their prison made him believe that he was right in being cautious. He smiled at the simple minded fear he could both see and feel coming off of the Phaedons, amused by their weakness. Still, precautions should be taken. The Ringmaster would make certain that when the final day came to open the doors of their wagon and march them with the other captives towards the coliseum, twice as many guards would walk with Biro and Csoda.

The sun and moon rose and set for many days before the time came for Biro and Csoda to be removed from their wagon. When that day came, neither Biro nor Csoda fought the many guards that were assigned to them. Csoda had recovered from the madness of anxiety though he was dazed and worn down. Stepping out of their prison brought him a strange euphoria and a sensation of being birthed from the confining barred womb and allowed to stand under the expansive sky.

Csoda experienced the events around him as if he was in a waking dream. The open stretch of the desert landscape reached out to touch the distant horizon in all directions from where he stood. Even passed Phaedon he could see the sand continue. He had been born from the cage into nothing but sky and sand.

Biro had a surge of adrenalin pulse through his veins as his feet felt the heat of the ground. Still, he was not planning on fighting the many guards, as that would have been futile. He had decided to save his strength for the coliseum as he still intended to live. For his amusement he did make a quick half lunge towards the guards as soon as he was out of the cage, just to see if he could make them back up, which they did. After that he contented himself with sneering at them as they bullied him into position to be chained to the rows of other captives.

Both Csoda and Biro welcomed the buckets of water thrown onto them to wash their bodies, and they consented to putting on the provided rope sandals and the simple, but fresh, canvas tunics. It seemed that even the convicts would be given matching attire for their parade into the city.

Csoda was still chained to Biro and placed directly

behind him. Their wrists were cuffed together in front of their bodies, the cuffs then chained to the shackles at their ankles, and all of them had heavy leather belts placed around their waists that were linked to more connecting chains. Altogether the bonds allowed them enough movement to walk, but not enough to do much else. Successful regular movement of the whole group relied upon the synchronicity of their unified steps. For this reason on either side of the captives two drummers walked, hitting the drums in regular unison to direct the captive's gait. Those who refused to walk or who fell out of rhythm were attacked with whips and flailing chains. Those who weakened and fell were unchained and pulled away from the group to be openly beaten and sometimes killed. The brutality of the guards soon affected the remaining captives, who responded in precise disciplined footfalls as they followed behind a line of guards dressed in polished mesh armor and meticulously clean black and grey uniforms.

Despite the chains and the dreaded events that awaited them, despite the terror and the bullying of the guards, both Csoda and Biro felt relief at being pulled outside of the wagon. This was not freedom, but it was movement, it was change. The sensation of the open air around them and the sand shifting under their sandaled feet filled them with a surge of energy. Walking in a continuous direction, with no walls and ceilings blocking the sun or the sky, created a mad exhilaration in their bodies and their minds.

Their group was led to an elaborate parade that would travel into Phaedon and end at the coliseum. They were directed to fall in behind a legion of grey horses wearing indigo blankets under silver, brass and polished leather saddles. The beast's foreheads and eyes were masked with silver decorated shields and round sections of mesh over their eyes allowing them to see. Each rider wore a gleaming white linen tunic and a flowing hooded cape, their individual faces covered with expressionless masks of gold.

Ahead of the golden masked horsemen, rows of light and nimble leather and wood chariots pulled by swift steeds darted and zigzagged in elaborate formations. The chariots were painted in multiple colors and carried drivers that wore short military indigo blue tunics, tall leather boots, and polished hammered silver helmets that reflected the sun and scattered that reflection into multiple tiny spheres that glinted like diamonds tumbling across the sand. Thin poles rose up from the sides of the chariots, holding aloft long snaking flags that flicked high above the driver's heads.

A legion of the brutal guards surrounded the chained captives. They stuck to a strict formation unless one was moved to viciously attack a straggling prisoner with swift punishment. Otherwise, their backs stayed straight and their faces stern. The cheek and nose guards of the ridge helmets that they all wore mostly masked their individual identities. Their grim, forbidding countenances contrasted with the graceful movement of long sprays of feathers that erupted from the tops of the helmets to dance in the desert wind.

Through the drumming rhythm that kept them in step, they could hear the bellows of the oxen pulling the cages of roaring lions, the groans of camels, the jingle of the acrobat's bells, the hollering of orders from the mounted guards that rode along the side of each section, their whips cracking. Behind them the towering, newly painted black carriage of the Ringmaster swayed with each pull of the slowly driven elephants. Dancing women, dressed in bells and carrying flowing silken scarves, circled around his carriage, their movement constant and fluid. His elite guard in their usual hooded capes and white masks lingered directly alongside, turning from side to side in slow rotations as they moved with the procession, their eyes constantly scanning.

The Ringmaster stood tall on his open platform, his towering frame regally overseeing the proceedings ahead of him. From there he moved like a mythical conductor, his long accentuated arms sweeping dramatically. With his movements the assembled parade maneuvered across the open desert valley towards the distant towering walls of Phaedon. It snaked like an elaborately colored dragon covered in swaths of bright silk, brass, silver and gold. Each unique section found its pace within the pulse of the marching drums and the melodies of the music that erupted from the accompanying musicians.

On the opposite side of the stretch of open desert the people of Phaedon spilled through the town gates into the outskirts of their city walls, fanning out to create two swarming lines of cheering faces and waving hands. A wide space was left open between the two crowded rows so that the parade could move through the center. There they waited to informally guide the spectacle into their city.

The Ringmaster held his hands high above and turned his head towards the sky. He called out in a booming voice, announcing into the air, "Phaedon! We have arrived! The Grand Kirkos now begins!"

His direct words were heard only by those closest to him as his voice was drowned out in the menagerie of other sounds, but his announcement could be felt, rippling through the air along the spine like shape of the marching parade. Csoda felt it, a sense of electricity that flashed through his body and forward towards the open gates of Phaedon. The crowds ahead felt it rush between their bodies at the same time that they saw, in the distance, the distinct figure of the Ringmaster, standing upon his platform, hands aloft in the air.

They responded to his call with crazed applause. Their cheers and cries could be heard across the sand, mixing with the wind. The sound hummed and buzzed over and through the parade into the ears of the proud Ringmaster. He smiled slightly upon hearing it and took in a deep breath, expanding his broad chest as if he could inhale the very sound.

18

———

The march across the sand to Phaedon seemed short to Csoda, who was distracted by the events that unfolded before him. He could not see the entire parade as he was blocked by the mounted guards and the bodies of the captives chained around him, but he could see flashes of chariots darting ahead through the formation of the white cloaked horsemen. The wheels on the chariots kicked up clouds of dust and sand behind them that occasionally drifted back to him, keeping him from seeing and breathing and sticking to his sweating skin. Through these clouds of dust he could see the drummer marching right ahead and to the left of his group. The drummer kept the rhythm on a single bass drum to which he and the other men stepped. He could see the side of the drummer's face, his stoic expression defying the movement of his animated arms and hands. He lifted the drum mallets high into the air, spinning them dramatically, before allowing them to fall, reverberating, against the leather drumhead with a monotonous boom.

It was this rhythm that Csoda connected with, its sound

reminiscent of the drums he was trained to use as a shaman. He allowed the beat to connect him to a place of peace in his mind, calming the terror of the coliseum that weighed on his soul.

Biro walked ahead. His back was straight and strong, his head never turned to look around, his steps were precise and militant. Csoda could now see that his friend's intimidating height and broad size was not an illusion produced by the small wagon cell. Next to these other captive men, Biro was a broad and powerful force. He was also a veteran of this insanity. He walked both as one who knew what lay ahead, and as one who had steeled himself against the fear of it.

The other captives surrounding him were of different races and different lands. The rare words spoken by some of them were in foreign tongues that he could not always recognize. As they marched and Csoda fell deeper into his calming trance, he witnessed the men's fear. He saw their isolation as they scanned the group, their eyes begging for a familiar face. Their brief, foreign words were desperate attempts to connect with someone, anyone, but their voices only drifted into the wind, away into the parade, garnering no recognition, no response.

While Biro remained solid and unwavering, others walked defeated, they shivered, their steps stumbled, their eyes and heads darted quickly around, or hung down in defeat. Csoda, unable to witness such fear without compassion, took deep breaths. With each breath he imagined a pulsating light emanating from the sides of his powerful friend, mixing with the rhythm of his calming trance. He imagined the light expanding beyond Biro and surrounding the men, one by one. Moment by moment, Csoda's covert magic took affect. As they walked, the men around him found their hearts, their memories of bravery, their indi-vidual stories of power, their peace with death. One by one, in each of their own minds, they chose to face their unknown fate with resolve. No longer did they scan desper-ately for familiarity. Instead they met each other's eyes with a fatalistic acceptance of their situation, united in a brother-hood of humanity, if not culture.

By the time the parade entered the walls of Phaedon and the captives, guards and entertainers were wrapped in the deafening roars of the awaiting crowd, the men chained to Biro and Csoda walked with straight backs. They walked with bodies unshaken, their eyes focused ahead, unwaver-ing. Their faces held the determined gaze of men going to battle, instead of to slaughter.

This group of proud and brave captives did not go unno-ticed. The citizens of Phaedon who looked down on the parade from building balconies and roof tops commented to each other on how powerful this group appeared. They declared that the group must have been assembled together for a special event. Perhaps, they were from a single culture of warriors? Or maybe, this year, some of the captives were being trained for battle to improve the quality of the sports? These assumptions jumped around from the balconies and rooftops and became full blown rumors within the crowds on the streets, until they had formed multiple trails of gossip, anticipation, and excitement about the first Grand Kirkos of the year.

How proud, how lucky they were to be citizens of Phae-don. The greatest city next to the Capital in all of Critias, chosen to be the first to witness such spectacular events. How grateful they were to their leaders. How loyal they felt to the distant Emperor Coracis. How easy it was to forget any ills that plagued their lives, or worries they had for their futures. Here, right in front of them, marched a group of captives, unafraid. The site of them became a rush of excitement in the crowd, as if the bravery of these men was their own, peaking their bloodlust and hunger for the glorious Kirkos.

Through the gates of Phaedon and down the crowded city streets full of cheering citizens, the captive's bodies began to weaken. They were exhausted, overheated, their skin burned, their throats dry. Their feet, despite the sandals strapped to them, were blistered and raw. Even the group that Csoda marched with, while mentally stronger, showed signs of weakened legs. The tremors of exhaustion rippling through their muscles made them sway. Such was the strain on their bodies that some of them stumbled and slipped as they tried to adjust to the hardened cobblestone streets that led them to the coliseum gates. Even the guards seemed tired, reducing their discipline to a few angry snaps of their whips or hoarse shouts as they responded to the faltering captive's missteps.

The towering white marble walls of the coliseum rose high before them. On all sides they were surrounded by distorted and glowering faces of multiple statues depicting men, Gods and beasts. These stone figures peered down on them from the edges of the streets, entrances, and from high perches on the top of the coliseum walls. Their giant forms and frozen eyes watched the parade as it entered the coliseum through two massive arched wooden doors to be engulfed in a cavernous dark opening.

Through the opening the captives were led, and the bright light of the sun dimmed dramatically as they were pulled down a wide ramp into the depths of the coliseum. Here the air turned cold. The walls and archways, built with blocks of insulating stone, revealed a maze of hallways and caverns that split out ahead of them. The guards quickly began to move different groups down separate hallways towards partitioned holding cells. Csoda and Biro's group was pulled far down a side passage, the light growing darker with every step away from the entrance, until they were herded into a shadowed space that was more like a cave than a room. Their chains and bonds were forcefully taken off as, one by one, they were pushed into a large group cell, a heavy iron door shutting behind them.

Biro moved to a corner and turned to face the group, his back against the wall. Csoda followed him and stood by his side. The exhausted captives settled themselves into the space. Some of them simply collapsed where they stood. When it was apparent that the men were merely going to rest and did not seem determined to fight each other, Biro, too, slid down the wall to sit on the floor, his knees bent, his arms crossed on top of them. Csoda sat next to his friend, his body ached but he did not feel tired. He looked at Biro and grabbed his attention with a quick wave of his hand then wrote in the dirt next to them. "Sleep. I will watch." Biro lowered his head and squinted his eyes to better read the words in the dark. When he did his guarded façade broke momentarily, revealing his own exhaustion. He nodded, leaned his head back against the wall and closed his eyes, falling asleep immediately.

Csoda sat, looking out onto the group of men, many of which had already fallen into different states of sleep, some curled like children on the floor. Their ability to sleep was a testament to their exhaustion and not to the comfort of the space itself. The cell echoed with the sounds of roaring animals, yelling men and the grinding cranks of rolling chains and pulleys, all emanating from the multiple corridors and cages hidden behind the stone walls that contained them.

In the dim light, even as his eyes adjusted, Csoda could not see the ceiling above them. The cold walls seemed to go up forever, disappearing into the dark. He could, however, hear the sounds of pounding hooves and what he guessed were chariot wheels reverberating on wood. Loosened dust, shaken by the thundering activity, fell on him. He could guess that the open arena was directly above them, simply by the logic of how they had entered the coliseum and the sounds that he now could hear. Everything else about where he was, the time of day and what laid in store for him and the other men in his cell, was shrouded by the darkness and the impenetrable stone.

By the time Biro came out of his sleep with a sudden intake of breath, the noises had quieted to the occasional roars of beasts and the anguished sobs of captives. The thundering above had ceased and the dim light that existed before had been extinguished by, what Csoda could only guess, was the presence of night. He could hear Biro speak, but could no longer see him.

"Csoda?" He whispered, and Csoda patted the ground next to him with a short rhythm of taps in response. He felt Biros hand tap his own as he identified where the sound came from and then the deep voice continued, "Thank you, I have slept, now you must too. The games will start in the morning. Sleep now."

If Biro's words disturbed him, it did not matter. Csoda's own fatigue overpowered his ability to worry. Time disappeared, lost in the black light of a dreamless sleep. Almost instantly after hearing Biro instruct him to rest, he was hearing his friend's voice alerting him to awake.

"Csoda," Said Biro, "Wake up... it is time."

19

———

Pushed from their stone waiting cells by guards with pointed spears, the mass of convicts grouped together into a narrow dark hall. The sheer number of men being pushed into the space forced those who had already entered to move forward, down the hallway, until they were finally funneled into a wider room where they crowded together and waited.

High in the darkness above their heads the heavy wooden ceiling pulsated with thundering movement. The sounds of racing horses and chariots, along with the deafening shrill hum of the cheering crowd rose and fell like ocean waves flooding through the darkened space, washing over the captive's fearful souls. A mist of dust released from the vibrations above, filling the air with a musty choking smell.

More men were pushed in through other adjoining passages, gates slamming behind them as they entered. The space filled until there was barely any room between them. Men stood shoulder-to-shoulder, belly-to-back, the air thick with the stench of sweat, urine and fear.

This, thought Csoda, was the darkest place he had ever been, even though there was a trace of light that played with the grey shadows and reflected upon the shoulders and cheeks of the men around him. Csoda could see the white of their eyes, the flashing fear on their horror stricken faces. This place, confined and helpless, stuck in the masses of the condemned, where he could find no rhythm, no way to escape, ignited claustrophobic fear in Csoda's heart.

He stifled the fear by focusing on the only task that made sense to him, making sure he did not get separated from Biro. They braced themselves alongside of each other, allowing no one to be pushed between them. Csoda was suddenly keenly aware that he was no longer physically chained to Biro. That thought, at this time, in this dark place, was more frightening than liberating.

Biro, too, was determined to stay close to Csoda, but he also made a point of moving and wedging himself forward. Inch by inch he moved, trying to gain a position in front of the pushing mass of men that faced a slash of light hovering ahead of them at the top of a steep ramp. Csoda followed his lead, moving along with his friend.

They succeeded in getting to the base of the ramp, the pressure of bodies too tight ahead of them to move any further. Biro braced himself with wide legs, his arms spread out from his body in order to keep the convicts from packing themselves too closely to him. Csoda did the same. The light ahead of them was a slit between two massive doors that Csoda assumed would open into the arena. For now, while they waited, they risked being trampled by the men who shared their fate as more and more of them were still being pushed into the space from behind, their haunted faces on the verge of panic.

"Steady," stated Biro and Csoda did not know if he spoke

to him or to the room in general. The inpouring of more captives from the back hallways stopped, and no longer being pushed forward by the prodding guards, the mass of confined men seemed to all hold their breath. Their eyes intent upon the closed door, they stood, braced, waiting.

The flood of voices coming from the cheering coliseum crowd still resonated through the door they faced, but now the sound adjusted and took on the rhythm of a chant. Csoda could not tell if the chant consisted of specific words, but before he could try to isolate the meaning, a rumbling new sound erupted from behind them sending a vibrating chaos through his chest and up his spine.

Biro reacted quickly to the sound. His body stayed braced while his head snapped to look behind them. Chains creaked through iron pulleys, the rumbling shook the ground. The men in the back of the room were all trapped and started to panic, pushing forward, clawing and yelling in frantic screams as they crashed against the men in front of them who blocked their way. Csoda looked behind, but could not see past the panicked faces surging towards him. The mass of men became an unforgiving wave of flesh as they tried to move away from what sounded like the groan of opening cage doors, followed by bellowing snorts and the roll of thunder.

A wall of hysterical captives soon crashed against Csoda and Biro and, despite their braced stance, pushed them into the men in front of them. Csoda felt a hand grasp his forearm and over the yells of the masses he heard Biro bellow, "Grab my arm!" He looked to see the hand on his forearm was his friends and clamped his hand onto Biro's forearm, locking them together as their bodies were shoved towards the closed door. Men fell before them under the pressuring crowd and there was nothing to stop their bodies from being trampled once they were underfoot.

Just as the chaos seemed un-navigable, just as both Biro and Csoda were being catapulted up the ramp towards the solid door in front of them, just as the force of panicking captives became a chaos of frenzied screams and Csoda imagined himself to soon be pinned against the door and crushed, a loud blasting sound of crashing metal rang from ahead and the doors to the arena swung open.

"Jump!" Biro yelled and Csoda, still locked in arms with his friend, followed his order.

They both leapt high into the air. The rushing captives that pushed against their backs stampeded towards the open door. Biro and Csoda, caught in the movement of the stampeding men rode upon their frenzied shoulders out into the arena.

Flung forward into the open air and blinded by the bright light of the mid morning sun, both Csoda and Biro unlocked arms and leapt forward. They hit the sandy ground running. The crowd of men that had unintentionally carried them out onto the coliseum floor spread out, running in all directions. Csoda ran as he had never run before in his life. He could hear the cries of the men still echoing from the dark hall behind him mixed with what seemed like otherworldly bellowing roars. He ran, even though his mind had no destination, and his eyesight had not adjusted to the bright sun. It was impossible to see what lay in front of him.

"Left, go left!" Biro barked at him. Csoda, his eyesight still straining against the bright light, shifted the movement of his body towards the left, following Biro's orders blindly. His feet were barely touching the packed sand surface as with each leaping step his legs catapulted his body forward, far off the ground. He ran into a chaos of roaring and flashing, unidentifiable sounds, shadows and light. Everything around and within him seemed to be surging–his bursting lungs, the turbulent clouds of stinging sand, the rumbling ground, the searing desert heat, his heart. Everything swelled and burst into a collage of violence erupting around him.

When his eyes adjusted to the light, he saw an expanse of open space in front of him. In his peripheral vision he thought he could still see Biro. He felt they were still close, swore he could hear his friend's feet pounding the ground near him. Otherwise, somehow, they had pulled away from the crowd of other men, who he did not see and could not hear amongst the drowning waterfall of cheers that reverberated from the watching crowd.

He could see the crowd now, merged together like a massive plague of hissing locusts clinging to the arena stands. He was running past the middle of the arena, to the left of where they first burst out through the door. The distance was closing quickly between him and the side of the fifteen-foot tall arena wall. He was close enough to its surface to see the remnants of past bloody battles still coating its merciless stone face with a slick sheen of oils and dark stains.

Guards in featureless iron masks lined the top of the wall. They were as still as the stone they stood upon, their legs apart, their left hands behind their backs, at ease, their right hands holding simple, thin, towering spears with glinting sharpened points that reached far into the air above their heads.

He could still feel the thundering vibration that had filled the captives with panic, but before he could think to turn his head and see what horrible terror had chased them into the arena, he heard a rumbling coming from behind him. A loud snorting breath vented behind his right hand leaving it moist with the exhale of a creature who was now directly behind him to his right. Biro was nowhere to be seen. Csoda arched his back and flung his body to the left to try to avoid the oncoming creature. Just as he did a sharp horn skimmed across his waist, tearing his tunic, but missing his skin.

The creature shot past him. A ton of rippling muscled, black coated flesh, snorting and bellowing with anger. Csoda had avoided the horns from behind but now couldn't stop his forward motion. He flew directly towards what he now saw was an angry black bull that spun in front of him with a surprising amount of nimble grace for its behemoth size. It spun so that it could face him head on. Its eyes were deep, empty black pools that rolled upward in manic fury and then widened, flashing a bloodshot red light as the bull focused back onto Csoda. The beast lowered its colossal head, swinging it back and forth on a thick neck, muscles rippling like iron ropes from the base of its skull to its broad, stiff shoulders. It aimed two arching bone white horns that had been tipped at their ends with silver pointed metal directly at Csoda.

Csoda, still plummeting forward from momentum, felt for a moment that he was floating–his body poised in midair as the bull moved slowly before him. It pawed the ground and then lunged towards him in a determined charge. In that moment, Csoda memorized every hair, every nuance of form of the creature before him. He could see the texture of the bone like horns, the wetness of the flared nostrils, the solid broad haunches that tapered down into agile, ebony hooves. It was as if he observed a dream, or an expertly carved sculpture that had come to life in front of him. It was all a mere illusion of life, created by the desert heat, his pulsing heart, and his own exhaustion.

Then it hit–the impact of over a ton of charging flesh and bone.

The thick skull bore him down into the dirt, the horns did not pierce his flesh, but scraped the ground on either side of his chest, pinning him between them as he was plowed across the arena floor. Everything became a collage of flying dust, a chaos of thundering pressure, stamping hooves, and the bellowing thick breath of the angry bull. Then, something, another form or shadow, suddenly flashed before Csoda's eyes. The crushing pressure of the plowing bull was pulled off of his body, just long enough for him to instinctually curl into a ball and try to cover his head to shield it from the blows of the animal's hooves.

To his surprise, the blows did not come. The bull leapt to the side, snorting angrily, pulled away from Csoda as it refocused on the intruding shadow. Csoda risked lifting his head away from his shielding arms. There before him, less than five feet away, he saw Biro, arms wide, legs braced and slightly bent, his upper body leaning forward as if he was about to pounce. Biro facing the fierce recalculating bull.

Like an expert wrestler, or a snake charmer facing a giant cobra, Biro swayed. His movement matched the dance of the outraged, if now hesitant bull. It swung its lumbering head from side to side, displaying its menacing horns, backing away slowly from Biro's predatory stance with rumbling snorting grunts and pawing hooves.

Csoda was crawling backwards, sucking in great gasps of air, otherwise unaware of any injuries the bull's charge had caused him. His body reacting instinctually to move away from what was before him as fast as possible. Yet his eyes were unable to look away, locked on the deadly dance between Biro and the bull.

The bull continued to back up, Biro held his ground. Then the creature, with a solid huff of breath, braced its back hooves, leaned into its haunches and, with its skin rippling over coiled flesh, launched forward, aiming its charge directly at Biro's stomach. Right before the mighty bull was about to ram into the man and before its rugged charge slammed the crown of its solid head into his mortal flesh, Biro, with all of the precision of a fine athlete, reached out with both hands and grabbed the bulls horns. Leveraging the energy behind the bulls up thrusting head, he matched its movement with his own calculated leap. Biro catapulted up into the air, his legs extending out to either side, the bull charged directly underneath him as he released the horns. Biro, to the delight and the surprise of both Csoda and the now ecstatic crowd, leapt over the charging bull.

A shocked laugh burst from Csoda's throat, his lack of tongue distorting the sound. A laugh both of relief and amazement at his countryman's adept feat. The bull had run far away from them, its full speed charge carrying it forward without stopping until it reached the far side of the arena. Biro landed on his feet, turned quickly and ran up to a delighted and shocked Csoda, who had briefly forgotten the imminent danger they were still both facing.

"Are you okay?" Biro bellowed over the deafening cheers of the crowd. Csoda, barely remembering that he had been pinned below the crushing bull's weight minutes before, beamed at his friend. His fear and panic destroyed by Biro's trick and the resulting surge of adrenaline that coursed through his blood.

Biro, confused by his friend's insane grin, quickly

surveyed Csoda's injuries. Seeing nothing completely debilitating, he grabbed Csoda's shoulders, giving him a small but firm shake. He growled an order, "Csoda, you must live. Do you understand? We must live!"

Csoda nodded and jumped up to stand with Biro, surprised by his energy and lack of fear. He pulled in deep breaths of air, and with each breath he could feel the entire crowd in the stadium surrounding them. Their cheers flooded into his lungs and traveled through his skin like electrical charges. The energy pushed through his blood and into his muscles. His skin tingled, and his bones seemed to lengthen and crack into alignment, making him feel taller. His face was still beaming a broad smile, when he saw wisps of delicate light shooting out from Biro's heart. Like tiny thin translucent red arrows they shot into the coliseum stands. He marveled at seeing them. He wished he could explain to Biro what he saw. Wished he had time to show his friend that he, Biro, had activated The Pull.

Where Csoda had learned to activate the magic through meditation and music, Biro apparently activated it through kinetic action and heroism. Csoda, if he had not been a fated mute, could have talked for hours about the uniqueness of this moment, but he had no way to speak to Biro. That and they still needed to face the terrors of the arena. So instead, he smiled with an irrational grin at Biro, who seemed unable to see the wisps of light.

Biro, was confused by Csoda's frenzied expression, but had concluded that neither of them were badly injured. Upon grasping Csoda's shoulders, he too had felt a surge of energy, a jolt of untamed courage. His own muscles seemed stronger, his senses heightened. He felt the cheers coming from the stadium crowd, cheers that traveled through his ears and seemed to enter his blood. His heart swelled and pushed an intensified rise of energy though every inch of his body, even as it cleared his mind of distress.

For the first time since they had been catapulted into the stadium, Csoda and Biro actually found themselves looking around and surveying their environment. The charging bull that had attacked them had joined the rest of the bulls in a giant stampede, running along the outer right wall of the arena. The bulls ran madly, trampling the scrambling captives that had the misfortune of being caught in front of their pulverizing hooves.

Behind the running bulls, three large, wide, red painted war wagons entered the stadium. Each wagon carried two soldiers, a driver and an archer, and each was pulled by two armored horses. The soldiers wore armored tunics that shielded their torsos and upper legs. They each also wore silver, gold and bronze helmet like masks with exaggerated and menacing facial features that gave them the appearance of otherworldly demons or beasts. Long arched noses, raptor beaks, horned ears, scaled textures, or snarling, dog like muzzles, differentiated each mask from the other, giving each driver a unique look so the crowd could tell them apart.

It was apparent that the goal at the moment was to drive the rampaging stampede over the escaping captives with great flare, mowing down the majority of the men. However, swords hung in scabbards at their sides, knives were strapped on their belts and while one drove the chariot, the second man in each vehicle held a bow, a quiver of arrows strapped to his side. This weaponry hinted that they would act as more than herdsman in this bloody spectacle.

Csoda observed the weaponized charioteers. He had already been attacked by one of the rampaging bulls and survived. Now, with the help of Biro's act of bravery, he could feel the ancestral magic of his people vibrating through his skin in a way that he had never expected. Thin tendrils of silver energy were stretching unseen through the air. These lights of silver thread connected him secretly to the surrounding crowd and, while the connections were wispy and weak, the sheer number of them gave him a surge of strength and confidence.

In this ring of death, for the first time since the horrid day that he was knocked to his knees and had his song stolen, here, Csoda remembered exactly who and what he was. He was the leader and poet of revolutions. He was the singer who could ignite the crowds. He was a Shaman of the ancient Törzsi Nomádok.

He felt the energy of the sacred magic, the connection of the cheering crowd, Biro's friendship, and even the powerful force of the rampaging bulls. Here, his ability to connect with the spiritual merged with his physical reality. Here, in this place of destruction, the severed bond between his soul and his body began to join together and heal.

He found that the hopeless mayhem and death that he and Biro were surrounded by was not only less frightening, but did not require his analysis or judgment. The past revolutions and his culture had crumbled. His people were scattered–but he was still alive.

This violent and surreal arena was where he had been placed. This was where his life had led him, and a strange acceptance of his circumstances settled into the depth of his being. Here he could remember the song of his soul. Here his song might affect the world around him, even when he could no longer physically sing it out loud.

The stampede was at the far end of the arena, turning along the edge of the ring so that the chariots were driving the angry herd back towards Biro and Csoda's position.

There was no shelter near them. The cliff walls of the arena edge had no noticeable crevices or niches that they could duck into or climb to avoid the stampede. The arena itself was void of anything except for the crushed and bleeding bodies of the hundreds of unfortunate men that had been released into the coliseum with them.

A few straggling survivors, who had escaped the storm of hooves, were huddled in the middle of the arena together as if their numbers would protect them. Others, scrambled within the alcoves of the four arched stone entrances placed around the outer walls on the north, south, east and west sides of the arena floor. In these recesses the captives scratched and pounded at the locked gates, trying to retreat back into the caverns and cages. Finding the gates locked solid they reverted to using the bars of the doors to climb upwards, only to be poked at through the bars by the attending guards with spears from the other side, until they fell on their backs and were left to scramble in the dust or return to pounding frantically on the doors once again.

Both of those options, huddling with the mass in the middle and scrambling to return to the prison they had just left, seemed futile to Csoda. Running away from the obviously faster armored wagons and bulls seemed just as hopeless. He looked towards Biro, who still stood next to him, braced for action, but also seemingly unclear as to what form of action to take. Their eyes met and Csoda could see the determined will of Biro. Biro in return, noticed the calm peace that had washed over Csoda.

Csoda reached out his hand to his friend, grasping it in a firm shake, just in case this was their last shared time on earth. Then he nodded at Biro, released his friend's hand and walked directly towards the oncoming stampede.

Biro watched as Csoda moved away from him. At first he

was confused, yet he could feel the electric surge of the magic coursing through his body. He felt it increase as Csoda shook his hand. He felt no desire to leave Csoda's side. Trotting a few steps at first to catch up, he moved next to his friend so that they could walk beside each other and meet their fate.

What had begun as a spark in Csoda's heart became stronger, more tangible, as soon as he chose to move towards the oncoming stampede. The wispy tendrils of energy that he could feel between him and the crowd were visible to him as a web of shiny threads that reached from the center of his chest outwards to the people.

"I am you." He thought quietly, sending the thought vibrating through the strings, outwards to all. "You are me." He thought, and again imagined the vibration on the strings.

The bulls had closed half the distance. Soon he and Biro would be taken over by them, but before he focused on the herd, he thought one last thought, sending it to the crowd.... "My glory is yours. My victory is yours. My death is yours." Then, taking in a strong breath, he sensed the crowd leaning towards him with the inhale, heard patterns of thoughts whispering through the air that were not his own. His body filled with a new found electric charge and he ran–straight towards the center of the oncoming stampede–and as he ran he felt a shift in the air as the entire silenced crowd gasped at once.

20

The massive billowing strips of canvas high above the coliseum stands worked as awnings for the velarium, shading the crowd below, shifting in each changing wind. The breeze normally funneled upwards, through the coliseum corridors and up through the center of the arena towards the open sky. Now, the awnings fluttered as a gentle, but steady, downdraft pulled into the stadium from above. Men were positioned along the top outer rim of the coliseum walls to man the complex ropes and pulleys that adjusted the awnings to suit the needs of the crowd below. They tightened and wrenched the controlling ropes as they looked upwards to the sky to try to see what weather had changed the breeze. Above them, the sky was a clear eternal blue, no clouds or weather to address, but the wind–the wind seemed of a different nature.

Below the tapered awnings in their rib like shadows, the crowd lustfully cheered the site of the many captives being crushed before them. They held up cups of thick, sickly sweet wine and toasted to the rampaging bulls. Some growled jokingly at the carnage as they tore at pieces of roasted pig, letting the wet grease coat their lips and chins.

They leaned forward to better see the chariot drivers, their horses and their masks, and in animated conversations they picked their favorites. Some declared their choices to each other as they raucously laughed, defending those they favored with confident bets. They grabbed at bowls of fresh grapes or olives and pushed handfuls of the fruits into their mouths. They leaned back contentedly, lounging in the shade and breeze, dabbing their shoulders with scented water on moistened cloths to cool their skin.

Yet, now the wind had shifted and the heat of the sun was pulled down into the stands. The individuals in the crowd moved their attention away from the driving chariots and onto the figures of two men–two men who moved calmly towards the center of what was surely their certain death–two men who only moments earlier were witnessed dodging an aggressive bull.

One of them, to the crowd's great surprise, even leapt over the creature as he saved the life of his companion. The crowd's attention shifted, and with it their demeanor also changed. Their ravenous shouts and side conversations quieted as each of them leaned forward, trying to better see the two men. The heated breeze warmed the backs of their arched and stretching necks, making them sweat. Their mouths fell open slightly agape. Their breathing slowed until the majority of them held a soft, frozen expression of quiet surprise.

In the Eastern stands, in the Imperial box, sat the royalty of Phaedon, along with the attentive Ringmaster. Below them the bulls smashed their way through the turn. Some moved too slowly and were pushed by the rest of the stampede against the arena wall, crashing and bellowing. The war wagons raced behind them, nimbly taking the corner, the backs of their wheels spinning up a cloud of sand. The privileged view of the royalty allowed them to watch the majority of the captives run straight toward them, be overtaken, and then killed by the angry bulls. Now, the herd was being driven away from them and directed towards the leftover survivors.

In spite of the spectacle the bulls made, it was not the retreating stampede that peaked the Ringmaster's curiosity. He had expected the thundering effects of the herd of bulls upon the panicking captives. It was not even the encounter he had noticed of one man at the far end nimbly jumping over one of the strays from the herd, though he had found the feat impressive and smiled at the increased cheers from the crowd. It was not uncommon for a captive to show a level of athletic prowess and agility, to dodge a few first oncoming attacks and, therefore, increase the entertainment value of the entire event. Such feats of strength and skill were to be expected on occasion by men whose lives were in danger and, to some extent, he counted on this to please the crowd. The Ringmaster found that even if that same captive died before the event was over the crowd would praise him, the Ringmaster, for the excitement they had gleaned. It was as if he was responsible for the creative and noble feats of any man or beast that successfully achieved any act of daring. In the end, the more daring the captives, the better the show, the better the show, the happier the crowd, the happier the crowd–the more powerful the Ringmaster became.

No, it was not the captives that caught his attention. What made him stand and walk to the edge of the Empirical seats to better see, was the change in the crowd. The Ringmaster was adept at reading the crowd. His existence relied on anticipating their shifting moods and sometimes fickle attention. He scanned the stands and all throughout. On all sides, the heads of the men and women were turned to look in the same direction. Their rowdy natures were now quiet and they were all focused like a flock of birds ready to take flight.

He tried to see what they focused on, but his view of the arena floor was slightly blocked by the now retreating stampede. He could not see clearly past the cloud of dust, the driving chariots or the crashing bulls to view what held the crowd's meditative stare. What he could do was feel a change of energy. It was a change he thought he'd experienced before, even if he could not remember where or when. His eyes furrowed at the sensation as he tried to understand the tugging at his heart.

"Something...." he thought, as he placed his hands on the stone wall that protected him from tumbling into the arena and leaned his weight forward towards the action, "... something is happening." But he could not identify nor predict exactly what.

21

Emperor Coracis let his formal upright posture slip as the day with the Senators dragged on, relaxing himself against the cushions that supported him while he leaned lazily onto the broad right arm of his wide marble throne. The fingers of his right hand, his resting hand, unconsciously traced the designs that were etched into the stone of the royal chair.

The dull speeches had waxed on longer than normal. He could call this event to an end, it was in his power to do so. Still, despite his own physical discomfort, he found an amusement of sorts in knowing that the Senators were also uncomfortable, probably more so, since many of them were older or of weaker physical stature than himself. Therefore, he allowed the day of speeches to continue under the guise of dedication to his post. The entire time he entertained a private venom by watching the assembly of Senators shift and maneuver uncomfortably in their hard, wooden bench seats.

In front of this heightened throne and its flanking Imperial Legion Guard, was a small circle of open marble floor which served as the forum stage. The Senator's seats curved in three crescent rows facing him on the opposite side of this stage. Each one of them waited for their scheduled turn to leave their appointed seat and stand in the middle of the circle. There they presented the Emperor, and their fellow Senators, with their specific concerns and important information. Only he, the Emperor, spoke from his seat. This way there was never a man who sat or stood higher than him, and never a moment where he was not protected by at least two armed guards.

Most of the speeches were about mundane matters, regular reports on the success of certain crops, tax collections contributed, requests for repairs, or the creation of public roads and other types of infrastructure. The mediocrity of the subject matter did not keep the presenting Senators from delivering their messages in elegant fashion, with animated gestures and dramatic posture. Even the most restrained of the group carried themselves with regal pomp and enough self-importance to cause the Emperor to occasionally sneer in pure disgust. He would scan their benches with his eyes, pausing on the few he knew to be his enemies, observing their movements and facial features. He had dreamt of many of them, watched their robed shadows move through the halls of his mind while he slept. He knew that any one of them could be his undoing if he let his guard down. As much as this group of men claimed to represent the concerns of the people that lived within their districts, and touted their full devotion to him as Emperor to his face, he was fully aware that they had other agendas. They were landowners and traders of foreign goods. They had their own alliances and strategic plans. He was also aware that many of them, old and grey, dressed in expensive well made cloth, their bodies well oiled and massaged, their lands harvested by slaves, had survived more years in their place of influence than most of the Emperors who had preceded him. For this reason, he hated them.

Just before Coracis' attention fully pulled away from the matters at hand, when he was sure he could not stand another moment of these proceedings, Senator Tiburtius from the bordering lands of the Nagy Föld approached the stage. His demeanor was serious. His brow furrowed in deep concern as he swallowed and took in a dramatic breath of air before making his first announcement.

"Emperor Coracis," he began, presenting a low bow towards the throne. He swept his right hand wide to the side, raising up slowly, then turning to face the Senate, he bowed again, this time not so low, "Gentlemen of the Senate..." he continued, "the day before I left my humble farmlands to join you for this gathering, a small troop of soldiers, far from their original Legion camp, came to my home seeking help. Upon speaking with them we found that they had been captured by a tribe of nomads from the depths of the Nagy Föld while pursuing a group of thieves."

The Emperor rose out of his apathetic slouch. The Senators drew in deep breaths of concern. Some groups of them fell into disconcerted murmurs, quick conversations between each other.

Tiburtius paused, waiting for them to quiet, then continued, "I am sure you are all aware of the concerns I have, both with how to react to this group of soldiers who were captured and then released alive, but also as a Senator of lands bordering the Nagy Föld. My utmost concern is, of course, for the farmers and simple citizens of the Empire who may come under harm by the Nomads." He paused again, this time for effect, and then, turning slowly, his arms opening ever so slightly, as if to try to physically hold their attention, he bowed his head. His breath drew in as he shook his head slowly from side to side, as if unable to believe the depth of the problem he was about to reveal, "But these concerns seem small after I gleaned more information from the Captain, Captain Abelardus. It seems–his own words–I report–he told me that they were kept in the Nomadic camp and before their release the camp was visited by Queen Zenobia of the Hidden Desert Canyon Lands. Captain Abelardus claims she addressed him and spoke to him directly."

The Senators broke out, this time in loud conversations. Their shock and concern echoing between each other. The Emperor leaned back into his throne, his arms crossing before him, his brow furrowed, his eyes became slits. What did this mean, and what, if anything, should he say on the matter directly to the Senate? He chose to stay silent for the moment, his eyes fixed on the speaking Senator who had ducked his head down as he waited for the voices to quiet around him. Instead of being allowed to continue, Tiburtius was bombarded with questions from the agitated Senators.

"What kind of soldiers are these that come back from an encounter with the barbarians alive?"

"To be captured is a disgrace to our Legions."

"Who are these men if they are not spies?"

"Why would a queen speak with a soldier from our Legions? Our Ambassadors visit her kingdom regularly. What interest does she have in the barbarians and our military?"

"What Legion did they come from?"

"What Legions are stationed in the borders of the Nagy Föld?"

"What were they doing there?"

It was the last few questions that alerted Emperor

Coracis to the need to control this ignited conversation. He knew of the Legions dispersed throughout the borders of the Nagy Föld. He knew of the battles, raids, and surveillance they conducted on the Nomadic tribes. He knew how their maneuvers helped them get closer to the southern borders of the Canyon Lands. He knew, because he had ordered these operations. The Senators, on the other hand, were blissfully unaware of these activities. Before the conversation turned in a direction that would raise even more questions, the Emperor took control of the dialogue. To be safe, he focused it back on the morality of the soldiers themselves. After all, it was a disgrace for a Legion soldier to not die in the line of duty. Even a small handful of men captured and returned without injury by tribes of Nomads the Empire considered barbarians, was a sign of potential moral decay.

"These Legion soldiers. Where are they now?" The Emperor questioned, his baritone voice rumbled against the marble, quieting the Senate. Senator Tiburtius turned gracefully to fully face the Emperor, bowing low as he responded.

"The soldiers I told to stay at my villa, under a respectful house arrest until I was able to speak to you. I would have returned them directly to their Legion, but they refused to tell me where it was stationed. They are being well cared for, but remain under guard. Their leader, Captain Abelardus, is with me here, waiting in the plaza. He has asked that he be blamed entirely for any misconduct. He takes full responsibility for the failure of their duties and for the capture of his men. He has asked to be punished alone, his men spared persecution or public humiliation."

Tiburtius' words calmed the Emperor's concern for the moment. The soldiers had not revealed their Legion's whereabouts, a fact that would have surely led to questions. Coracis took in a deep breath. The entire room was quiet, waiting for him to continue. He let the depth of the pause sink in, allowed himself to feel his personal power over them in their silence. Senator Tiburtius stood with his head bowed. The Emperor watched him like a hawk, eyeing his insecurity as it revealed itself over the drawn out silence. Tiburtius' body swayed in the depth of the quiet, time stretched out, his thick, fidgety fingers stroked the side of his robe.

The Emperor did not like Tiburtius, though this could be said for the majority of the Senators. He knew that Tiburtius had inherited his lands. He knew that Tirburtius' father quietly expanded his lands by buying one farm after another cheaply from poor families, families who were often suffering from the absence of the fathers and brothers who had been sent to war by Coracis' predecessors. The absent men left their crops unharvested from lack of healthy laborers, rendering their wives and aging parents helpless. However, it was not concern for the poor that ignited Coracis' displeasure. It was the fact that he knew this man came from a long line of opportunists. Coracis recognized in Tiburtius' delicate speech, that this important information, these soldiers and their fate, was seen as a potential opportunity, even if he had not yet calculated how to use it to his advantage. This calculating was what Coracis hated. So he let his brow furrow, and the silence settle, and he stared at Tiburtius' ducked gaze until he could hear the nervous shifting movement emanating from the Senator's fidgeting hands.

Coracis reached for a silver cup of freshly poured wine and drank slowly. Then, with a voice smooth and cold, as a slow moving reptile he asked, "Senator Tiburtius. Why did you choose to present this information here and now? Don't you think the information about these men should have been presented to our military leaders and not to an open panel of Senators?"

The other Senators moved in their seats. They all believed themselves to be worthy of this information, higher placed than the rank and file generals the Emperor held dear. Any one of them would have presented the information in this forum with that thought in mind, but they also knew of Coracis' wrath. They could hear the disgust in his voice. They could not, would not, speak up against him for a small group of simple Legion soldiers. Tiburtius was on his own with this mistake.

"Emperor, Emperor Coracis," Tiburtius fumbled, stuttered even, recognizing that despite all of his calculations he had misstepped, at least in the eyes of the Emperor, " M–my Grace... highest of high–" he continued, diving into a full flourished and panic stricken bow, "–forgive me if I have made a mistake. I was presented with the men before I traveled to the forum. The time was limited–and forgive me–many of the esteemed generals were away when I arrived here." He bowed again, lower still, stuttering, "–an–an–and while I considered bringing this matter to you in private... I–I know your time is more valuable–h–has more–I mean, you have more pressing matters to attend to than for me to bother you with wi–with such a trivial matter. Forgive me... forgive me...highest of high...if you find f–failure in my hasty decision...."

Coracis waved his hand, a gesture for silence. Tiburtius instantly quieted, dropping to one knee in an attempt to bow even lower.

The Emperor's lips curled in a small smirk. This opportunist, with his swooping gestures and exaggerated pauses was, for just a moment, impressive to Coracis. So quickly had he concocted his reasons. So instantly had he explained himself. His skilled diplomacy at justifying his reasons, his political aptitude for self preservation was a form of art, of theatre. Coracis was amused.

The amusement, even with its rancorous edge, saved Tiburtius from further focus. Emperor Coracis was awakened from his apathy and simply told the Senator, "Very well, bring us this Captain Abelardus who has so patiently waited in the plaza. Bring him now."

Tiburtius, relieved to be finished with his dangerous moment in the spotlight, prostrated himself on the ground. Then he sprung up and, without words, backed away from the throne to exit out the door. Outside, free of the Emperors noxious glare, he turned and moved swiftly to the plaza, his robes a flurry of rich fabric, to find Captain Abelardus.

22

———

Abelardus sat at the fountain edge, marveling at the water that sprung from the mouths of leaping stone dolphins and rippled around the feet of a sculpted wild eyed nymph. Crowned in a flowing headdress of seaweed and shells, the nymph leaned lovingly against the broad legs of a muscled and robust mortal image of Pontus, the sea-god.

He marveled at the art of the fountain but was mostly in awe of its ingenuity. The fountain was a gift from the aqueducts that carried fresh water through the Capital of Critias. Connected to distant rivers, they redirected the water into and throughout the city. Some of it was directed here, to this pool of clean water that expanded out from the sculpted Gods in the middle of a public plaza. He scooped a handful of the flowing water to his mouth, its taste as clear and cool as the water from the river's edge it came from miles away.

The soothing sound of moving water helped wash away his concerns. His men and the potential punishment he may have to face for being marked as a soldier who allowed the enemy to take him alive weighed on his mind. Only a month before, the shame of being labeled by such a failure would have been enough to make him consider taking his blade and cutting open his own throat. Yet, since the strange incident in the nomad's camp when the smoky creature was pulled from his mouth by the shaman, Abelardus had felt very little shame or regret. Instead, he felt a solid sense of duty to ensure the safety of his men, but for himself he felt only an acceptance for whatever his fate.

He sat next to the fountain totally relaxed. He could relate the feeling to the redirected water, which had traveled across miles of engineered structures so that it could cascade among the marble figures of spectacular creatures and immortal Gods in this central plaza. It was as if his life was simply another resource, redirected from a distant land to be a service, or at the very least a novelty, for the Empire and the fickle Gods to use at will. He recognized the fatalistic nature of his thoughts and, yet, he was content. Content that everything he faced was exactly as it needed to be and if that meant severe punishment for still being alive after facing an enemy...well then, so be it.

He had waited most of the day in the central plaza, as Senator Tiburtius requested, watching women from the town gather around the fountain, carrying large, empty, wide bellied pottery jugs that they held like babes in their arms, balanced on full hips. Gossiping quietly amongst each other they dipped the empty vessels into the gift of clean flowing water. A gift they would balance on their shoulders in those same robust jugs to take home and share with their children and family as they cooked spiced lamb over hearth fires.

By the time Tiburtius returned to the plaza to retrieve him, Abelardus had spent quite a few hours unintentionally meditating on the abundance of flowing water that sprang from that fountain. He'd been reminded of his frail existence in the hot sun and felt deep gratitude for the cool miracle that existed beside him. One simple scoop of the fresh liquid quenched his thirst and battled the heat. He even found himself chuckling when he lifted the water to his mouth, remembering that it was his need for water which had led him to the pond in the fog. He felt at peace with his fate. Surely there were outside forces, Gods at work in these strange events, moving him where he should be. First they had diverted him and his men into the great grasslands, then led him before the foreign warrior Queen, and now he had been escorted straight to the very center of the Empire's Capital.

Abelardus' acceptance was in direct contrast to the flustered and disturbed Tiburtius who retrieved him from the fountain, addressing him sharply and ordering him to follow him back to the Senators forum. The two of them walked back towards the Senate hall. Tiburtius, a flurry of fidgeting robes and sweating red skin, mumbling to himself and distracted to the point of nearly running into the occasional pillar. Abelardus, walking swiftly but calmly, his hands humbly clasped behind his back, his alert nature gratefully taking in the marvels of architecture, masonry and sculptures that filled the halls and buildings surrounding them. Tiburtius rushed past and ignored the entrance guards, even as Abelardus nodded politely at them as they passed through.

Abelardus was led through the final corridor where two arched doors flanked by royal guards swung open before him, revealing the circular floor of the Senate hall. The Senators perched like strange birds in their wooden stands on his right, leaning forward with stretched necks as they peered at him and Tiburtius when they entered. To his left the raised throne of the Emperor hovered over them all, and on it Coracis lounged like a well fed leopard, his eyes steady and focused directly on Abelardus.

Tiburtius walked ahead, his flustering movements exaggerated by the rustle of his thick robe that echoed in the otherwise deathly quiet hall. He dropped to his knee, his head bowed and never looking directly at the Emperor, announced, "This, my Emperor, is Captain Abelardus,"

The Emperor motioned Tiburtius away with an apathetic flick of his hand, as if shooing a fly. Tiburtius, seeing the signal, moved quickly back to his seat. Abelardus could hear him release a sigh of relief as he scurried past.

Abelardus, not completely schooled in the manners of court etiquette, did the only thing that seemed appropriate. He moved forward to the center of the marble circle. Facing the Emperor directly, he dropped down on his left knee, his right knee pointed at the middle of the throne. With the precise and strong movements of military gestures, he saluted the Emperor with his right hand then clasped it into a fist and brought it firmly to his chest over his heart, bowing his head. He did not speak, he did not really know what to say. Here before him was the man he had been raised to serve, the leader of his proud nation, and of all that he had been taught to hold dear. If meeting the Queen of the distant lands was like a strange dream, finding himself before the revered Emperor was like being embedded in the stories of the traveling bards that roamed through his homelands when he was a child.

He stayed bowed, and while the Emperor's earlier extended silence made Tiburtius fidget, the same silence now aimed at Abelardus seemed to calm him. For Abelardus, the silence allowed him to appreciate what he considered a sacred moment.

This captain's manners were not lost on Emperor Coracis. He stared in silence for many minutes at Abelardus, but not out of a vindictive need to make him suffer under his gaze. Coracis actually found himself in the rare position of admiring this soldier who bowed before him. So different was this captain from the rolling, squirmy, fat maggots that called themselves Senators, who swayed and peered from their seats behind him. So quick this soldier had bowed before him, facing him only, his back to the politicians. He had not announced his name, had not soiled the quiet with a flourishing and self-appreciating speech, or a flood of nervous apologies for his crimes. Instead, this captain simply bowed, his only flourish his strong salute, his fisted hand landing to rest on his chest above his heart with a solid, single strike before he ducked his head. How rare it was for the Emperor to see a man bow before him who actually became more illustrious instead of inferior.

"Captain Abelardus," announced the Emperor, "you may stand."

Obediently, Abelardus rose, his gaze aimed forward, not at the Emperor directly, but straight ahead, as military men do when standing at attention. The Emperor enjoyed this, too. Coracis smiled from his throne, planting his feet firmly before him so that he could lean forward and focus more intently on the soldier. Coracis imagined ordering this obedient and capable soldier to take a blade from the attending guards and slaughter the Senators like squealing swine. He held on to this fantasy for a moment as he glanced over the faces of the waiting Senators. Their eyes looked yellow and small, their skin frail, their jowls flaccid. He leaned back into his throne, imagining how they would scramble, their cries of privileged protest, their piggish eyes wide with shock and horror. Then, shaking off his mental diversion, Coracis returned to the matters at hand. He addressed Abelardus.

"Captain, it has been brought to our attention that you returned from capture by one of the barbarian tribes. Is this true?"

"Yes Emperor, this is true." Abelardus replied, giving a brief nod of his head.

"Then, if that is the case, your situation has brought to light some concerns. First...I am most curious about one fact. Senator Tiburtius told us that you claimed to see a member of royalty from one of the neighboring lands in the nomadic camp. Tell us who is it that you saw during your capture."

Abelardus nodded, raising his head to speak, " My Emperor, I saw Queen Zenobia of the Hidden Desert Canyon Lands."

"And how could you be so sure that this woman you encountered was our kingdom's neighbor, Queen Zenobia?"

Abelardus looked up, somewhat shocked that the Emperor assumed he could be fooled by an impostor. He answered precisely. "Emperor, she carried the royal flag of her land, was accompanied by flanking soldiers in the uniforms of her country, all of which, including herself rode upon the rare Jeweled Horses. The nomads addressed her by her title and name and she introduced herself as such to me when we spoke."

The Senate broke their silence, murmuring among themselves, even as the Emperor continued his questioning.

"You spoke with Queen Zenobia?"

"Yes."

"In passing or in depth?"

"In depth. She invited me to have tea at the nomad's

campfire." This news ignited a new wave of concerned murmuring.

"Why would a queen talk to a soldier?"

"What was she doing in the barbarian's camp?"

"What has this Captain Abelardus told her?"

"Why was he captured and kept alive?"

The Emperor raised his hand, quieting the Senators. He paused while he considered the best way to continue. On one hand, he thought he may be able to use the information gained here to his advantage. On another, he was concerned that in this open forum, the captain may say something that could expose his more secret military activities. He decided to end this questioning, at least for now.

"Captain Abelardus, I believe your situation and its significance to the Empire should be looked into further. However, we have had a long day. We shall reconvene in three days time." Then, addressing his attention to one of his flanking guards, he stated, "Avitus, find the captain some adequate sleeping quarters. Make sure he is well fed and cared for, and since he has been through so much already, make sure he is not disturbed."

The Senators all stood, glad to be finished for the day. Even though they were agitated by this latest news, many of them quickly turned their thoughts and discussions to the thrill of acquiring a good meal and some wine. The Emperor stood, turned, and left the hall first, his guards flanking him on all sides, except for Avitus who went straight to care for Captain Abelardus. Only after The Emperor had left completely and made his way to his private villa did an attending messenger return to the hall to signal that everyone else was now free to leave.

23

There was no time or space for planning. There was no assurance that death would be overcome. Csoda simply ran, and Biro joined him. They were two men running into the violent storm of an oncoming stampede, and as they ran forward they connected to their past. They had been born on the open fields, surrounded by the nomadic herds and, like the wind, they were at home within the storm of thundering hooves, the tornado of the stampede. Even in the confined towering walls of the stone arena where the herds movements were manipulated by the oncoming fury of war wagons and the snapping whips of masked drivers, both Biro and Csoda understood the movements of the charging bulls. When they finally met the first line of horned beasts, they instinctively leapt and dodged, barely missing the crushing hooves and lowered horns.

The chaos crashed around them, but in the pounding rhythm Biro and Csoda found a way to maneuver into the middle of the herd. Biro changed directions, rolling against the side of a moving bull, using the animals motion to spin him 180 degrees so that he now ran with the flow of animals and not against it. Csoda moved towards the oncoming chariots. Two snorting bulls running beside one another left enough of a narrow gap for Csoda to race between. The bulls, caught up in the movement of the herd, ignored him, even as he leapt up, using the animal's close proximity to brace himself on ether side to scramble onto the backs of the condensed herd that surrounded him. Running upon the backs of a raging sea of angry bulls, jumping over the thrashing heads and horns, Csoda focused on the middle of the oncoming wagons and ran directly towards it.

The people rose in the stands, all eyes glued on the two men as they ran into the thick of raging beasts. The crowd sucked in a collective gasp, some cried out, their hearts aching as the chaos of the herd hid the men from their view. Then, in an instant, their hearts rose to their throats as they witnessed Csoda leap out of the abyss and run along the backs of the beasts.

The men roared out, the women wept. Many reached out their hands as if to try to hold him up and keep him from falling into the crushing black mass below him. His movements dazzled them, for in them was a world of visual contradiction. He seemed both graceful and clumsy, skillful and foolish. Each time he leapt clear, his feet landing true, the crowd cheered, and each time he stumbled, his weakness and humanity revealed, they gasped and cried out and held their hands into the air asking the heavens to lift him up.

The cries and prayers of the crowd were answered as Csoda made his way to the oncoming wagon. Their supporting roar and lifted hands seemed to fill his legs with strength and each leap looked less like a stumbling puppet and more like the graceful spring of a determined panther. He reached the backs of the bulls that ran directly in front of the frothing mouths of the horses. From there he took an unrestrained jump from the last bucking bull and flung himself forward, crashing against the slick sweaty neck of a galloping steed. He scrambled and clung even as the horse attempted to rear but was kept from doing so by the bonds that held it to the wagon. The horses swerved dramatically and nearly hit the wagon driving next to them.

The masked driver steadied himself and the team, but the wagon's side still crashed into the stadium wall. Control of the team of horses was handicapped by Csoda who clung fast to the horse's neck. Csoda swung one leg over the animal so that he rode on its front shoulders, facing forward.

Ahead of them the herd of bulls had pulled away as the wagons slowed in an attempt to regain control of their formation. The bulls, free of the pressure from the oncoming driver's charge, split into two stampedes. One group moved ahead in the original direction and the other circled into the center of the arena moving towards the other side. At the fork of the splitting herd an empty space widened to reveal Biro, who had survived running amongst them. Upon seeing Csoda on the neck of the oncoming horse, he braced himself in front of his friend's position.

Csoda clung tightly to the horse, and took the chance to take in deep gasps of air, trying to ease the pressure from the explosive beating of his heart. His ears filled with the grinding growl of wheels behind him, the sharp rattles of armor plates that covered parts of the horse's bodies, and the pounding of their iron shod hooves on the compacted sand. He heard drivers yelling, and the quick deafening snap of one of their long whips spit in the air close to his head, nearly licking his ear with its cutting leather tip. Through it all he focused on Biro, and upon the sea of sound that flooded the arena from the ecstatic crowd. From their cheers he gathered strength and felt the energy from their wailing cries push itself into his body and mind.

Csoda's hand slid up to rub the horses neck, he leaned to the side, hugging closely, until he could see the large liquid eye of the animal under its brass armored blinders. The eye rolled back to look at him, wide in its socket, the whites flashing in panicked fear as it charged ahead. Its mouth was parted wide, huffing, red at the corners where a stiff bit pulled violently against its skin. The whip cracked again, this time slashing against Csoda's leg, and the horse's eyes widened from the sound as Csoda grimaced from the biting pain.

Still, Csoda focused. Biro was close ahead, Csoda whispered in his mind words directed at the wide eyed horse, "Shhhh, friend, I am not who you should fear. Please, carry me to my brother." As he thought these words he reached forward, grabbing the reins that pulled on the bit in the horse's mouth and loosened them so that the chariot driver no longer had control of at least this one horses head. The horse responded to the loosened rein, its head stretching forward like an arrow. The horse next to it responded to the increase in speed and the team ran straight towards Biro in thundering chaos. Csoda reached forward and out with his hand, Biro reached up and as soon as the horses got to him he grabbed Csoda's forearm. Csoda clasped onto his friends arm and pulled, swinging Biro up into the air then behind, where he landed on the back of the horse behind his friend.

Without hesitating, before the driver's whips or the archer's bow could be aimed at him, Biro leapt up and turned to face the masked men in the chariot. Placing his feet on either side of the steed's broad back, with bent knees and strong balance, he moved quickly to stand in front of the streaming tail and then leaped into the air meeting the driver head on with a crashing force as he fell into the wagon bed.

The leather tendrils of the newly freed reins slithered and snapped through brass rings as they left the opened hands of the masked driver. The force of impact had surprised him, and he flailed and scrambled to reach the dagger that was sheathed at his waist. Biro's intensity was driven by desperation and matched with his own strength and skill. Not having a weapon of his own, he saw what his enemy was reaching for and grabbed at it for himself. Yet the driver was not his only concern, for the accompanying archer in the chariot had swung his bow behind his back, pulled out a short sword and moved to stab at Biro while he struggled with the driver.

Biro, who had defied death many times before, both in the coliseum and in his past life as a free nomad, had done so by being ever vigilant and aware. He kept conscious of all weaknesses, both his own and his attackers. His obvious weakness now was his lack of physical armored protection and weaponry. He knew that one strike from the falling sword would be all that was needed to finish him. His less obvious strength was his quick observation of the attacking archer's position. The archer now faced the opened back of the jumping and jolting wagon bed and the swinging motion he took with his sword put the majority of his balancing weight directly above Biro's body. Taking advantage of the archer's stance, Biro reacted. While snatching the coveted dagger from the belt of the driver with one hand, he reached up to grab the belted waste band of the attacking archer right as the archer's arms and weight fell forward to swing the sword down on him. Before the archer realized that his forward momentum was being used against him,

Biro rolled onto his back, pulling the archer's waist up and forward and kicked out his legs, tripping the archer's feet and catapulting him into a devastating roll right off the back of the wagon. The archer hit the ground, rolling and broken in the wake of the scattering sand and dust of the coliseum floor.

Biro was now dangerously exposed to the driver who was recovered from his initial shock. The driver was positioned on his hands and knees, facing Biro like a crouched cat ready to spring. Biro slid to the side, bracing his back against the stretched and tightened leather that served as the wagon wall. The driver had missed his chance to push him off the back with the archer, but Biro could see that his enemy had located a second dagger, which he gripped in his right hand. Vulnerable in his simple tunic, holding nothing but a dagger, Biro was now face to face with the brass armored driver. The driver's face mask that served as his protective helmet, made him appear to be more creature than man. The mask's features were hawk like with a large curved and pointed nose that arched out under the sculpted brass folds of an exaggerated, furrowed brow. The top of the mask arched over the top of the driver's head, its slick surface ending in the middle of the back of his skull. There it attached to a layer of spiked metal mesh that fell past his shoulders and gave the appearance of dragon like scales. His torso was protected by solid breast, shoulder, and back plates of brass that were painted and tinted with white, green and black designs, continuing the illusion of reptilian skin.

Biro could see no immediate weakness in the armored warrior who was so close that he thought he could smell his breath even through the clouds of dust. They stayed facing each other, the wagon bouncing and rumbling uncontrollably around them. His own weakness was obvious to him, his bare arm held out in front, grasping the stolen dagger in a clinched hand was his only shield. Its muscled size was made of penetrable flesh. Yet, the dragon armored man with the hawk nosed mask did not attack, did not move, did not push past this meager dagger shield to tear him apart. Mere seconds had passed, but that was enough time for Biro to ask himself, "Why? Why doesn't he attack?"

The answer was revealed in a tremor in the driver's arm that shuddered from his shoulder down to his hand in a spasm of unintentional movement. Biro saw the tremor, squinted and looked past the mask into the eyes of his attacker. There he saw the impossible. Fear. Fear rippled in the whites of the man's eyes and after Biro recognized it, he saw that it moved throughout the man's body. It became obvious in the way he held his dagger, his coiled crouch was less like a leopard about to leap and more like that of a shivering animal trying to hide.

Fear? This perplexed Biro, not because he had never felt fear, but because he did not imagine a man with so many advantages over him to have it. He had not witnessed himself racing upon the backs of the bulls and leaping towards the wagon, his arms stretched out like a lion jumping towards its prey before he crashed against this man. He had not seen the whites of his flashing teeth and the snarl that had taken over his face, a snarl that contorted his features into a manic, crazed, menacing smile.

It was impossible for Biro to feel the cold determination that pummeled into the driver's heart when Biro's angry eyes had drilled into him. Biro had not seen his own speed nor watched the swift maneuvers he had used to grab the dagger and throw the archer off the back of the wagon. Biro did not see himself now, his face smeared with sweat, dust and blood, his hair matted with wind and years of imprisonment, his thick muscled hand and arm holding a stolen dagger in defiance. He did not see his own terrifying gaze as he quickly sized up his now frozen opponent. Biro could not see and did not realize that he was a fearsome figure. Where this man's armor gave the illusion of an otherworldly beast, Biro's flesh, blood and will was the real thing.

The wagon had slowed, though it still moved forward at great speed, its chaotic jostling had settled as it followed a straighter line. Biro could not tell why, since his view of the horses and the arena were blocked by the wall of the wagon bed that he crouched within. He did not have a solution to his current state of limbo. And while he recognized the fear in his opponent, he could not see a way to strike without exposing himself to an inevitable gutting.

He considered leaping off the back, leaving the driver behind, but he did not want to give up his position in the wagon. Plus, he believed that Csoda was still riding the horse, and Biro leaving would allow the driver to recover and perhaps give him the chance to kill his only friend in the world. So he sat frozen with the enemy, calculating every outcome he could imagine.

Then, in the midst of the air he caught a sound, a growing powerful hum. He thought he saw something in his peripheral vision, tendrils of mist or cobwebs aloft in the air that shimmered like silver and vibrated with the sound. The hum took shape and form and Biro, stuck staring at the fearful man shaking in his beastly armor, realized that the sound was coming from the arena crowd. Their cries were growing every moment towards deafening, blocking all other sounds as they roared in unison. The armored driver looked away from Biro, turning his head sharply towards the front of the chariot, his hawk beaked mask arching to the sky, his eyes wide in disbelief.

Biro saw his chance.

He jumped forward and cut at a sliver of the man's exposed throat with his dagger, grabbing at the nose of the mask and wrenching it backwards to try to expose more of his pale neck. His attempt missed the mark, and instead of cutting the driver's neck, the blade slid through a weaving of leather straps that held the mask on the mans head. They struggled, and in an unplanned twist of fate, Biro wrenched the mask helmet right off the driver's head as he rolled over him, all the while trying to protect his vulnerable abdomen.

Yet the expected gutting did not come, and Biro found himself up against the opposite wall of the wagon, the hawk masked helmet in one hand and the dagger in the other. The driver's head was exposed. His short cut hair was tawny and curled close to his head. His reddened face looked overly flushed against the black paint that had been applied around his eyes, paint that accentuated the fear in his eyes. His narrow face and clean shaven jaw shocked Biro, for he saw who he truly faced was only a young man. This young man looked back at Biro with divided attention. He braced himself up against the opposite wall of the wagon bed, staring at Biro, his eyes occasionally darting up towards the front of the wagon.

Biro, concerned, tried to see what kept taking the driver's attention away from him. Without turning his head, he quickly glanced to the side and saw Csoda, the back of Csoda, holding the captured reins of the chariot horses high in the air as he directed them. His friend's body was in front of the wagon itself and he leaned slightly back. By the movement of his body and his position, Biro knew that Csoda was braced with one leg on each horse as he took charge of their movement. Csoda's head was raised high and Biro knew that if he had still had his tongue, he would have been singing.

This was why the crowd grew so loud in their cries and applause. This was what distracted his opponent. Intense power and unity filled him, a feeling Biro remembered from long ago when he was in battle with his own people. The feeling made him lose all calculation in his plans. With no forethought, he simply moved towards the frightened boy and with a powerful and unabashed shove of his foot, pushed the driver off the back of the wagon.

Biro now stood in the wagon bed alone with Csoda directly ahead of him, driving the horses that he stood upon. The crowd grew almost riotous when they saw him like that. Food and drink toppled off of tables as the people climbed on top of them to get a better view. If Csoda could not sing then Biro would add his own sound to the event. He held the hawk mask high in the air, as if it was the decapitated head of an enemy, and let his voice roar into the sky. The crowd roared back and Biro, in great flourish, pulled the hawk shaped helmet over his own head. He held his hands high in the air, one hand clenching the dagger, the other wide open and, again, he saw a mist of silvery lines that fluctuated in the air then disappeared. A surge of electrical energy moved through him.

On either side of them the two other wagons moved into position. Their horses were neck in neck with those that Csoda drove, and Biro could see the archer on the right quickly draw, aim and shoot an arrow directly at Csoda's exposed back. Csoda instinctually dropped out of range, sitting on the left chariot horse's back while he pulled on the reins. His quick action caused the horses to slow dramatically and, whether inspired by luck, by the will of the crowd, or by his innate skill, the move saved his life as the arrow flew harmlessly over his head. The wagons on either side of them tore ahead, their drivers too slow to adjust to the sudden change in speed. Then, before their enemies could regroup, Csoda rose back up on the horse and, keeping hold of the reins, leapt into the bed of the wagon to join Biro. Protected by the walls of the chariot, he flicked the reins, encouraging the horses back up to speed.

Ahead of them the two enemy wagons were turning around to face them, crossing each other's paths in two wide arches. The clouds of sand and dust sprayed out from their wheels creating a gold tinted haze. Csoda stood slightly ducked in the wagon, trying to shield himself while still seeing enough to drive the horses. Biro stood more raised up, surveying the movements of the wagons ahead, his newly acquired helmet providing him with a bit more protection from the threat of the archer's arrows. He wished he could get hold of one of the bows, and growled a private curse to himself for not trying to take them off of the archer when he threw him off the back of the wagon. The other wagons now surged head on towards them, bound to either collide with them or to part and have each one pass on either side, exposing them to two attacks at once.

"Give me the reins!" Biro shouted.

Csoda complied and ducked down completely in the chariot bed. Biro held the reins in his left hand, pulling back to slow the horses, allowing him to direct them more precisely, aiming for the center between the oncoming enemies. It seemed that the three teams of horses were bound to collide. The powerful animal's muzzles frothed madly, their noses flared and their manes snapped in the wind, giving them the appearance of creatures driven mad by the chaos, beasts willing to crash into each other at full speed. The driver's masked faces grimaced from the war wagons. One had the exaggerated snout of a boar complete with silver tusks and a ring of whisker like hair encircling his neck. The other was a distorted fanged dog with heavy copper brows. Next to them the archers stood ready, arrows set in their bows, their own masks wide eyed facades with manic grins and gritting metal teeth.

Right before the charging hooves of the horses were set to flail against each other in a thrashing storm of a violent crash, the two oncoming wagons parted, going to either side of Biro's team. Biro urged the horses to full speed. Quickly, he handed the reins down to Csoda to hold as he stayed ducked in the bed. Biro gripped his dagger in his right hand, his eyes darting from side to side beneath the hawkish mask, as he tried to calculate his enemy's attack, as well as his own.

The oncoming horses slid by Biro's team, so close their sides nearly touched, their necks arching, ears back and teeth bared as if they were about to reach out and bite each other. The dog masked driver was on the right, the boar masked driver on the left.

The archers in each wagon pulled back and let fly two arrows aimed directly at Biro and then quickly prepared the next arrow to shoot. One arrow skimmed the back of their horse, sticking into the side of the wagon bed. The other barely missed Biro, skimming along the side of his mask close to his eye.

Biro lunged to the right and lifted himself so that he could hang from his waist over the edge of the chariot bed. Leaning far forward, he met the startled face of the closest horse whose eyes grew wide, throwing its head up in the air trying to avoid him. Before it could move out of his way, Biro grabbed its bridal halter around its nose with his left hand and, with the dagger in his right hand, he cut the halter free letting it drop before the horse and leaving it free of the dog masked driver's control.

The horse, startled, pushed away from Biro, forcing the other horse and the wagon to swerve far to the right and away from Biro's wagon bed. The loose halter fell into the horse's legs, tangling with slackened reins among their feet. The driver struggled to regain control and attempted to slow them down in order to keep the animals from tripping in the free flying leather straps. His wagon and team of horses was rendered useless.

Biro had leapt to the left of the wagon to face the boar masked driver and his accompanying archer. Their horses had already passed Biro's wagon bed, beyond the reach of his halter slashing dagger. The beds of the wagons were almost side-by-side.

Again, Biro leaned far out over the edge, his intention to attack the driver head on. He was so focused on his attack that when an arrow pierced his right shoulder, solidly embedding through his muscled flesh, it only shocked him for a moment. His mind wavered briefly, then a clear understanding overtook him and he quickly switched the dagger to his left hand.

That which had always been within Biro, a deep-seated anger, kicked in and what had seemed like heightened focus paled in comparison to the determined release of fury that engulfed him. For, to a man like Biro, pain was more of an incentive than a deterrent, triggering all of the wrongs and suffering that he carried deep in his being, giving release to his pent up rage.

The golden haze of the coliseum dust and the decorative bronze masks–the red flushed skin and green eyes of his attackers–the blue sky above and the multicolored collage of the cheering people in the stands–the red flags snapping high up on the walls—to Biro, all these colors faded, until all he saw was a spectrum of black and white images, their intricate details called out by dark contrasts. Instead of seeing the blinding glints of sunlight off of the armor, the colorful elements of design, the distractions of decorations, his vision now isolated the architecture of the forms in front of him.

He saw the system of straps and clips holding onto the helmets. He identified the joints and spaces in the armor plates. He saw the pulse of a heartbeat from a sliver of exposed flesh, tucked under the metal boar mask's jawline.

All the while his body stretched forward, trying to bridge the gap of space that separated them. His arms spread wide, the dagger he held glinting in his left hand. The wagon beds met, ready to slide, side-by-side, their churning wheels nearly touching. The driver pulled out a dagger of his own. The archer leaned out of Biro's reach on the far side, pulling back on the bowstring, another arrow in place, ready to be aimed and released.

Collision. They met head on. Biro and the boar headed driver clashed, and Biro took on the spirit of the eagle mask that he wore. The dagger in his hand became a deadly talon, his eyes focused precisely on the delicate exposed skin at the jaw of the mask. He drove the knife blade into that space with savage precision, releasing a fountain of blood that rained onto him as the wagons movement pulled him through the encounter. The dagger wedged in the flesh of the neck, between the metal, and was pulled from his hand. Now weaponless, he fell back into his own wagon bed, dropping down to the floor as the arrows flew over his head.

He was cut. A dagger slash deep across his left arm bled heavily, but did not seem to bother him otherwise. The arrow still deep in his right shoulder was his concern. With a deep throated growl that emanated from the base of his throat, he snapped the back of the arrow shaft off so that it would not protrude out so far.

Their wagon moved past their enemies, but they both stayed low as two more arrows shot through the air. The horses, running without a driver's direction, headed for an open space, free of wagons and roaming bulls.

Csoda could see that the other wagons had fallen off. The boar masked driver slumped over the rim of his wagon bed. The archer was attempting to recover the reins that were still clenched in the hands of the slain boar masked man, but they were pinned between his lifeless body and the wagon wall. Realizing that the archers were far off and not focused on attacking, Csoda stood and looked out onto the coliseum grounds.

Upon seeing him, the crowd roared. The pounding of their feet and hands on the wooden floors and tables reverberated through the air. He looked down to Biro who was alive, but obviously injured. Biro looked up for he too heard the crowd, and in response he took in a deep breath and stood up.

The pounding increased, solidified into a strong rhythm, a wall of sound. The barrage of voices and cheers found a common word and they repeated in unison, in line with the pounding, "Sal-UTE, Sal-UTE, Sal-UTE…"

24

The Ringmaster leaned so far forward and pushed so much weight into the stone wall, the gravel texture pressed deep into the skin on the palms of his hands. He took in a deep breath to regain focus, and only then became aware that he had been holding his breath. He stood up straight, turning his hands to look at the palms where he could see the dappled pattern of the stone and tiny marks of red that marked the torture he had just imposed on them.

He shook his head and instinctually looked back into the arena stands to observe the crowd. The faces of the individuals, some flushed, some pale, revealed the earlier rush of excitement and frenzy that had overtaken the stands. The people glowed. Their eyes were bright, their mouths turned up on the edges in satisfaction, they wore ecstatic smiles. Their eyes were still focused on the two captives who had taken over one of the war wagons, and they were still cheering for these men with voices turned hoarse from their earlier howls. Their cheers had shifted from the chaos of sound of a few moments before, and were now unified, metered out in a rhythmic chant, "Sal-UTE, Sal-UTE, Sal-UTE…"

The two captives occupied the only war wagon that was still on the move. One of them wore the hawk like mask of a defeated driver and stood straight and strong despite the back of an arrow protruding from his shoulder. One of his thick, blood covered arms was raised to the sky, his broad hand clinched in a fist. The sun glinting off the beak of the mask made him look more like a demigod than a man.

The bulls had settled into the middle of the coliseum, milling like a peaceful herd. The meager remnants of surviving captives stood cheering in the still locked, gated alcoves. The two other wagons were stopped in their tracks. One driver was dead, a dagger embedded in his throat. The other two drivers, one with his head exposed, and the archers, were fumbling about their wagons and horses in a dazed stupor. Their custom armor made them look more like dawdling fools than warriors.

The Ringmaster felt a surge of satisfaction. The intoxicating mixture of adrenaline and joy pushed through his body, creating a tremor in his stomach as his heart pulsed in a flutter of leftover excitement. The feeling confused him, as he had grown numb over the years to the general rush that came from watching the events in the coliseum. He had long thought himself immune to the thrill that could engulf other men. This, however, *this* feeling was different. There was something in the air, an electric surge, and the Ringmaster considered that this excitement could be coming from more than just the events that had played out moments before.

"What did I just witness?" He thought as he pulled in a deep breath of air to calm himself. He knew what he had *watched* but–what–what had he *seen*?

The victorious captives had moved with fearless speed. They leapt with animal like grace and precision. The large man, the one wearing the hawk mask, had attacked with the speed of a diving falcon and the strength of a bull. They had not only defended themselves, they had also attacked. They had not only faced both animals and men, but they had done so with flare and dramatic showmanship. Yet, even these dramatic feats of skill and athleticism did not explain everything to the Ringmaster. He had seen many skilled warriors and acrobats in his years. This was, although exceptional, nothing new.

What the Ringmaster could not explain was the emotion he felt, the pull and expansion of his heart. He could not explain how he had lost track of all time, how he had been so focused on the captive's activities that he lost all awareness of everything around him, including the pain in his hands as he grasped the stone wall as if his life depended on it. He could not explain how deeply he had wanted them to survive. Nor could he explain why the sight of them driving the chariot, far across on the other side of the coliseum, made him feel more than relief–but pride–as if he had accomplished the deeds with them.

All of this flew through his mind as he looked back at the crowd and knew, by the tear streaks on some of their faces and the sweat on their brows, that they felt the same thing.

He would have stared at them longer, reading their expressions, except that they cried now, in unison, hundreds of people, "Sal-UTE, Sal-UTE, Sal-UTE..." and he, as Ringmaster, must respond. Their unified cheer was a call for the Ringmaster to honor these men for their victory. The crowd was demanding that they be freed from that which they had been marked for, freed from meaningless death. The crowd wanted to lift them higher in rank and purpose. The Ring-master listened to the crowd, but these things were always delicate, and his mind clicked through what his next actions should be.

He turned to walk back to his seat, to find the closest runner he could send off with a message. When he did, he was faced with the nobles that were seated near him. Even this group, one prone to indifference, had been inspired to leave their seats. Their hands stretched forward to shake his hand. They patted his shoulders and, beaming with approval, flooded his ears with their words of adulation and awe, praising him for the successful intensity of the first Kirkos of the season.

———

25

The open courtyard, though small, served its purpose in filling the rooms of the cozy house with sunlight and a fresh breeze. It was spacious enough and pleasant, but it was not lost on Abelardus that this particular house was void of windows or balconies facing the outside streets. While this was not a particularly rare architectural decision in many houses within the larger cities, it was a reminder to him that his rest in the Capital was a luxurious form of imprisonment.

His presence and his encounter with Zenobia and the tribes made him an odd piece in a very abstract puzzle, one that he did not completely understand. He could only hope that he had a more useful role to play than a troublesome one, at least as far as the Emperor was concerned. He feared the latter might mean being ripped from this comfortable retreat and swept away to some much less friendly cell, or worse, flailed and beheaded. This possibility kept his sleep restless. Though the Emperor's guard had brought him here, he was still alive, and the servants of the house treated him as if he was a wealthy merchant home from a long and successful trading run. They kept his plates full of rich food and a mug of water or wine always close at hand. So he resigned himself, for the time being, to calm his concerns with the luxuries being offered.

For a day and a half the only people he saw or spoke to were his attending servants. He knew he was under guard, having seen armored men standing at attention when the servants swung open the heavy wooden front doors, and watched the same guards inspect the same servant's baskets when they returned from the market.

Yet, it was only the servants that conversed with him, and then in only the limited manner that was the way of servants and slaves. Would he like water, wine, or perhaps a light mead? Is the bath water hot enough or perhaps too hot? Would he like to take his meal in the courtyard or perhaps inside? When Abelardus occasionally attempted to talk about more, even on such neutral subjects as the weather or his admiration of the house, they listened politely, but offered very little feedback of their own opinions. The formality of it all convinced him even further that the isolation and restful peace allotted him was not truly for his well being. Rather, these comfortable quarters were meant to hide him–along with whatever secrets he might carry.

"Perhaps," he considered, "perhaps they are hiding the shame."

Void of conversation and activity, he drifted into quiet contemplation. He lingered mostly in the sun of the courtyard, observing the delicate lines and subtle colors of an expertly painted mural that adorned one of the walls. In the painting, a flowering tree reached its long limbs all the way to the opening above, where the painted sky married itself with the blue of the true sky. The painted tree branched out wide, a canopy that spread near the top of the wall. Its mirage of limbs were accentuated with impressive details painted in gestural strokes. The limbs carried a thousand surprises, camouflaged birds and creative renditions of exotic flowers, berries, and fruit. At the bottom, the tree's trunk widened and became a maze of spreading roots, thick and solid, coiling deep into the rich earth and anchoring the tree next to a shimmering clear pond full of bright fish and watery plants.

As Abelardus let his eyes linger on the painting, he began to see the images hidden behind the brighter surface. Behind the leaves and fanciful birds, darker shadows appeared in the spaces. The form of a hidden panther hovered on a high branch. A coiled snake wrapped close to the trunk. Earthworms, beetles and other insects wove in and out of the dirt that the tree was rooted in and, sometimes, in all the secret shadows and spaces, he could find the eyes of unidentifiable creatures staring back at him. The depth of the painting became more fascinating the longer he looked into the details. While he explored the image, trying to decide if a specific dark section hid another of the shadowy creatures, he heard the front door open. A quick flutter of voices erupted from scurrying servants, echoed through the halls and ended quickly as they fell to their knees in reverent bows.

Abelardus stood and turned to greet whoever was soon to enter the courtyard. There, to his great surprise, with no guards or attendants, the Emperor emerged alone under the doorway arches. His tall stature, purple tunic and gold sash announced his presence even before Abelardus could make out his facial features. In an instant Abelardus dropped to one knee, his hand held out in salute, his head ducked humbly.

The Emperor came in a few feet and surveyed the court-yard briefly, observing the last scurrying shadows of the servants as they disappeared into the far reaches of the house. Then, when he felt assured he was alone with the captain kneeling before him, he spoke.

"Stand Captain Abelardus." Abelardus stood and the Emperor gestured towards the chair he had lounged on while viewing the painting, "Sit, Captain, I simply wanted a chance to talk to you in private. We are alone, are we not?"

Abelardus nodded, sitting down, but not in the lazy manner he had before. He sat with his back straight, his feet firm in front of him, facing the Emperor, his head still slightly bowed. The Emperor nodded, accepting his alert posture for respect and again surveyed the courtyard around him, but this time in a slower more casual manner. His eyes finally fell upon the painted mural of the detailed tree and as he did he began to talk, his voice drifting strangely, its tone quieter than it had been in the Senate hall.

"Ahhh, yes, this house is small but I remember this courtyard, this mural. Did you know that the man who painted this was from the distant canyon lands? The home of the lovely Queen you had the pleasure of meeting. Her people can be crude in manner, but some of them do have talented hands. Have you heard of their abilities in the arts?" Abelardus nodded, but the Emperor was no longer content with his silent responses, "Captain, you can speak. Tell me, what you have heard of Zenobia's artisans?"

"Only that which the average man knows, Emperor. They are rumored to have much talent. Forgive me sir, until viewing this painting, I do not believe I have ever witnessed their work."

The Emperor paused again, raising his eyebrow slightly

as he looked deeper into the painting. "Yes, they are talented. So then, your conversation with the Queen did not include a discussion on the arts. Funny, that seems to be the only subject she is content to discuss when in my presence." Abelardus nodded. Again, his quiet response was not enough, "Come Captain," The Emperor coerced, "If not the arts, what did our neighboring Queen wish to discuss with a soldier of our Legion. What subjects did she find so fascinating that she was willing to travel into the dangerous hands of the nomadic warlocks and endure the stench of their filthy camp?"

"Emperor, sir, the Queen wanted to know how I had come to be in the hands of the tribe. She wondered towards my safety and the safety of my men and negotiated our release. She told me that she had been hunting for sport along her border and noticed the campsite fires the night before. She speaks the nomad's language. She came to look into their activities."

This time the Emperor nodded silently. Abelardus did not hesitate in his response, he did not pause nor stutter, he seemed to be telling the truth. For a moment, Coracis relaxed and moved to a seat in the courtyard, sitting down across from the soldier, clapping his hands loudly as he did. From the distant halls a new flutter of activity erupted and soon a servant stood alert on the fringe of the courtyard.

"Bring us some wine, some bread and fruit," the Emperor ordered. The servant jumped to action, running towards the kitchen to fulfill the Emperor's wishes.

They ate in the courtyard together and the casual nature of the Emperor surprised Abelardus, who never could have imagined being in such an environment alone with the leader of the Empire. The servants rushed in only to bring food and wine, then as quickly and quietly as possible they darted away, heads lowered, averting their gaze from both the Emperor and Abelardus.

The Emperor Coracis, upon relaxing in the warmth of the sun, eating and drinking wine, fell into a sort of one way nostalgic dialogue. He explained to Abelardus that this particular house they were in was where he was tutored as a small child. Here he had learned the basics of knowledge, reading and writing along with math and music. He explained that his Uncle had commissioned the mural, and that he was there, as a young boy, watching the painter, this artist from Queen Zenobia's land, day after day, paint the intricate masterpiece.

Abelardus listened respectfully. His shock at being addressed as the Emperor's old friend was dulled slightly by the warmth and the wine. That and the Emperor's calm voice proved to be somewhat hypnotic.

"His way of working was different than I have seen other artists since then," Coracis explained, lazily holding his hand up as if he held an invisible brush and making stroke like motions directed at the painted wall. "He did not start with outlined forms in a fully conceived composition, but instead seemed to paint an entire painting in full detail and then paint the next layer of images directly on top of what was already finished." He paused, confused for a moment, then continued, "The mural you see now is a collage of multiple older paintings, images hidden in the background and shadows, all pieces and hints of the first works." Coracis paused, leaned his head back, his eyes gliding over the image in its entirety, his voice drifting off slightly as if lost in thought, "Very strange way to work...time consuming...."

Abelardus nodded, again looking deep into the mural. He could see now that the painting was built up in layers, increasing the dimension and depth of the work. The

Emperor's description of the techniques used made him peer even deeper into the shadows, trying to imagine what some of the first layers of paintings looked like before they were covered.

Coracis paused for a moment, taking a slow breath, then continued, "I was here watching him every day as a child. I remember each painted layer. It is the first one I remember best." He moved up slowly from his slouched seated position and stood, facing the center of the mural, spreading his arms in front of him as if he could pull the paint layers away as easily as opening a heavy curtain. "It was a wide vast grassland, dusted in fog, with infinite skies that were the deep amber colors of a red setting sun..."

Abelardus sat up straighter. The Emperor's description reminded him of the fields he had entered the day he was captured by the nomads.

The Emperor continued, "That was all, just a vast open landscape, except for one figure standing far in the distance. In the very center of the plains, obscured by the fog..." The emperor moved forward towards the wall, his eyes scanning the center of the painting, searching, "There... there it is..." He moved forward reaching his hand out to point at what he saw.

Abelardus stood up and moved closer to the painting, trying to see what the Emperor pointed at. Beyond the shadows of the tree's lower branches stood the stoic image of a noble white stag staring directly towards Abelardus. He smiled upon seeing it. It was startlingly obvious once sighted, but had been camouflaged effectively from his earlier observations. Its antlers blended into the tree's branches, its white fur at some angles could be mistaken for rays of dappled sunlight. Yet, there it was, a white stag hidden in the negative space of the regal tree, looking at him with wide open eyes.

Abelardus gave a slight surprised laugh as he exclaimed, "Oh...a stag. Ingenious! I stared at this very spot for a long time, but I never saw the creature."

"No," replied the Emperor quietly, "Not the stag... look at its eyes."

Abelardus leaned forward, gazing into the large glossy eyes and there, as if viewing the reflection of what the animal stared at, was a distant figure of a tall, lean man walking through the thick grass. This man's head was slightly bowed, his hair long and black, his tunic a strange patchwork of colors. Abelardus was struck in reverent silence. The detail in the mural was overwhelming, surreal—even supernatural. The figure in the eyes of the stag was small, yet delicately detailed, and though the features on the figure's face were not precise, Abelardus felt that if he knew this man, walking far off in a field, there would be enough detail for him to recognize his form.

A span of silence passed where both Abelardus and the Emperor stared at the painted figure. Then, in a hushed voice, as if they spoke of a secret, Abelardus asked, "Who is he?...Who is this man?"

The Emperor shook his head as he replied, "I do not know." His manner and carriage making him seem like a simple man, despite the royal purple robes he wore. "All I know is that he was the first and only human figure painted in this mural. A man walking in a vast grassland, alone." The Emperor turned, his back straightening, reclaiming his royal status physically. He walked away from the mural, back towards the center of the courtyard, slowly grasping his hands behind his back.

The light of the day had shifted in their long time

together. The sun no longer shone directly above and was hidden by the walls of the home surrounding the courtyard. Long shadows stretched across the floor, reaching it seemed, towards the center of the painted tree. Abelardus was still lost in the details of the mural, caught in the depth of its mystery, trying to find other secrets it had hidden from him. Its distraction kept him from noticing that the Emperor's mood was changed. The informality was falling away and now, along with the long shadows, the face and eyes of Coracis had also darkened. The hallows under his eyes deepened, his broad cheekbones and jawbone became sharp as his cheeks seemed to sink in. The intake and outtake of his breath produced a subtle rasping sound. The color in his eyes seemed to fill with a sheen of dark smoke.

"Captain Abelardus..." the Emperor began, his voice reclaiming its deepened tone of authority, "We have more important things to discuss."

Abelardus responded quickly to the Emperor's change of voice. He turned away from the painted wall swiftly on his heal and snapped into place, standing at attention as a soldier to face his Emperor.

"Captain," the Emperor continued, "You were captured by the nomadic tribes and failed in your duty to apprehend the thieves you chased. For reasons I do not understand, you were simply set free by the nomads under the random request of the visiting Queen, who you say informed you that she was out hunting for sport out on the fringes of her lands, a place I might add, in case you are unaware, that is very far from her capital and palace. Why did the nomads choose to capture you in the first place? What did they gain by keeping you alive and then releasing you?"

"I do not know, sir." Abelardus' voice was steady but he was internally shaken, the swift change of manner and the darkness on the Emperor's face had come out of nowhere. The change was drastic enough that the long hours of lazy informal discussions that ended merely moments before already seemed like a hallucination. Still, Abelardus was a Captain of the Empire's Legion and he had been trained to adjust when needed to any situation. Instantly, he washed away his thoughts of Coracis as a mere man, a casual friend talking about his childhood and the painting. Abelardus the soldier stood in front of the leader of the Empire of Critias and he was still on trial for his involvement in the strange circumstances that had brought him to this place.

"Yet, you my dear Captain, are very calm and relaxed... considering there are multiple reasons, according to our laws and your testimony...to have you hung." Coracis watched Abelardus' face closely as he made the threatening remark, but no flash of fear announced itself. Instead Abelardus nodded in stoic agreement. Coracis continued, "You know that your failure to capture the thieves is enough?" Abelardus nodded. "You are aware that you sitting down and eating at their campfire makes you look much like a traitor?" Abelardus nodded again. "Do you realize that your conversation with Queen Zenobia could be interpreted as a sign that you, my dear Captain, are perhaps one of her spies? A full fledged traitor to your rank and the Empire of Critias?"

Abelardus shook his head, he had not anticipated the last accusation, " My Emperor, sir..." he took in a deep breath, "I understand my failure to–"

"Don't explain yourself, Captain. I do not intend to have you killed, and I do not believe you to be a traitor. However, I do believe you should tell me, from start to finish, exactly what happened to you from the day you began chasing the thieves to the moment you found yourself standing in front of me and the Senators. I want you to tell me every single detail. Do you understand?"

"Yes, sir," Abelardus answered.

"Good," replied Coracis. He clapped his hands, ordered the servants to bring more wine, and settled into a comfortable seat to listen.

26

———

The shadows from the velarium awnings had shifted across the arena floor. The men who controlled them heaved on the ropes and pulleys, directing the heavy canvases to stretch far towards the center, their girth widening and dropping much needed shade onto the stands. The wind was now funneled upwards, and the hot air of the stadium flowed out of the top making the entire space cooler and more comfortable. With the changing wind through the heaving awnings, the crowds unified demand echoed, "Sal-UTE, Sal-UTE, Sal-UTE..."

Below, Biro and Csoda pulled their wagon to a halt. They were far from any combatants and bulls. Csoda held the reins, ready to signal the horses to move, but for the moment, he did not know where they should go. Biro stood tall, but the wounds he suffered were weakening him, an arrowhead still embedded in his shoulder. Fighting the pain with a wincing sneer, he gripped the edge of the wagon with one hand to balance himself even as he used the other to wave to the chanting crowd.

The other wagons and horses, along with the archers

and drivers, were being cleared from the arena. Led out, somewhat roughly, by a group of armed guards who had burst through one of the alcoves closest to them a short time ago, rendering the arena free of direct enemies that either Biro or Csoda could see.

The herd of bulls was settled. No longer being pushed by the wagons to continue their stampede, they were exhausted by the event and meandered around the center of the arena, only occasionally butting at each other out of confused frustration. The majority of surviving captives were huddled into the alcoves next to the closed gates, purposefully avoiding the temperamental herd of bulls. They too had been pulled into the cheering. Many of them stood on the fringes, holding their fists up into the air as they joined with the crowd in the stands, "Sal-UTE, Sal-UTE, Sal-UTE..."

Csoda felt the cooling air cross over his skin, but he was aware that the relief of the breeze was caused by more than the shade that fell from the velarium above. The sound had shifted as well and even though the crowd still cried their unified chant and the bulls still snorted and bellowed, the overall sound of the arena receded into the background. The air around him quieted.

"Now what do we do?" Biro asked.

Csoda smiled at the question. His friend had put Csoda's thoughts into words. He looked at Biro, who still held one hand up in the air waving to the crowd. His face was mostly hidden beneath the surreal hawkish mask. His arms and tunic were streaked with sweat, dirt and drying blood. Biro still bled from the arrow embedded in his shoulder and Csoda knew his strong companion would need care soon. Csoda shook his head and shrugged in reply, for at this moment, he did not know.

Across the arena grounds, farthest from where they waited, Biro and Csoda could see the purple and red canopies and flags that hovered above the royalty. They could see the swaying tall triangular silhouette of the Ringmaster within the group. His height, elaborate costume and headdress always distinguished his presence, even at a great distance. He was signaling with great swooping gestures. To whom or what he was signaling was not obvious to them.

Yet, soon after his signals, the large gates in the alcove below the stands where the Ringmaster stood began to open. The cranking sounds of rolling chains and heavy doors could be heard as a muffled rumble from far away. The bulls reacted dramatically to the sound. They recognized the opening gates as the sign of their potential freedom from the ring. With snorts and excited kicks they turned and loped towards the wide opening, their heads shaking menacingly at the gateway as they charged out of the arena. The prisoners who had fearfully hidden in alcoves were also allowed to retreat back into captivity, as guards swiftly cracked open doors and directed them into the cavern of cells they had been taken from earlier.

Soon, the herds of beasts and humanity had funneled through the exits, emptying the arena floor of sound and movement–all except for the pawing hooves and bobbing heads of the two horses that stood eagerly awaiting the command to move from the reins in Csoda's hands.

It was Biro who made a decision. He knew the crowds were calling for them to be honored instead of killed. He knew that the Ringmaster now had to appeal to the cheering hoard with, at the very least, a show of acceptance and fanfare. He also knew, from his past experience that the fanfare may not last beyond the arena wall. After all, he had achieved honors once before when he herded the lions before the Emperor, but he had also been thrown back into the cage when the show was over. Still, despite his mistrust of what was about to unfold, Biro recognized that it was the crowd, the masses, that could save them. Their cries of 'Salute' and their attention was the their only hope.

"Move us forward," he told Csoda, "Directly down the middle of this place. Aim towards the platform ahead where the Ringmaster stands."

Csoda nodded and signaled the horses to move, pointing the chariot towards the opposite end of the arena. Biro leaned forward on his strong arm to brace himself. He arched his back and waved triumphantly to the crowd, still hiding his pain.

He continued talking to Csoda while looking out over the crowd "Not too fast... can you make the horses prance? We must make a show of this." And then he turned to briefly make eye contact with Csoda, staring at him seriously from the depths of the hawkish mask, saying, "If you have any magic left brother...use it now."

Csoda nodded. The crowd waved and yelled. In the distant stands special flags were raised above the Ringmaster's platform. Signals, he assumed, of some change in his and Biro's status within all of this chaos.

He followed his countryman's direction, pulling in slightly on the reins, not enough to stop the horse's movement, but just enough to tuck their noses down close to their broad chests. In response, their necks curved in muscular arches like powerful springs, their backs straightened, and their weight shifted to their back haunches so that they marched in spirited surging steps.

He directed the proud team down the center of the arena, and when he felt the horses find their rhythm and their path ahead was clear, he took in deep breaths and shifted his attention to the crowd. Finding particles of strength within, he focused on the air around him, on the space between him and the individuals in the crowd, and even upon the openness between him and the distant silhouette of the Ringmaster.

The horses pranced forward regally. Biro stood straight and proud, displaying his full broad size, the hawkish mask helmet increasing his height. Csoda stood straight as well, his eyes fixed over the heads of the prancing horses, aimed towards the Ringmaster's platform, but focused on something else. In the air, with each inhale of deep breath, Csoda again saw the wispy threads of light that he had noticed earlier. First they were subtle, slight glimmers, but as his concentration intensified the strands became more solid in form. The entire arena filled with these delicate strands, crisscrossing above and around Csoda in an intricate web. Each thread stretched from an individual in the crowd and, as Csoda took in deep breaths and exhaled, the threads stretched through the air, straight into his own chest–into his heart.

As the number of lightly humming threads connecting to him increased, the slight vibrations built on each other. The hums accumulated until the feeling and sounds that Csoda experienced internally became a shaking, deafening roar. He was weakened by the arena event and had already used much of his strength to connect with the crowd earlier–but still, he focused. He stayed held onto and overcame the violent vibration and, with the roaring hum building in his ears he formed his own thought, a powerful but simple statement. With a strong exhale he sent that thought as its own vibration, down through the individual threads and into the many hearts of the crowd in the stadium.

"Our glory is your glory." That was all he had the strength to send, but it was all that was needed.

The crowd surged forward. Those sitting instantly stood. Those closest to the edge of the stands, leaned their bodies precariously over the sides, their arms stretched forward as if trying to touch the two men in the wagon. All the people moved forward, pressing themselves against each other, trying to get as close as possible to the center of the arena. Even the guards stood transfixed, ignoring their normal duties of policing the crowd, frozen, watching. The chant continued, louder and more desperate than before, it reverberated throughout the stands, "Sal-UTE, Sal-UTE, Sal-UTE…"

The response of the crowd pushed energy back towards Csoda and the violent vibration within him became a force of strength. His pain left him and his fatigue was removed, so that he felt light and strong. The energy overflowed from his own form, washing over Biro and the horses. Biro stretched his body up towards the sky and roared out at the crowd. The horse's prancing intensified, their muscles rippling with each parading step.

At the other end of the coliseum the Ringmaster stared straight at the wagon and the men who drove it towards him. Even he felt a surge of emotion and pride, the corners of his eyes slightly wet with tears.

By the time the wagon had made its way across the stadium and pulled to a stop before the awestricken gaze of the nobles and the calculating eyes of the Ringmaster, Csoda and Biro's injuries were forgotten. They showed no signs of weakness or fatigue. They appeared larger than before, the air around them glowed.

The large alcove gates situated before their chariot under the stands of the Ringmaster rattled and groaned as their heavy doors swung open again. This time, instead of bulls, a flurry of silken robes and flags flooded out of them. The sound of drums and a waterfall of chiming bells, along with the heavy smell of incense and thick sweet perfume filled the air.

Here, to Biro and Csoda's surprise, came not a legion of soldiers, but a parade of women, dressed in bright flowing costumes. Some carried hanging brass censers that swung before their movement on sparkling chains, releasing thick musky incense smoke through intricate carvings. The scented smoke swirled around the women, entangling itself in their swaths of flowing fabric and long hair, billowing out into the air above them.

Other women danced on the outside of the group, long scarves swirling in great circles far above their heads as their bodies twisted and turned. The dancers and the incense bearers parted in the middle, revealing five striking women in golden robes. Two held out their arms laden with platters filled with grapes, and two others carried large clay jugs with fresh water spilling out over the rims. Four of these women hurried to the sides of the wagon bed, holding the offerings up towards Csoda and Biro. The fifth carried two ripe apples, which she offered to the curious horses.

Biro took the jug of water first, lifting it out of the delicate hands of the dark eyed woman who offered it to him. He raised it high, tilted it to his mouth and drank heartedly, to the great elation of the crowd.

Csoda was met by a woman with red hair that curled tightly to frame the sides of her fair skinned face. Her lips were reddened and her green eyes were highlighted and framed with thick, dark eyeliner. She raised up the platter of fresh fruits and entreated him to eat. He hesitated for a moment, struck not just by her beauty, but by the thread of light that connected her to him. Her close proximity made the ethereal connection of the magic more pronounced and powerful. He saw her head turning up to him, her eyes locked on his, her body moving forward as she released a sigh of awe.

Her reaction to him was intoxicating, but he purposefully focused on detaching himself, even as he mechanically reached for the grapes and tried to keep the magic focused on the crowd. To some extent it worked, the woman moved back a few steps and Csoda returned his gaze to the Ringmaster. Still she swayed in his peripheral vision, her eyes transfixed on him, her thread of light reaching gently through the air towards him.

"You! Those who have defied all odds! Those who have faced the wrath of the arena and survived with triumph!" The Ringmaster's voice boomed from above, his words accentuated with great hand gestures so that all could see he was addressing Biro and Csoda. "We salute you as being blessed! We salute you as being worthy!" The Ringmaster held his hands out in front of him then pulled them both back swiftly to pound on his chest in a dramatic salute.

The crowd cheered, the women surrounding them danced around the chariot and sang out in high trilling voices. Drums beat all around the stadium. The woman who fed apples to the horses took them by their halters and led Biro and Csoda's wagon, surrounded by the dancing women, through the alcove gates and out of arena. Behind them the sounds of the cheering crowd were highlighted with trumpet blasts as the heavy doors closed.

27

The nobles around him sang his praises, for he, the Ringmaster, was always credited for the quality of the Kirkos. Its acrobats and entertainers, the glorifying acts and the memorable deaths were all, in the end, seen as his ultimate creation. He was the composer and the choreographer of the Kirkos. He was the Master of the arena and the show, the hand behind the fabricated brutal spectacle that the ever-hungry crowd and the blood thirsty nobility craved.

Of course, he received their admiration. He had felt the awe that lifted the crowd out of their seats, the feeling that urged the people to reach towards the two victorious captives. He had seen the showmanship and the flourish the two men added to death defying acts. He recognized their skill, their presence and what he could only describe as a fierce determination to not only live, but to defy odds. Yet, he had also sensed that there was something untouchable about the essence of the men who he ceremoniously saluted in front of all. It was this that made his thoughts spin through his mind, calculating risks and ultimate rewards that he might glean from this day's surprise.

Normally, this type of situation received a much simpler response. Captives who showed such skill and ability to not only survive, but also captivate the crowd, were valuable. The Kirkos and its parade moved from city to city and did not consist only of hoards of slaves that were sent out to die. There were other more notable and even famous individuals and groups, acrobats and animal trainers, warriors and musicians, contortionists and illusionists, who lived within the ranks of the Kirkos. Almost all of the special acts had been created and carried out by captives who were chosen to live after displaying impressive skills. Many had received the blessing of the crowd's desire to salute their accomplishments.

In any other case the Ringmaster would set the captives apart. He would publicize their names and virtues and give them the gifts and lifestyle that their higher rank and fame deserved. New acts would be created and these entertainers would become key components in the show, and though most all of the acts still carried the risk of death, these special performers were raised above the common slaves and carried their names to special graves, immortalized even to the end.

To add new names to the Kirkos this early in the season, the Ringmaster could guarantee the popularity of upcoming events. He knew that news of the latest Kirkos heroes would reach the future cities long before the parade arrived. Normally, the Ringmaster welcomed such new additions to the ranks and benefited from their inclusion. Yet, the situation with these men was slightly more complicated.

Before the bulls had even been released from the arena the Ringmaster had sent runners to identify the notable captives. By the time the wagon had pulled up to a stop in front of his platform his efficient guard had gotten back to him with those names. These were the two nomads, the ones marked specifically by the Emperor for a dramatic and brutal death. These were the two captives that the Ringmaster had isolated and chained to each other, kept in a sealed off separate wagon, to ensure they would not influence the other slaves.

This was Biro, the man who a year before had herded lions in front of the Emperor, an act that might have won any other man's life, but who had also roared in anger and defiance enough to shake the nobility.

This was Csoda, a known revolutionary, a man they said could raise up armies out of ordinary men with his heart filling songs. A man who the Emperor considered a direct enemy, a man whose songs the Emperor feared so much that he ordered his guard to sever his tongue as soon as they captured him. The Emperor wanted both of these men dead. Both were supposed to die as nameless captives in the death acts of the arena, just one of many, for fear that individual executions, even done secretly, would make them into martyrs.

Normally the Ringmaster would not defy the Emperor's wishes. But today, even as he ordered the dancers to retrieve them, even while he saluted them in front of the whole crowd, the Ringmaster's thoughts were flying, calculating, discreetly scheming.

These men had more than acrobatic skill, more than showmanship. The reaction from the crowd and even the reaction he had felt himself, was not ordinary and it was not an accident. There was something working for these men, an untouchable quality or magic he could not identify. He even considered the possibility that they were favored by a strong deity, one whose wrath may be worse than that of any mortal Emperor. At the very least, the Ringmaster recognized that what these two men had was powerful. For him, being a shrewd businessman above all else, powerful meant valuable–very valuable–if used to his advantage.

Normally he would announce the newly redeemed captive's names to the crowd during the salute. But today, he did not. He chose to salute them without names–for now.

28

———

Over the canyons, the clouds melted into the fog of the horizon, hiding a distant view of the Sea of AyRuh. The painted cliffs that followed the carving, twisting river far below were streaked in red, grey and slate blue, highlighted with stripes of sagebrush and evergreen trees. The stubborn trees were determined to cling to the crevices wherever they found a vein of soft earth between the steep rocks. Their branching forms twisted out of the rock faces and then curved up towards the sky, like the claws of a woody beast stuck under the stones.

Zenobia knew this land, knew each crevice and cave, each delicate and dangerous ledge, and the trails that nimbly danced around them. She even remembered trails from the past that, after holding out for years in the howling wind and merciless rain, finally gave out and crumbled into a pile of rubble far below, or disappeared into the raging river, falling into the white foam and fast currents.

As a child she had scrambled up these cliff sides, climbed these rocky walls and ducked into countless small crevices. Sometimes her curiosity had revealed surprises, small entrances into the rock that opened up beyond the surface and revealed vast chasms and caves, or dark underground rooms that lit up with sparkling surfaces when they were hit with the light of a small lantern. That same small lantern revealed chandeliers of stalactites, human sized stalagmites, crystals and sometimes dark reflective pools of water that were always deeper than they appeared.

"It was a wonder I ever found my way out," she said to herself as she sat upon the top of the canyon ridge surveying what had been her childhood playground.

Through her adult eyes she recognized the danger a young girl, makeshift lantern and curiosity in hand, might have faced in exploring these deep unmapped chasms alone. She laughed, remembering that at the time she never considered danger, never even thought of the exploration as foolish. Instead, she followed the shear joy of discovery and she had to admit that she could not muster up a single inch of regret while she reflected on those memories. It had been many years since she explored the caves. Ever since they lowered her father's body into the deep earth she had lost her love for dark caverns.

Yet, she did still enjoy looking out over the cliff sides. Of course, as the responsible queen, she stayed on the more stable trails and sturdier ledges. Here she could look over much of her fertile kingdom.

On a clear day she could see across the striped fields worked by humble farmers, all the way to the seaside. She could see the bustling merchants in the nearest town, moving like industrious ants taking their goods from one place to another. She could see the multitude of stone stables scattered throughout the towns, all of them holding rare horses, The Gifts of the Sun, the pride of her people.

She could watch the many native falcons that nested in the high cliffs, crisscrossing and diving through the sky.

Seeing her lands and her people from this vantage point always helped her keep her perspective. At this point in her life she was truly in service to them, and not the other way around. Her father had taught her well, that a leader was a servant, and should never forget their duty to the people that depended on them. She had learned that lesson, and because she knew it so well, she was filled with worry.

There, behind the lazy clouds and heavy fog, across the Sea of AyRuh, was the Empire of Critias, the lands of Emperor Coracis. It was the largest, most powerful kingdom known by Zenobia, and though a treaty still stood between them, she knew it was disintegrating.

The Emperor was fickle at best, vengeful at worst, and always untrustworthy. She had danced a fine political line by defying his requests to shun trade with the nomadic tribes as well as others, even though she'd defied him politely. She had ignored or stood up against too many of his unreasonable demands. After her meeting with the captives of his Legion, and a brief discussion with what was left of the tribal leaders of the nomads, she was sure that the Emperor had already focused his greed and wrath upon her, her people, and her kingdom.

While the Legion soldiers had not revealed from where they came, the tribal leaders were able to tell her what lands the Emperor's armies now patrolled. They were no longer staying in the confines of the Empire borders. They were secretly pushing into the neutral nomadic lands, lands now emptied by the Empire's persecution and war against the tribes. They were close enough to her kingdom for her to see their threat.

Nearby, the smallest of falcons, a kestrel with red and

blue wings, landed in a tree near where Zenobia sat. She admired the bird, let her concerns rest for a moment and observed his tilting curious head. His smart marble eyes under the smooth slate blue feathers that decorated the top of his head stared directly at her. His body was light and small, but still powerful and swift. His feet were curved talons, his beak a sharp hook. He was a bird of prey and he carried himself as such. His diminutive size did not take away from his strength. He watched her for a moment as she watched him. Then, as if deciding that she was no threat, he took off from the branch, soared out into the wind ten feet in front of her past the ledge drop off, and tucking his wings to his side, he dove down, straight as an arrow and fast as a lightening bolt, alongside the edge of the cliff.

Zenobia laughed. Her love for her kingdom's famous horses was closely followed by her love for the many breeds of canyon falcons that glided through her kingdom's skies. She moved towards the edge slightly to see where the small falcon had gone. She expected to see him triumphantly gripping a small rodent or snake, but instead, she could not see any sign of him.

"He must have flown away…" she thought, but before she moved back away from the edge she saw a flurry of movement far down on a minuscule rock ledge that protruded out from a sheer section of black slate.

There, popping his head out of a tiny hole, the little falcon revealed his home. Behind him a nest full of screeching young and his flustering mate could be heard tucked into their cave. Zenobia laughed again, the distraction making her feel less heavy in her heart. She moved back and settled into her previous position, scanned her eyes over the vast canyon before her and returned to her political concerns, but now with a striking idea forming in her mind.

29

—————

Sweat streamed down the sides of Coracis' face, mixing in with the curls of hair along his temples. His body ached. He had a bruise on his arm and a small cut on his hand. He laid on a large, well cushioned, rectangular couch, his upper body slightly elevated on its sloping headrest. He had stretched out along its entire length, moving his head from side to side, trying to lengthen the muscles that were now tense in his neck.

The adrenaline still moved through him, making his skin vibrate, his breathing fast, his heart pound. He opened and closed his mouth wide, in a purposeful yawning motion, making his aching jaw pop as he tried to calm shaky nerves.

He reached up with his uncut hand to remove the fat roll of leather that now laid loose between his back teeth, its edges protruding out the corners of his mouth like a flimsy horse bit. He looked at it momentarily before laying it down on the table next to him, noting the deep impression of his teeth marks that now riddled its surface, and the darkened color of the compressed leather created by his own drool.

Except for the discarded roll of leather, the table next to him was empty. The jar of wine, plate of food and even the burner of incense that used to be there were now scattered across the floor, the jar shattered, the incense turned over but still smoking, the puddle of wine expanding on the floor nearby, threatening to douse the final burning embers. He looked at the cut on his hand, the new bruise on his lower arm and tried to determine if it was the wine jar that had been the culprit of these injuries or the table itself.

A door on the far end of the room began moving slowly as someone cautiously opened it.

"Leave me!" Coracis shouted, catching the incoming servant before they had fully stepped into the room. A rustle of quick panicking movement could be heard on the other side of the door, a swift flutter as they escaped down the hall, eager to avoid his wrath.

Yelling brought up the excess phlegm in his throat and the strain of using his voice now sent him into a spasm of wet coughing. His head ached. He laid back against the thick pillows, trying to swallow, breathing deeply through the coughing in an attempt to stop it. He closed his eyes, his head felt foggy as it always did right after a seizure. He knew it would ache for the rest of the day.

He tried to remember what he had been doing before the tremor set in. He barely had enough time to bite down on the plug of leather before being sent into uncontrollable spasms. By the soreness in his jaw, his throbbing headache, and the look of the now scattered items that his convulsions had swiped off the table, the leather had surely saved his teeth from the violent clenching of his jaw.

For a moment he regretted sending the servant away, considering that he would now like a drink of water. Yet, the desire for a drink did not outweigh his exhaustion, and the energy to call for service escaped him. Plus, he didn't want to look at a servant right now–didn't feel like watching their nervous scuffling as they moved around him, fumbling. They always fumbled–always gave him a reason to hate them. Their darting eyes, shallow smiles and trembling hands were annoying.

Instead of calling for service he sat upright on the couch and stretched his neck again, leaning his head from side to side. The movement sent a sharp pain up behind his ear causing his face to grimace harshly, and with the sharp pain he thought of her name, *Zenobia*.

"Zenobia," he quietly uttered out loud. This was the name that lingered in his mind.

Her name had haunted him regularly for the past day–the Queen and her kingdom, her suspicious behavior, her incessant refusal to follow his decrees and suggestions when it came to running her tiny, ridiculous kingdom. Insisting, as if she was half the leader that her father had been, that she knew best and basically ignoring him, the Emperor.

All the while her foolish people praised her, sung songs of her beauty and wisdom and wrote long intricate poems of their beautiful lands. They painted intense giant murals on buildings and canyon walls portraying her larger than life, full of power, her intense eyes glowing. In these paintings she was usually accompanied by grandiose images of giant falcons and the revered Jeweled Horses. Yet he, the Emperor of the largest kingdom known, the son of the most powerful line of men out of history, he was belittled by the same artisans. They made fun of him and his kingdom in their foppish plays, and she, this little queen, did nothing to stop them. She did nothing to appease Emperor Coracis.

Now her name, her insolence, had brought on his affliction, this weakness that he hated. Zenobia. This name, this queen, everything about her was unacceptable to him.

He leaned forward, bracing his elbows on his knees, letting his aching head fall into his hands. The shift forward helped the blood flow to his head, he could feel its movement pulse through his neck with the throbbing rhythm of his beating heart. His back ached, he closed his eyes and cleared his throat, uttering quietly to himself with menacing disdain, "Zenobia".

His discussion with Abelardus had done little to relieve his sense of growing distrust of Zenobia. The report from Abelardus had confirmed many rumors, which were already a concern to him.

First, Queen Zenobia was on such good terms with what was left of the nomadic tribes that they provided her access to a captured Legion general. Yet, she had convinced the tribes to release his soldiers and she claimed to have only come across the captured men while on a hunting excursion. No, he did not think Zenobia was innocently passing by, he did not think anything the Queen did was un-calculated. How could it be? How could she have denied so many of his demands without harboring a plan against him? Such plotting needed to be squashed, quickly.

Second, and perhaps more disturbing, was Abelardus' description of a supernatural event. A shaman and a specter of smoke that hissed and called itself Uralom? The story haunted Coracis. He had never heard of such magic or any type of mythical being that matched what was described. The possible meaning was concerning, the power of the shaman, threatening.

Could the Captain's experience have been a hallucination? A dream brought on by a drugged drink given to him by the nomads? The Emperor considered such a trick, for the tribes were full of tricks, but deep down he believed that the story was not a mirage of the steady Captain's mind. If it had been a dream then the Emperor believed it to be a prophetic one. No, this story stirred fear deep in the Emperor's spine and he believed the tale, believed the Captain had seen a real phantom.

Coracis also had no reason to believe that Abelardus had fabricated a lie. He believed the Captain had actually been part of the events he described. This Legion Captain was straightforward, trustworthy and not prone to exaggeration. If asked, Coracis would even have admitted that he liked the sturdy Abelardus. The man was smart, but at the same time stoic and simple.

Coracis, did not like many people. That, however, only made the fantastic story more of a problem and the thought of it gave the Emperor a slight twitch in his right eye.

He held his hand up to his head, rubbed his temples slowly as he stood up. First, he would get some water. Then he would make more decided plans against the problematic queen.

30

The coliseum doors shut, instantly blocking the sunlight that poured in from behind them, muffling the cheers of the crowds in the stadium and the blasts of the trumpeting horns. A few narrow streams of sun leaked through the rafters and doors and mixed with the flickering fires of five pillar shaped pits that burned high above them. These flaming pillars lined the edge of a long, dark, private balcony that stretched far above the reach of the animals and men as they left the arena floor.

As soon as the doors shut, Csoda collapsed like a puppet whose strings were unceremoniously cut. He sat slumped in the chariot bed gasping for air, unable to move. His magic spent, his connection to the crowd blocked, he was reduced to his body, still weak from past torture and captivity, robbed of all strength.

Biro weakened as well, though not as noticeably as Csoda. His shoulders slumped, weighted under the heavy helmet he had carried earlier with ease. As he leaned his weight against the edge of the wagon to keep himself from falling, his body began to shake and sway. The pain of his wounds and a large loss of blood was taking its toll.

The woman that had led the wagon inside, unhitched the horses and moved them out of the hall towards the distant stables. The wagon bed now sat still, angled against some blocks of wood to support the braces that used to connect to the horses. The open aired glory of the arena energy was now gone, reduced to the dust of the shadowy hall. Here the air was ancient and musty, mixed with the smells of livestock, hay, sweat, smoke, perfume and incense. Smells so thick it made it difficult to breath.

The rest of the women who had accompanied them out of the arena still moved quickly around them, though with less flourish than they previously displayed before the crowd. They settled into the rhythms of an efficient troupe instead of a dancing harem. The bells in their clothing filled the hall with delicate, echoing sounds, dangling rhythms that trickled through the air.

The almond eyed beauty who handed Biro water in front of the crowd, now placed a delicate hand tentatively on his bracing arm. Her soft touch sent a vibration through him, his breath escaped in a weighted sigh as the helmet he wore grew even heavier. It had been a long time since a woman had touched his skin, so much so that the longing it produced in him was almost physically painful. She spoke to him, but he did not know her language. With slow calm gestures she guided him to turn, so that she could better see his wounds. She noted with a nod where the arrow had punctured his shoulder. Then, raising her eyes to meet his, she gently lifted the heavy mask from his head and signaled for him to sit. His tired body gladly lowered to the bed of the wagon next to Csoda.

The red haired woman knelt by Csoda's opposite side,

attending to his crumpled frame with a dampened cloth that she used to wipe the dirt and splashes of blood from his face. Her attention was sincere, her touch tentative, and Csoda could still see the smallest, faintest wisp of a silvery thread darting occasionally out of her, through the air and towards him. He was too weak to think about it. He was no longer trying to invoke The Pull, yet this woman with striking green eyes continued to connect to him.

Her touch was calming, the dampened cloth left his skin cool. His breath deepened and slowed. He watched her face as she looked over his arms, scanning him for injuries. The corners of her heavily made up eyes winced when she found a bruise, her lips pursed in deepening concern, her hands shook slightly. Occasionally, she would turn away, the cloth lifting up to her face quickly before she turned back towards him.

"She is crying..." he thought to himself, the idea of it intrigued him. He closed his eyes to relieve her of his gaze and allow her to attend his wounds, all the while thinking, "What torture this world is to those who are kind."

Exhausted, the two friends were only capable of focusing on the women who attended their injuries. Neither Biro nor Csoda heard the sounds of heavy doors opening and closing far above on the overlooking balcony. Nor did they hear the methodical steps or see the arching shadow that the fire pits threw against the back balcony wall and ceiling as the Ringmaster stepped towards the edge.

His muscular arms, banded with ringlets of precious metals, were crossed. His tall, wide shouldered silhouette stretched regally, a glint of a sheathed dagger at his belt line. His head was cocked to one side, his chin raised slightly as he peered down upon them. He stood there, quietly perched above them on the balcony edge, watching the women work on their broken bodies. His view of their weakened forms slumped against the horseless wagon was so different from the God-like figures they had embodied only moments before. He didn't call down, didn't announce himself or their fate, but simply watched, calculating–always calculating.

When the women finished tending to their wounds and determined that Biro and Csoda could move, they entreated in foreign tongues and gestures, for them to stand. With a light touch they led them to the end of the alcove. Both men now followed, like tired horses being led to their stable, heads down, their feet barely lifting above the ground. They did not struggle, did not have the energy to will themselves to care. They let the women lead them to the end of the alcove and through an open door, out from under the watchful gaze of the Ringmaster.

31

———

There was a voice in Csoda, a voice that came to him long ago in the tall grass of his roving homeland. It was a voice that could not be contained. It sprouted from the fertile ground to flower in his cries as a small child. It reverberated through his youth, strengthened his movements, focused his mind. As soon as music was introduced to him Csoda found a playground for his voice in the deep vibrations and drum beats, and what had started as voice frolicked in the world as song.

It was his voice, dancing in the wind as song, joining with the distant thunder of storms that hovered and moved across far off horizons and raised the attention of the Nomadic Shamans and other leaders of his tribe. It marked him as a candidate who would be trained to learn more and to become more connected to that which was within him.

The Shamans took him to the forest and helped him feel the vibrations that came from the trees. They sat him in the vast pastures and taught him to interpret the vibrations that spoke through the wind and in the swaying ocean of grass. He learned to interpret the storms, the stars, and the rays of the sun as it rose and set on the horizon. He learned to join the vibration that rippled off the wings of the soaring falcons and hawks that were common sights across the grasslands. He learned to connect and to see behind the eyes of the roaming packs of wolves and in the racing herds of horses that moved with them through their lives.

In learning to join, to connect, to see, as well as hear, the vibration–the voice–he learned to be intensely sensitive to the changes in the world around him. He could not necessarily predict the future, but this sensitivity allowed him to feel when change was moving towards him, and this power protected the tribe.

Csoda could feel the ground and know that distant armies moved, feel the fire of distant campfires through the wind, see the fire makers through the eyes of passing falcons and understand their intentions through the messages sent to him by howling wolves. In this way he learned and lived, until he grew so adept that what had started as a voice and vibration manifested into the vision of thin strands of light, often silvery in color but also taking on multiple colors that related to the intensity and nature of the connection. He learned that when he could see the strands of light, he not only felt the vibration, but could amplify it towards others, even to the point of sending messages directly to them.

The Shamans taught him that this powerful vibration was available everywhere, to everyone, yet he, for whatever reason, was adept at hearing it, amplifying it, and helping others join with it themselves. This was the very essence of the Art of the Pull, his ability to connect.

This was his beginning, before his people were pushed into multiple wars and tempted into lifestyles that stripped them of connection and their internal voices. Even when the Empire of Critias and neighboring kingdoms tried to suffocate his people's hope, he learned to connect with the vibration and send it out to those around him. In a deep, rumbling combination of voice, poetry and song, drumming and trance, he could lift them out of their fear and confusion, setting fire to their passionate souls.

He campaigned against the forces of imprisoning change that the Emperor Coracis imposed on the nomadic tribes. He stood up to the encroaching borders that were forever shrinking around them as the Empire and neighboring kingdoms attempted to slowly steal their territory.

For some years his efforts proved successful against the incoming forces of war and dark shadows. His people lived freely and continued to move through the lands, holding fast to their beliefs and family ties. For a while, even after larger clans had fallen into war, were enslaved by nearby kingdoms, or had disappeared unheard of again, dissipating like weakened clouds, Csoda believed that his direct clan would survive.

Eventually, his clan was specifically targeted for their rebellion and independence. Their beliefs and his song were labeled a crime and they were hunted down by large armies. His clan both eluded attack and successfully fought the many armies for more than a year, which was a great testimony to their skill and abilities. But over time they were weakened under the constant attacks and the drains of incessant war. They were pushed into unfamiliar lands and ambushed by former allying kingdoms that had been pressured by the Emperor to outlaw their way of life. Then came the day that they found themselves surrounded, outnumbered and overwhelmed by an army ten times their size. The Legion armies overtook them, and as they fell, a giant bonfire was built.

His Shamanic teachers were set afire first. His people's

massive herd of horses were destroyed and added to the flames. The tribal men, women and children were tortured and killed, but given no burial ritual. They too were fed to the fire. The smoke that came from this horrific destruction thickened and swelled like a growing creature, spreading from one edge of the horizon to the other, blackening out the sun.

Csoda was able to fight off and break away from the armies, briefly. He led a small group of his surviving people secretly past the fighting, trying to help them escape into a nearby forest. The thickening fog of hissing smoke entered his lungs as he scrambled on the edge of the field. He tried to push magical strength into the few survivors of his people as they slipped into the slight protection of the forested hills. But the terrible smoke of his dying tribe filled his lungs and, for the first time in his life, the vibration fell silent and the smoke choked out his voice, leaving him gasping on the edge of the forest where he was captured.

They lashed him to a wagon full of dead bodies, the bodies of his family and friends, and pulled the wagon to the base of the fire where he was to be thrown into the flames alive, fed to the ominous oily smoke.

The soldiers, who callously moved the bodies into the flames, pushed the wagons themselves into the fire, keeping it fed while avoiding getting too close to its growing heat for fear that they themselves would ignite. One-by-one, wagons filled with dead nomads were pushed from afar, rolling madly into the ravenous furnace to crash and ignite against the mountain of burning dead that fed the rolling waves of carnivorous smoke.

Csoda was overwhelmed with the smell of burning skin and hair that suffocated him. The smoke entering his nose, mouth and eyes hissed menacingly, cackling like evil laughter. The heat was all encompassing, reddening and blistering his skin as the wagon he was strapped within was moved to the edge of a slight hill, positioned to be pushed into the bonfire.

He could no longer hear the screams of both humans and beasts being killed. Their struggle had gone silent. No longer could he sense the energy of his people flowing towards him. Beside him he saw the familiar faces of family and friends, contorted in the macabre masks of pale death, their eyes shallow and empty of life, their skin colored only by the nearby flames.

The intake of smoke filled his lungs and he felt the choking deep within, in his heart, whispering his shame to him. He had failed to protect them, failed to anticipate this horror, failed to fight off this destruction, and his shame made him weaker, made him crave the coming destruction of death.

Yet, there was an inch of hope that lingered behind his ashen tears. He had led the small group of men, women and children to the edge of the forest. He had seen them disappear into the thickening trees right before the smoke blinded them to him. He had sent his last breath of magic towards them, trying to protect them, before the soldiers grabbed him. That memory held a small sense of hope and purpose.

When his eyes caught sight of a soaring hawk through a small hole in the ink black cloud, gliding so high above the mountain plume of smoke, it appeared to be only a sharp winged dot in the graying sky. Csoda gathered together that tiny hope. He tried, one last time, to connect to the vibration that he could no longer hear. His purpose was only to see through the eyes of the soaring bird one last time. To see if he could use the bird's lofty perspective to see beyond the smoke, where he might be able to watch the remnants of his people escape, even as he himself turned to ash.

He focused on the small dot of the distant bird, his blue eyes flashing with his last wish. He began to sing, a guttural hum, a harmonic growl that started deep in his chest and rose through his lungs, clearing his throat of the ashen phlegm. The sound, though a shallow mimic of the strong vibration he had always known, still produced the slightest wisp of a coppery silken thread.

As delicate as a single line from a spider's web, the thread glimmered for a brief moment, moving with his growling voice. He sent a wish out on that coppery thread, to see the survival of his people, his tribe, his culture. Yet, before the wish was sent high to the soaring bird the ink black smoke filled the opening view of the sky, blacking out the vision of the hawk above.

The hard silhouette of an armored soldier stepped before him. The soldier's dark, uncaring eyes looked into his own, and the coppery thread, the vibration of hope, suddenly flashed up and away from Csoda like a minuscule arrow of light, his wish upon it. This small arrow of hope did not fly to the far off soaring bird. Instead it pierced directly into the soldier before him. It disappeared into the man's dull eyes.

For a moment they stared at each other, Csoda's heart sinking, the smoke reentering his lungs, his sense of failure overwhelming. The soldier glared, his face a rock of inhumanity, his eyes a reflection of the deadly fire before them. Then, briefly, the soldier's eyes wavered, his blackened pupils lightened with a slight copper flash and, quickly, the armored man reached down to Csoda, cutting his bonds and pulling him off the doomed wagon, just as the rest of the soldiers pushed it forward to career wildly towards the burning abyss.

"I recognize this one. He's one of their leaders!" The soldier shouted to the others. "He's still alive," he stated, as he wrapped a strap of leather around Csoda's feet and hands, binding him. He threw Csoda towards a patch of open grass, the ground surprisingly cool against his body. "A good gift for the Emperor."

Losing his tongue was the aftermath of that horrific event. That and the maddening captivity, but he had already lost the sound of the vibration before they mutilated his body. He had lost the vibration when the corpse fed smoke entered his lungs and, until the arena, until the events of the deadly Kirkos, he had not seen the connecting threads.

He lay in a cool room of stone, led here by the hands of a kind woman who had lifted cool water to his lips and fed him fresh fruits. He had tasted fruit. Something he thought was impossible without a tongue, but he could taste the sweetness of fruit as it touched what was left of his tongue in the back of his throat. It was now healed from the mutilation, the pain gone.

He lay in this room alone, free of shackles, his body's exhaustion enough to contain him—for now. He did not know his future, but he had seen the vibrating cords in the arena. He had felt the strength of the crowd. He had seen his countryman, Biro, leap with great power over the bull and battle upon the chariot. He had felt the herd, the pounding hooves of the charging black bulls, looked into the eyes of the chariot horses and felt their power surging beneath him.

He was alive—and if he and Biro survived, then there was hope that others did as well.

The voice, it still existed, he was sure of it, even though he could not exactly hear it. He lay still in this cool room of stone. His memory of the fire and destruction that happened so long ago brought tears to his eyes, but it was also urging him to focus. Something deep within him was telling him to listen and reconnect. As he focused, a deep rumble emanated from the back of his throat.

If the voice could not frolic as harmonic song, he would help it live as the low resonating rumble that now moved out from deep in his chest, vibrating in the back of his throat. He pushed the guttural sound out to echo against the walls of the room. The depth of the sound, the shear thickness of it, pleased him. It reminded him of the songs of other tribes, fellow kinsmen, those he had met long ago. Men who let their voices rumble from deep within so the sound echoed across the open plains, joining with the sounds of the wind and flowing water. He let the sound rumble for a while, playing with the fluctuations in tone he could create. Then, feeling tired, he let the sound drift off, let its echo quiet, and let his eyelids fall.

32

"Father?... Father?" The voice lingered in the air, light in tone, drifting in and out on a heartbeat rhythm. "Father..." it uttered again, and again.

Csoda, half asleep, had to truly digest the word, fully comprehend that it was being addressed to him, though he knew he did not have a child.

Csoda opened his eyes, but the darkness of the room where he laid was as black as the world behind his closed lids.

"Father?" The voice came again, and this time with his eyes open, Csoda could sense that the voice was coming from a presence to his right.

Comfortable, yet still unable to move his body, he tried to move his eyes, but only darkness revealed itself. Darkness, and the sense that someone stood near, close to his hand laying flat by his side, palm down on what felt like a silken blanket.

The voice had awakened him, but for a moment he could not place where he was sleeping. There was no movement of wheels on rough gravel and sand rocking his body, no thick smell of musty horses, oxen and men, no layer of scratching dirt and straw against his skin, no discomfort. This was not the moving prison wagon that he had been trapped in with Biro for so long. This room was still, its air cool, the presence of a breeze caressed his face, the surface he laid upon was silken and soft. Without moving and without seeing he realized that the breeze did not touch the skin of his body. He must be covered with a light blanket.

Waking, his eyes adjusted to the dark room, giving him glimpses of navy blue shadows and slight variations of minimal light. He remembered where he was, the room he had been led to by the green-eyed woman. He remembered the coliseum, the chant of the crowd, the exhausted collapse he had fallen into when they were led into the alcove after the event with the bulls. He remembered the taste of clean cold water, the taste of fresh fruit and grains before being left alone to rest. He remembered creating the resonating sound from deep in his throat, a substitute for his broken song. He remembered the moment just before he fell into a deep sleep on the cushioned bed he laid on now.

He was alive.

"Father?"

This time the voice startled him, for Csoda was fully awake. He had already brushed aside the previous utterances as the remnants of a forgotten dream drifting into his mind right as he awoke. Yet the words came from out of the dark, clearer than before. To the right of him in the blue shadows he could see the form, not of a child, but of a man.

To his surprise he did not feel fear, only confusion, as he attempted to look at the stranger. Csoda turned his head towards the man, keeping the rest of his body perfectly still.

There, standing against what appeared to be a solid wall was the lean silhouette of a man wearing a tricorn hat and dressed in the checkered costume of some type of acrobat. The man shifted his weight and cocked his head to the side, he held his right hand up before him pounded his chest briefly and then moved his hand towards his face making elaborate, graceful, and seemingly meaningful gestures. The man's hand signals were an attempt to communicate, but Csoda could not decipher their meaning. At the very least they did not seem threatening.

When Csoda did not react to the signals the voice came again, a young man's voice asking, almost begging, "Father?"

Instinctually Csoda raised his right hand from his side and reached out to the young man, who, upon seeing this, quickly moved to Csoda's side. The man knelt, dropping down to grasp Csoda's upraised hand, his head bowed.

"Father. It is you!" The young man gasped, his voice catching as he held back a sob.

Csoda could make out the young man's face, strong but lean, handsome, with striking greenish blue eyes framed by ebony eyelashes, brows and thick black hair, his complexion slightly darker than Csoda's. The young man spoke in Csoda's tribal language, the same one that Biro spoke, but he did not look like Csoda or his direct kinsmen. This young man did not look like anyone Csoda had ever known. Yet, he was so familiar.

Even the young man's clothing seemed foreign to him. His well worn tricorn hat was made of brown leather, burnished at the edges and tattered at the brim. His clothing was a strange combination of acrobat costume and armor, a checkered patchwork of well sewn pieces of leather and thick cloth.

Though Csoda did not recognize this man, he felt a sense of trust in this stranger, and he was sure that the young man sincerely felt that he knew Csoda. He called him Father.

The young man looked up at Csoda with tear filled eyes only to duck his head back down to Csoda's hand as he cried. Csoda simply stayed in place, observing, until he noticed a shimmering golden light spiraling though the air between him and the young man, a golden cord that solidified with each deep breath and moved between them like a tiny, floating stream of liquid sun. The golden cord spiraled and danced through the air, stretching between the two of them until it simultaneously entered both of their hearts.

Csoda's chest expanded, his heart swelled almost painfully. Suddenly, he knew this young man, and despite what his memory told him he saw this stranger as his son.

He drew in a quick breath, his eyes tearing up, he reached across his body and placed his left hand on the young man's shoulder pulling him towards him to hug him firmly. His emotions overwhelmed his logical mind. They embraced for a moment then Csoda moved out of the hug, grabbed both sides of the young man's face and peered deep into his eyes. He searched for meaning, understanding, logical recognition to match the emotions he felt. Who was this?

"Father. It is you. You do recognize me," the young man said. A sense of relief washed over his face as his eyes connected with Csoda.

With all of his will, Csoda searched the young man's eyes for answers. The words formed in his head, the golden light vibrated in the air and Csoda tried to send his question into the young man's thoughts, "Where am I?"

The young man nodded, acknowledging Csoda's confusion, seeming to receive his question. "You are in the ruins of Phaedon," he answered.

Csoda took in the words, let them move through his thoughts, but he was more confused than before, "Ruins?"

The young man choked down tears, leaned back still holding Csoda's right hand, he sighed and steadied himself. Taking in a deep breath he quietly restated his answer, "I'm sorry, I misspoke. You, Father, are in the city of Phaedon." Then, with a firm squeeze he continued, his voice slightly breaking, "I am in the ruins..."

Csoda still did not understand the reply, yet he settled into a state of calm and observed the stranger for a few moments. As he did the young man visibly relaxed. Csoda sat up in the bed, his feet swinging to touch the floor, he reached out his left hand to join his right in warmly grasping the young man's hand.

They stood up together, facing one another, their hands clasped. They were the same height. The young man was strong and steady, his crystal green-blue eyes revealed a mind that seemed sharp and alert. Csoda felt proud of him.

In the edges of his sight Csoda could see the darkness of the room shift. The light of dawn trickled in overtop what seemed to be the edges of crumbled stone walls. The floor beneath his bare feet changed from polished marble and momentarily became roughened earth and barren stone, an unhampered wind moved through the room, moving the young man's hair but not his own.

"Ruins?" Thought Csoda. Far in the distance, behind him, Csoda could hear the sound of delicate bells, the haunting beat of a distant drum.

The young man squeezed Csoda's hands again, and with a relaxed smile he said, "Father, I love you."

And then the crumbling walls of the room seemed to reform around Csoda. The wind ceased to blow, the floor solidified into polished marble tiles and the young man, who had been as solid as the stone, faded away right before him, his voice echoing quietly, "Thank you."

Csoda was used to visions, was used to exploring mysteries of the unknown. He had seen and performed feats that could only be described as magic. He had been trained by powerful Shamans, spoken to the mystical Taltos in life and in visions. Even still, this moment, when he was so suddenly alone, his hands folded in front of him out in the air where they had moments before been holding the hands of a stranger who called him Father, he felt a shivering aftermath of shock, disappointment, loss.

He let his hands fall to hang still folded in front of him. He stood still. His only movement was the turning of his head as he looked over the room. Solid walls on three sides, the only opening a small window directly in front of him. The window was too small for a man to get through. Heavy wooden shutters were closed in front of it, letting in only a small glow of light. He moved forward and swung one shutter open, revealing a setting sun, the light of dusk, not dawn. Through the window he could see the glowing city of Phaedon, a city alive with lit torches and celebratory music, the walls of the coliseum towering nearby.

Behind Csoda the sound of bells and drums had grown louder, now accompanied by the harmony of other instruments mixed with voices and laughter.

He turned to see the only door in the room. The music and drums he heard were leaking in through its edges. He moved towards the door, tentatively reached for the handle, expecting it to be locked. He pulled aggressively and almost fell when it swung open so easily on solid hinges. Opening the door flooded the small room with warm light and inviting music no longer muffled by the heavy wood. Before him was a hallway lit by small torches. At the far end of it an open room full of women and the intoxicating smells of roasting meat. He stood staring for a long while, his hand still warm from grasping the hand of a stranger, or a vision, one that had called him Father. Then, at the far end of the hallway, the young woman with the red hair and green eyes stepped into view and, with an inviting smile, gestured to him, inviting him to join them.

33

———

Dusk was long past and the Ringmaster was locked in his private chamber. For all intensive purposes he was alone, except for two of his elite guard who were positioned on either side of the door, far on the other side of what was an enormous space. Their presence hardly changed the feeling of solitude, their forms hovered quietly, never moving, their blank, masked faces staring straight ahead.

The Ringmaster leaned back on a well cushioned chair with broad armrests, his arms propped and legs extended, feet resting on a heavy wooden ottoman. He was relaxing, letting his eyes rest on the generous take of this season's first show. His armor, headdress, canopy like robe and sturdy leather boots were removed. All he wore was a regal tunic, simple but finely made, its edges embroidered with gold and copper threads in a delicate pattern that resembled the feathers of roosters.

In this vast space, dressed as he was, the Ringmaster almost seemed to be an ordinary man. His tawny hair was cut close to his head, slightly longer on the very top where it made a barely noticeable peak. His mid section was wider than it appeared when encased in the tightened leather armor. However, even out of his formal costume, lounging in a large chair, he was still a broad and tall figure. His body was still heavily muscled, his neck, thick. Tattoos and scars spiraled up his arms and chest, decorating his skin with marks of past endeavors–and mistakes.

The vast room appointed to him by the King of Phaedon always felt strange to the Ringmaster for the first few days. After over a year of quartering himself in the black wagon as the caravan wound its way throughout the land, he was used to movement and his opulent, if small, quarters. He missed the constant sound of beasts and men. The contrast was always drastic, the rooms openness always a bit unsettling. These vast chambers were filled with quiet, cool air that smelled of ancient stone and crushed herbs. The beds were massive, almost four times the size he was used to sleeping on, and they proved to always be uncomfortably soft to his hardened back. Still, he enjoyed being catered to, and he knew that these private chambers, one in each city the Kirkos performed, would be especially valuable to him on the days that the Kirkos was in full swing. Long brutal days and evenings when his oversight was needed constantly, and his presence was regularly requested by every king and nobleman and, eventually, the Emperor himself. At those times, he would relish the privacy that such quarters provided, and crave these moments of exhausted silence late in the evenings.

Before him lay a mound of gold and silver coins mixed with a few precious jewels. They were piled on top of a large stone table in the middle of the vast room. The treasure sparkled in the light of the oil lamps that were placed strategically throughout the space. He had not counted the treasure before him. Not now, not yet. He would save that for the next day.

He never counted the money on the first night. This was a tradition for him. One that he created long ago with the first meager earnings that he had obtained by organizing and promoting a simple cockfight in an abandoned stone ruin on the edge of the village where he was raised. He was thirteen at the time, and the earnings, which now seemed a laughable sum, had filled him with a surreal sense of accomplishment. He had barely been able to touch the coins that the bloody spectacle provided him. At the time, wealth was foreign. He had been content to place the money on a table in his room and gaze at it in quiet awe for the rest of the evening.

Thus the tradition was born, and he never denied himself this moment. Though, he had to admit, the sense of awe was never quite as overwhelming as it had been on that first night, an interesting fact, since the wealth he acquired now far surpassed his take from that first cockfight.

Through the years, this tradition had become a sort of private superstition, a form of spiritual focus. Instead of counting the wealth, he simply sat alone and stared at the bounty. He let its sheer volume and glory wash over him, all the while knowing that the pile would continue to grow. More and more wealth would pour in over the next few months. More wealth than most people could imagine would pass through his hands and be recorded in his vast archive of scrolls.

The attendance at the arena was only one form of income. There were slaves and animals that were bought and sold. Dancers and acrobats lent out to the eager nobles for private performances and as sexual escorts. Private battles between popular fighters would be arranged behind closed doors for the royalty's blood lusting amusement. Trinkets were sold to the masses, souvenirs and exotic cures for whatever ailed them. Locks of hair from humans and animals were popular. Clips of hair from the most beautiful dancers would go to their admirers, or to women wishing to use them to obtain better luck in love. Fur from the lions often went to men wishing to impress. Horse hair was braided and dyed bright colors and worn as good luck bracelets.

The carcasses of the animals that died in the Kirkos were skinned or mounted. Their pelts and taxidermy figures sold for high prices and decorated the walls and hallways of the wealthiest homes. Their flesh was burnt at the many temples that filled the city centers. Each God was observed, each high priest was satisfied. The Ringmaster was not of a religious bent, at least not in a traditional sense, but he understood the value of being viewed as observant to the Gods, both socially and politically. Most of all, he knew that the rest of the meat, that which did not go to the temples, would be cooked by skilled chefs at extravagant banquets. The wealthiest paid well to be fed like the Gods with meat from the Kirkos slaughter.

Indeed, the Ringmaster milked material benefit out of the spectacle. He worked every angle and enticed every penny out of the hands of the spectators, rich and poor. He gave them what they craved and in return they opened their pockets generously. The ability to see and fully embrace all potential opportunities to obtain wealth was one of the Ringmaster's true gifts. It was what had set him apart from the average fight promoter or slave trader. In a sense, he was a visionary, and this skill was, on this night, working overtime.

Upon the table along with the pile of gold and jewels,

lay the dragon hawk mask that had been ripped from the head of one of his trained warriors by what should have been an exhausted, unskilled and weakened captive. A captive that, along with another, had run along the backs of stampeding bulls and avoided the chaos of the arena like the most skilled acrobats he had ever known. More importantly, the two captives had pulled the crowd up out of their seats, moved them to tears and elation in ways he, the Ringmaster, had never seen. The answer was simple to the Ringmaster, embrace these captives, promote them into the ranks of the upper level performers. He would reward their skills, even train them, and in doing so, they would funnel the crowd's money into his hands. This was his plan. There was only one snag, one problem that hovered in the air–the identity of the two captives.

The name of the strong one who had worn the mask was a name he could easily obscure over time. The second one, the seemingly frail man who had somehow lifted himself into the air on thin legs and danced upon the backs of bulls, this one concerned the Ringmaster. It was this man, Csoda, whom the Emperor had insisted be killed like a dog in the events. It was the name of Csoda that the Emperor feared. For while the man lived, his name could be used to give energy to the Empire's enemies, and if this man died, his name carried the threat of potential martyrdom.

The Ringmaster gained no profit from disobeying the highest powers, and risked much more than money in being disloyal. However, his truest loyalty was to profit and wealth. His political connections were only to secure the same. The temptation to bend the political rules was too great. He saw the opportunity and understood the full volume of wealth that it promised.

It was the names of these slaves that was the problem.

The famous name, the feared name, and the feared identity of the mysterious tribes that both these men represented that he could not allow to survive this night. The men themselves, their skills and talents, their abilities that promised great profit for the Kirkos, those were things that the Ringmaster could not ignore. No, the men would live, their flesh and blood enslaved as great performers, and he would profit from them. Their identities, their names, their history, *those* would have to die.

34

The echo of a falling rock cascaded through the damp space long after the actual rock had ceased to move. With that echo came the voice of Erastos who stood nearby. She could sense him somewhere to her right, but the thick silk scarf that he had tied gently over her eyes prevented her from seeing where she was and where he stood.

"We are here, my Queen." He said, "May I remove the blindfold?"

Zenobia was eager to look around, but she was also cautious. She, more than anybody, knew that it was important for her to be ignorant of the details of her loyal guard's findings. "Yes, if you are sure there is nothing here that I will recognize."

Erastos touched her right shoulder reassuringly before he untied the scarf. "We are deep within the cave now, my Queen, and I have only one torch lit. I believe we are safe."

He lifted the blindfold and Zenobia's sight now revealed the flickering glow of the single torch that Erastos had placed in front of them, tucked firmly into a deep crevice of rock close to the cave floor. The light from that torch shone over a large open space as it reflected dimly against a distant wall to her right, then faded into a seemingly endless black void to her left, where she had heard the rock fall. She breathed the damp air in deeply, moist but fresh enough, as she took in what proved to be a larger cavern than she had expected. High above she could see the glimmer of large stalactites reaching down towards her, and around her their mirrored companion stalagmites reached upwards. The forms looked to her like odd miniature kingdoms and castles, strange ancient cities of worlds unknown. For a moment she fell silent, in awe, and was extremely grateful towards dear Erastos.

"Is this an illusion of light Erastos, or does this cavern open up to our left?"

"It opens up, my Queen, the space is much larger than what we can see right now. Even more importantly, it leads to other large rooms as well. This is a labyrinth of useable caves." He answered and Zenobia could tell by the tone of his voice that he was proud of his finding, excited even.

"This is marvelous, Erastos, you have done well." She replied, "You have done me, us, our whole kingdom a great service."

Erastos stood straight, his heels clicked together as he bowed deeply, "Thank you, my Queen." Again Zenobia could read the tone of his voice. She knew that he choked back his emotions, his eyes tearing slightly at her high praise.

Praise he truly deserved, she thought to herself, as she walked towards the darker edge of their torch light. It was only a few months since she sent him on this special errand. Entrusting him to explore the surrounding kingdom and lands for suitable hidden caverns.

She had sent him alone. Trusting only him with the

findings, insisting it be done in utmost secrecy. Even when he did find something she instructed him to take her there blindfolded and promise to lead her around the kingdom erratically until she was sufficiently confused and lost. She did not want to be able to identify where he had taken her. Now, she was here, in this massive cavern, and even though she had no traceable idea where she was, she felt a sense of hope for her people.

"I only wish I could see more of this great find, my friend," she continued, "but I think it is best that this is all I see." She moved back towards the torch and to Erastos' side who still held himself in a reverent bow. "Will you be able to work on the rest of the preparations alone?"

"Yes, my Queen, I have already started." Zenobia smiled, she would miss her dear guard. He and Alexius were unflappable in their loyalty and dedication and always proved to be capable at whatever task was thrown their way. She regretted putting so much on Erastos' shoulders, but knew that the less people involved in this undertaking the better. Even Alexius and herself would have to be in the dark.

"Very good Erastos, very good." She replied. "Now please, blindfold me again and let us leave before my own curious nature gets the better of me."

Erastos obeyed, sweeping himself gracefully up from his bow, he quickly moved to his queen's side. He placed the blindfold across her eyes and efficiently, but gently, tied it back into place.

"Take my arm, my Queen." He stated and Zenobia reached forward, finding his extended elbow and placing her hand on his forearm, she allowed him to guide her away.

35

It was one of many dreams Biro had of Zenobia. Rich in detail, her face as clear as life before him, her dark eyes hypnotizing, her voice rich. They were all surprisingly realistic and each time he woke slightly disoriented, trying to remember where he was. Yet now he awoke and she was still there, her naked shoulder peaking out from under the thick covers they shared, her dark hair loose, tussled and full, overflowed onto the pillow where her head rested.

Biro's heart raced, the reality of her presence trickling into his freshly wakened mind. He had just heard her voice, her question like so many dreams before, "Biro, what will become of us..." And here she was. How? How had she come to be here with him?

He moved in closely, desperate to feel his skin against hers. He reached out to slide his hand up along her waist when he noticed her skin was paler, her hair a different tone of brown. A thick smell of henna, incense, and perfume washed over his senses. His mind fully wakened, his memory of the previous night returned, and before him was not Zenobia, but the dancer he had lain with last night. His recent memories came back, drowning out the dream. With them came a throbbing pain in his head, making him groan as he turned away from the still sleeping woman and stretched out on his back.

The last few days had been full of food, drink and women. Days in which Biro fully indulged in all that was offered. His days of captivity had left him starving, and his senses were overwhelmed with the desire to partake of the abundant offerings laid before him. Now, after the dream, and faced with a thick and merciless headache, he wished he had been capable of at least some restraint–the kind that seemed to come more easily to Csoda.

It became apparent that the headache was likely to stay with him whether he remained on the bed or not. He chose to sit up. He swung his legs off the side, his feet finding a warm thick rug beneath them as they touched the floor. Biro scanned the room, still unfamiliar with its layout, uncomfortable in its luxury and size. At the foot of the bed was a large copper basin full of fresh water that would be cool to the touch, fresh from the spring, brought in by slave girls early in the morning so that he could drink and wash at his leisure.

Water. How often had he woke in the wagon cage thirsty, his throat dry, his skin covered with sweat, straw and a rough coating of grit and sand. The memory of the torturous conditions echoed through his body, and he craved that water now just as he craved it then. Yet now it was here in front of him–available.

Everything was available now. Everything except the ability to leave. It was true that he and Csoda now had two separate rooms to themselves, rooms six times the size of the cage they had been living in. It was also true that they could leave their private quarters and meet in a large living space that was between the bedrooms. They had attendants at their beck and call, always ready with food, wine or eager to fulfill their requests. They even had access to a large courtyard where delicate trees had been nurtured in the desert heat so they would grow tall enough to provide a wispy shade for those who sought fresh air. It did not take long for Biro to note that there were only two entrances into the space, and both of those entrances were locked and guarded from the outside. This is where their new cage ended.

Biro wondered where exactly he would go if the door swung open and he was free to run. For all he knew, his tribes no longer existed and Zenobia was now a queen with a kingdom. She was no longer the young woman he had left by the side of the shimmering pond, their secret meeting place. He could not be sure she would even acknowledge him now. And really, why should she? For all she knew he had abandoned her all those years ago.

Biro knew they were still captives, but by the extravagant treatment they now received he must surmise that their status within the Kirkos had changed. Though he was not sure what that meant for them in the long run, for now he would refresh himself with the cool water. He dipped the copper cup that sat next to the basin again and again into the shimmering depths and drank deeply, in hopes that the thirst that had sat with him for so long would be quenched.

Behind him he could hear the dancer stirring awake. She moved up behind him, her hands sliding up his back and onto his shoulder. Her lips came resting softly in light kisses on his neck. He was still thirsty but another desire now presented itself and he turned to face her, her dark eyes steady against his gaze, lined thickly with carefully applied makeup, the edges ever so slightly smudged from her sleep.

Her eyelids and cheeks were dusted with gold powder. Her skin was soft and warm to his touch. A thin scar made a curved line from the corner of her right eye and tapered to a delicate point below a well defined cheekbone making it look like it was an intentional decoration. He remembered her now. Remembered her dancing the night before, her hips shaking expertly to quick paced tabla drums, her belly softly moving and undulating above a belt of shimmering brass bells and red silken scarves. In the light of the evening and under the spell of the rich wine she had been an image of liquid fire, molten heat, and burning movement. Her dark hair and eyes reminded him of Zenobia, though he had tried to put that thought out of his mind.

Today, away from the firelight, his mind clearer, she was more human, but still beautiful. Her resemblance to the Queen was not as accurate as it had seemed in the night. Biro reached up to touch the delicate scar by her eye, wondering where it came from. He already knew they did not speak the same language, so he did not ask. Instead he let her eagerly push against him and he responded to her, pressing her gently down before him to attend to the hunger in their bodies.

36

———

"**A** Traitor!" Coracis announced, and the Senators before him sat up straighter in their hard bench seats, sucking in deep breaths of air and holding it behind pale, pursed lips.

The Senators were enwrapped in his tale of the Queen's secret undertakings and his description of the dark magic wielded by the nomadic Shaman told to him by Captain Abelardus. They were quiet for the entire speech, pulled into Coracis' tale like children before a puppeteer. They paused after their united gasp. Then, one by one, they stood from their seats and applauded vigorously, their draping robes fluttering madly with the movement, the echoing hall amplifying their hearty clapping.

Before his scanning eyes he could not see a single one of them that seemed hesitant or reserved about their support. Rarely did the Emperor's decrees meet with such absolute and whole hearted backing from a unified Senate. It was true that the Senators feared him and would often mask any complaints when they did have them, but on this day he did not see a single uneasy shifting of eyes or hear the repressed murmurs of whispered protest.

Today they were unified in their purpose. Queen Zenobia was a traitor who consorted with warlocks and rebels. It was his duty as Emperor of Critias to protect his land and people from the danger she represented. In protecting his country he would also be enriching it, freeing the fertile canyon lands from the grasp of this controlling Queen and opening them up for his own people to colonize.

Coracis looked over the applauding Senate and they did not seem so old and weak as he had known them to be in the past. "Perhaps," he thought, "These men could be pulled out of their greying apathetic years and become refreshed with new purpose. United with their Emperor they could dawn a new era of fruitful progress and glory for all of Critias."

He glanced down to the side of the stage. At the edge in front of his guards was the figure of Captain Abelardus who knelt on one knee, his head bowed, his right fist held firmly against his chest over his heart. The captain had remained in this frozen military bow for the entire speech, never wavering, a testimony to discipline. In this man, this soldier, this symbol of military loyalty, was evidence of the glory of Critias.

The Senators were still applauding. Their voices now joined the clapping, "Hail Coracis!", "Hail the Empire of Critias!", "Let's be free from Zenobia! Free from the false treaty!" They were ready for war.

Coracis himself would go to the edge of his kingdom. He decided this as he stood surrounded by the Senate's applause. He would see the loyal troops off into the remaining open lands of the Nagy Föld. He would remain nearby to receive their reports as they made their way into the hidden desert canyon land's southern border. He would lead Critias to glory.

The thought of it filled him with purpose. For so long he had hidden away in the cold empty estates of the capital. For so many years he had shuttered himself away from his potential, allowing the deceit and lower nature of those around him to chase him into protective isolation. Now he realized he was meant to lead and expand Critias beyond what the Emperors before him could manage. He, Coracis, was not meant to hide from the urchins around him, but instead, lead. Standing tall as Emperor he would pull them up with him or crush those who refused to match the glorious expectations of the greatest empire.

37

Five days. Csoda's finger drew a line across four other marks he had created in a light coat of dust on the arm of his chair. The red haired woman stood behind him. Her hands gently dabbed a cloth coated in a cooling medicine against the jagged cuts on his shoulder, neck and back. Injuries he most likely obtained in the arena when the bull pushed him into the ground.

Her name was Eir. She pronounced it, along with most of her words, with a slight melodic lilt and a delicate roll of the tongue that often made him unintentionally smile. He had ignored the other women. He knew they were slaves and their attentions made him uncomfortable. But Eir, even though she too was a slave, seemed different.

Her mannerisms stemmed from pure kindness. Her attention felt healing and, despite his attempt to stop the magic, there still existed a delicate cord of light that danced between them. At first this confused him, but after days of watching, he realized that it was Eir who had created the cord, not him. He did not know if she created the magic intentionally, but there it was, spinning slowly, ebbing in and out of translucency, connecting him to her. From it he could feel a warm vibrating hum that spun around within him, touching both noticeable and hidden wounds and softening their pain. He found her attention and ability to comfort fascinating and sincere.

Five days he and Biro had been kept in these extravagant quarters. Csoda could not help but wonder how long this phase would last. The first few nights of intoxicating feasting had noticeably tapered off. Regular food was still provided, and some of the attending women still lingered there in the evenings, but the overall intensity of the feasts was dulled.

"You're cold?" Asked Eir, her voice concerned. "Such a hot day, but your skin, so cold." She stopped dabbing his shoulder and reached up to touch his forehead with the back of her hand, feeling for his temperature.

Csoda smiled and gently took her hand from his brow, guiding it down before him. He was drifting in thought before now, not meditating exactly, but in a state that was distant from all that surrounded him. Perhaps such a state made his skin cold.

He held her delicate hand and brought her to stand in front of him. Her fingers were long and thin, her skin would have seemed paler except for the coating of freckles that made her appear tanner than she was. Her striking red hair and bright green eyes were exotic to him and he often found himself staring at her face longer than he intended.

Eir fidgeted under his gaze, but did not try to pull away. She was older than many of the women, beautiful, but older. He regretted his lack of tongue, his inability to ask her questions about how she came to be in this place. She did not speak his native language but she proved adept at speaking a few other languages, switching from one to another easily when talking to the guards and the other women. With him she spoke the trade language that many cultures used when working with the nomads.

"Even your hands," she said, "too cold." She furrowed her brow in concern. Csoda smiled again at her worry.

He reached forward and laid his hand on her belly causing her to cock her head to the side, confused. Then he pointed at her, tapped her belly again and made a motion as if he cradled a child. It took her a moment to comprehend what he was asking and then she suddenly became shy, her head ducking.

"No…" she responded, her head lowered, "I do not have a child." She looked back at him and raised one eyebrow, trying to gauge if she had understood his inquiry. Csoda confirmed her questioning stare with a nodding head.

"Do you?" she asked.

Csoda shook his head slowly then reached out and took her hand in his, patting it softly.

She smiled and then, ducking her eyes she stated, "I can't."

With her free hand she pulled at he waist of the long skirt she wore and exposed a portion of her belly as well as a long deep scar that cut under her navel. Csoda reached out to touch it instinctually. They stayed silent for a long while, Csoda's hand laying gently on her scar. Before him he could see the thread of light glimmering through the air, spiraling slowly.

Eir took in a deep breath, "Your hand is warm now."

She stared at his hand on her belly. Her eyes, he noticed, were tearing up. He lifted his hand, she was right, his palm was warm, his heart felt warm. Eir covered her belly and moved back behind him, falling into the task of tending his wounds.

"It is best," she said quietly. "This is bad place for children."

Csoda nodded in agreement and closed his eyes. His own thoughts drifted to the strange visions with what he now thought of as his future son.

Csoda allowed Eir to return to her nurturing. He knew he was still in a prison and most likely this comforting moment was a temporary one. He allowed rest because, at any moment, he might be pulled from it and his body and soul would be pushed to the extreme once again. There would be a price to pay for this rest and recovery–and for what they'd done in the coliseum.

It came as no surprise to him when later in the evening he heard boots of armored men move in unison up to the guarded entrance of their quarters. Biro heard the oncoming sounds as well, and came to stand near his friend. They glanced at each other, both of them feeling that the cost of their current luxury would soon be revealed.

As certainly as the sound of boots predicted the coming of guards, the sound of heavy latches scraping and clashing from the outside announced the inevitable opening of their prison doors. Free of the grip of the heavy locks and encouraged with a pull from the outside, the doors swung open. Two Phaedon guards were revealed, looking briefly into the room. They sized up Csoda and Biro, scanning the space with their steady eyes, then they signaled to the visitors that it was safe to enter.

The visitors hardly needed to fear for their safety. Gliding through the doorway the six broad figures of the Ringmaster's elite guards moved into the room. Their white faced masks peered out from under shadows created by the hoods of their flowing black cloaks, the blank expressions stared everywhere and nowhere at once. The cloak fabric clipped at their necks and opened slightly with their movement, revealing broad bodies completely covered in armor. They moved swiftly, carrying heavy broad swords and massive axes with unencumbered ease. Biro stood back on one foot, braced for what would surely be a hopeless fight. Csoda sat still, waiting.

The masked figures did not speak, nor did they attack. Instead they stood in two rows, three on each side, in order to make a path for Csoda and Biro's real visitor. Towering above all, the Ringmaster floated through the door, his cloak and headdress billowing in a breeze that appeared to push him forward. He had to duck through the entry before he walked between his special guards, but all of his movements, even in confined spaces, were full of grace and power. His costume, a mass of flowing fabric, emphasized the control he had over his own presence.

Eir and the other servants dropped to their knees, their eyes averting, their quick unison intake of breath held. The Ringmaster signaled, a swift fleeting gesture with his right hand, and the same women rose quickly, heads bowing as they backed away from Csoda and Biro. They gave wide berth to the Ringmaster as they left the room.

When the women were gone, the Ringmaster, swept his arms in a wide gesture again and two male acrobats dressed in the red and black patchwork costume of one of the many Kirkos troops ran in through the door. Each acrobat carried a heavy pile of folded leather and cloth, on top of which sat leather footwear and elaborate helmeted masks similar to the one Biro had worn in the coliseum. One of the acrobats ran directly to Csoda, bowing deeply and placing the costume before him. The other did the same to Biro. Neither of the nomads took their eyes off of the intimidating figure of the Ringmaster to look closely at the presented items.

After their delivery, the acrobats backed away from their gifts with elaborate steps and left the room, closing the door as they did. The white masked guards positioned themselves with their backs against the walls. Their expressionless masks made them more objects than men, their new positions lessened their intimidating presence as they blended into the walls. Though they knew it was an illusion, it seemed that Csoda and Biro were alone with the Ringmaster.

The massive man took a step forward. His two arms swept open and the long sleeves of his black tunic billowed out like abstract wings of a giant raven. Images of roosters fighting, expertly tattooed with dark black spiraled designs, wrapped around his muscular forearms and hands, which he now presented, palms open, as he pointed to the costumes laying at their feet.

Csoda continued to look the Ringmaster in his eyes. His expressions were cold stone, his jaw a chiseled testament to his strength and size. Csoda saw no dullness in the Ringmaster's eyes. In fact, he saw a flash of great intelligence and a glimmer of something else, a mysterious glint of moving shadow.

Csoda couldn't help but think that this man was not an illusion of costume and rank–not a dull strong man who operated by brute force alone–this man was dangerously capable in strength, mind and something more.

Unaware of Csoda's thoughts about him, the Ringmaster spoke, "I would have beaten most captives by now, for not bowing in my presence."

These were the first words out of his mouth, yet the threat was matched with a break in his cold features. The corners of his mouth turned up in a slight smile and his eyes squinted at the sides, making it apparent that while this statement may be true, right now it was said in jest.

Still, Biro tensed. Csoda could feel his friend's anger. Had he been suitably armed, Csoda was sure Biro would have attacked the man before them, despite the fact that the Ringmaster towered over Biro's broad size and was flanked by the expert fighters in his special guard. Csoda was not the only one to notice Biro's reaction. The Ringmaster's eyes shifted to Biro, his head slightly cocked, his smirk widened. He seemed happy to see the spark of fight in Biro's nature.

The Ringmaster ignored the tension that filled the air around them and continued, gesturing again to the costumes. "However, I believe you to be unlike most captives, and so I am giving you these gifts. These and one other. You, my doomed spoils of war, will have the chance to live... perhaps not how you imagined you would live when you were young men, but you will have the possibility of a new existence." His eyes moved slowly as he spoke, looking at both of them directly. First at Csoda, "A life removed from your past..." and then to Biro "...a life where your skills can be...repurposed."

Csoda heard the Ringmaster's hidden meaning, and he dropped his gaze down at the costume folded at his feet. The clothing was mostly white with splashes of bright colors. The helmeted mask was gold and copper and looked like it would cover the upper half of his face. It was decorated with simple designs–stars, moons and a running horse pulling a chariot, but this was not a warrior's mask. The designs were too simple and bright green tassels sprung up from the top of a pointed helmet. The eyes on the mask were accentuated in their width, black eyebrows raised high gave and overall look of shocked surprise. The bright accents in the cloth of green, red and blue were almost pretty and light-hearted. These were not the dark, intimidating colors of the warrior, at least none that Csoda had ever seen.

The Ringmaster continued, his voice steady, pleased, "I admit your performance with the bulls was impressive. The crowd was greatly pleased. I recognize great performances and, as I am sure you can testify, I reward great performers. I am giving you a chance to become more than the captives who were sold to me. I am giving you the chance to become great. The Kirkos in Phaedon is coming to a close in three days. You will be expected to perform in the Finale and, if you prove that your talents were not sheer luck, I guarantee you will be rewarded, again and again. This is what I am offering you."

Csoda raised his gaze back to the Ringmaster just as Biro spoke. His friend's voice was steady and defiant, "What if we will not perform?"

The Ringmaster tilted his head again, amused, "You will be put in the Finale one way or another. And if you don't perform, given the nature of the Kirkos, I am sure you will die." The Ringmaster, finished with the conversation, crossed his arms and smiled coldly, "Three days," he stated again, "You may want to make sure your costumes are of a good fit. Inform the servants if you need adjustments made." He turned and began to leave, the blank masked guards moved in unison away from the walls to walk behind him.

"He will need a drum," Biro called out. Csoda looked back at his bold friend, surprised.

The Ringmaster paused, turning his head to look over his broad shoulder, but he did not look at Biro. Instead he looked directly at Csoda while he considered the request.

"A round, hand drum, stretched with leather," Biro continued.

The Ringmaster continued to look at Csoda, as if trying to peer into his mind.

"We shall see," The Ringmaster stated. He broke away from his searching stare of Csoda to move his gaze onto the bold Biro. He half smirked again, "Beat... I would beat most captives for such boldness...for your sake I hope your performance in the Finale matches your brashness towards me."

With that statement the Ringmaster ducked out of the doorway. His guards swooped behind him and the heavy doors shut as they disappeared. The otherwise quiet room now echoed with the sound of the heavy bolts and latches clamping down.

Biro looked at Csoda, then down at the costume before him. He had not reviewed it before, his eyebrows furrowed in confusion as he reached down to pick up the large grotesque helmet mask that was his own.

While Csoda's mask had wide open eyes, Biros mask had an elaborately long and thick comical hooked nose as its main feature. The eyes were not wide, but small slits. The eyebrows were made of thick bushy fur and the helmet had a fan of boar's hair and feathers that stuck straight up into the air. The entire mask was tinted with red as if the face was flushed from drinking.

He looked over the strange features with some disgust, and then he looked at Csoda and said sharply, "I guess we will make a pair of deadly clowns for this ridiculous charade. That or lay down and die."

Csoda nodded. He reached down to pick up his own costume and carried it to his private quarters.

38

___

"My Queen, please drink some water." Zenobia slowed her steady stride at Alexius' request and looked down at the flowing river they had walked next to for the last twenty minutes. Behind her, ten thousand warriors followed. They did not march, walking behind her in an informal formation instead. Periodically, some of them stopped to take drinks from the river before they returned to keep pace with the rest of the group.

"Soon." Zenobia replied, "Soon we will take a moment to rest, together." He nodded at her statement and she quickened her pace.

It was not that the cold tumbling waters of the river did not appeal to her. Her throat was dry, her legs tired. It was that she knew a better place that she wished to rest for the day. Plus, stopping even briefly was counter productive to the driving determination that was her current state of mind.

They had been walking for miles, ever since they accompanied the last of her people and horses to meet with

Erastos in the distant deep forests. Under the cover of night, Erastos would lead her people away from the incoming invasion, while she and the ten thousand volunteer warriors would return to the canyon lands that they called home. This river was familiar to them all, it flowed from the canyon lands themselves. Reaching it meant that, if they made good time, they would be home in just a few days.

She already missed Inanna, both for the companionship and the convenience that the steed always provided. She knew that many of the men would feel the same about the horses they had left behind. Yet, none of her people argued with her choice. They valued the Gifts of the Sun and understood the decision to keep them out of the hands of the invading troops. Plus, the Gifts of the Sun breed was built mostly for speed and quick agility, they were not the thick war horses that would be accompanying the Legion troops.

Instead of the Gifts of the Sun they took with them only a few dozen normal horses to be used by scouts and to haul supplies. Zenobia had also arranged to join with a volunteer group of fighters from the nomadic tribes who would supply a herd of their stocky brave horses that could be used as cavalry early on in the battles. Those same horses could be released if needed and they, by their wild nature, would have the ability to run back to the lands of the tribes.

This was important, for Zenobia knew this was not a normal war. This would not be a long battle in the fields where horse's speed, strength and courage was invaluable. This would likely become a siege and, in all truth, the horse's need for water and food in such conditions would make them a burden.

Those returning with her to fight knew that this was a

potential suicide mission. They knew they were outnumbered. No matter the outcome, Zenobia would stay to fight, knowing that her warriors felt the same. If all of them ran, they would be hunted down and risked capture. If Zenobia stayed back with an army to fight, then the wrath of the Emperor would remain focused on her, giving Erastos time to move, hiding her people and their wealth. If her army was destroyed and she was killed or captured, then the Emperor may content himself with his victory over her. While her people may not be able to return to their homes, they might be kept safe from the fury of the Legion troops.

"Perhaps," Zenobia considered, "I am making a mistake. Perhaps...." But she kept these thoughts to herself, as it was her duty to do so. Her people were brave, her warriors fearless, but the Legions of Critias outnumbered her own army by a thousand to one. She knew a helpless situation when she saw it and her focus up until now had been to find a way to shelter her people and their culture from the inevitable horror heading their way. Now, with that concern behind her, she was focused on the upcoming battle.

It was another mile before Zenobia came upon the place she wanted to rest. She led the troops away from the river's edge to cut through the deeper forest until a small meadow opened up before them. There, on the far end of the meadow lay a shimmering pond with crystal clear deep water. Behind the pond was the edge of an old forest full of thickets and lush foliage. A massive ancient tree, growing close to the shoreline, seemed to guard the pure waters. Nourished through the many years by the spring fed pond it had grown broad and full, with a canopy of limbs that stretched far into the air and wide out to the sides, shading the pond and nearby thickets from the heat of the sun.

"Here," Zenobia told Alexius, " We shall rest here. Tell the troops that dusk will soon be upon us. We shall sleep well and leave in the morning. Tomorrow will be a long day."

Alexius nodded and gave a quick bow to the Queen before he jogged off to relay the information to the rest of the army.

Zenobia watched him go, then walked to the pond's sandy shoreline and sat down at the water's edge. She dipped her cupped hands into the cold water and lifted the liquid to her mouth to drink. The water here was always fresh. The pond was fed by a natural deep spring and drinking from it had always made her feel that she was drinking a strengthening tonic.

She drank her fill, then looked out across the crystal surface of water to the ancient tree, thickets and forest that bordered the opposite shore. Her memories were sad, but at the same time the nostalgia of the place brought to her heart a bitter peace.

This was where she used to meet Biro, in the thickets upon the opposite shore. Here her horse grazed in the meadow with his, while they swam and laughed in the healing waters and stretched on the warm sandy edge as they talked through the day and late into the evenings. Here she remembered watching the stars boldly shine above the tree's dark canopy when the sun dropped below the horizon, listening to the howls of distant wolves, and watching wide winged bats glide above the pond's surface, their leathery bodies glowing with the light of the moon's silver reflection that was mirrored in the water. She had decided to rest here on this day, giving herself one last time to sit with fonder memories before she led her army of devoted warriors to face the oncoming invasion.

"Perhaps," she thought, "This is the last time I will sit at the shore of this pond and drink of its pure waters." She closed her eyes to prevent them from tearing and took in a deep breath. Tonight she would stay awake longer than usual and look up at the peaceful stars, one last time.

39

Phaedon was on the edge of the empire, distant from the capital. Its population, while prosperous, lacked a certain amount of elegance and prestige. Its leaders were mostly of the lower royal families who did not have the connections to attain great notoriety outside of their humble local holdings. Situated in mostly a desert landscape, Phaedon supported a meager amount of farming that clung to the edges of a small river, which trickled along its border. The nearby desert hills were peppered with occasional shepherds who moved through the landscape herding the tough local breed of goats who had proven capable of bearing the intense heat and meager amount of water, somehow managing to sustain themselves on the wiry desert foliage. These scant food sources could not sustain the entire city population and Phaedon was dependent on the import and export of food, goods, and spices. Luckily for their elite there was one trade that was a constant source of the city's wealth—slavery.

The desert city was situated as the first stopping point into the Empire of Critias where slave traders could bring in captives they had gathered from wars in other kingdoms. The slaves were auctioned off in a large central plaza and sold to traders from the Capital and other large cities. Many of these traders worked as middlemen for the city's elite merchants who would not think of bothering to travel such a distance through the heat of the desert.

The slave trade was also promoted by the fact that Phaedon supported the first Kirkos of the season. The Ringmaster was an expert in slave trade and it was here that he would often switch out less impressive captives for finer choices that he could either include in his deadly events or trade later for profit when he brought them into the wealthier cities.

He was currently occupied with the purchase of an impressive captive–a wild man with a mane of matted hair, strong and fierce, captured in an unknown land – a man who seemed more comfortable with beasts than men. The Ringmaster was in the heat of negotiations for this slave when one of his runners burst into the meeting.

News. News was traveling fast across the desert sands, passed quickly by the many merchants who traveled upon the long, dry roads. News that the Ringmaster had to know, had to hear. News that cut his transaction short, making him offer the wizened toothless slave trader a quick and ample offer, free of bartering, for the purchase of the wild captive.

The roads to and from Phaedon stretched far across the desert to disappear into the high northern hills. Eventually the roads to the north connected to the interlaced web-like pattern of the Empire's infrastructure, joining with the many other main dirt paths and stone paved roads that crisscrossed the Empire of Critias. Because Phaedon's roads connected to the Empire, many traders, journeymen and travelers made the journey across their brutally expansive distance, but it was rare for these roads to be traveled by the Emperor's royal caravan.

This was the news that came so fast, spreading like a fire through Phaedon. The Emperor's caravan, his private coach surrounded by a legion of men, wove its way down the road straight towards Phaedon.

It was with great excitement that the news of his approach spread down these roads and through the city gates. News that Emperor Coracis, on route from important military endeavors, was making his way to Phaedon.

This excitement mixed with the feverish festivities that already surrounded the Grand Kirkos and encouraged the people of Phaedon to fall into maniacal riotous moods. The drinking doubled, the evening fires burned all night and there was a flush of spontaneous parades that sometimes ended in drunken song and sometimes in ineffective fighting amongst stumbling men and women. The guard patrols were doubled as well as the public feasts. The royalty spent extra time preparing their estates and their families for the possibility that the Emperor or his entourage may make visits or need them or their staff to help with entertainment.

The King of Phaedon rushed about, preparing the best quarters available for the Emperor and making sure to inform the Ringmaster that there was a good chance the caravan would arrive in time to view the Finale of the Grand Kirkos. In preparation, an extra pavilion was being built within the coliseum so that Coracis would have the best view of all. The Ringmaster, of course, agreed, and sent his own messenger out to greet the Emperor's caravan halfway, inviting him personally to join them for the first Kirkos Finale of the Grand Kirkos' tour through the Empire.

The messenger was well greeted, the Emperor being in

high spirits as other positive reports had been relayed to him earlier in the day. Reports telling of his distant troop's success in marching into the Kingdom of Zenobia unhindered by either the remnant nomad tribes or the Queen's own troops. It seemed that the people of the towns bordering Zenobia's empire had evacuated and, though it annoyed Coracis that the towns were empty, it was a good sign that the defiant Queen was in retreat. It was only a matter of time before the Emperor's troops made it to her Capital and secured her kingdom for Coracis. As for the retreating people and the Queen, Coracis was sure it was only a matter of time before his Legions hunted them all down.

The Ringmaster's messenger was given a positive reply, "Yes, the Emperor would join the King of Phaedon and the Ringmaster for the Kirkos' Grand Finale in which he looked forward to the rest and entertainment he was sure would be provided."

The special pavilion was raised, freshly painted with the royal colors, a canopy of perfumed silk shading it from the merciless sun. Placed so that its occupants were given the best view of the coliseum, while the rest of the crowd could, in turn, view their position. The flags of Phaedon were proudly raised alongside those of Coracis and the Kirkos, the Emperor's flag placed high above them all.

All of Phaedon crowded into the coliseum on the Final day, if not to watch the Grand Finale, then to peer curiously at the Emperor's pavilion. His caravan had come in, late at night, the torches lit along before him as they moved through the city. The citizens of Phaedon had looked on from their balconies, street corners and sidewalks, but the Emperor's coach was covered and guarded so that no peering eyes could see Coracis. Now in the bright light of day, Emperor Coracis lounged in view of them all. High on the new pavilion he rested, eating dates and drinking ginger spiced wine. Below him sat their own king, proud and anxious, waving to the stands and smiling broadly.

The Ringmaster stood on the edge of the coliseum wall, his costume of deep black accentuated with white feathers crowning his shoulders, his headdress a tall cylinder upon his head, ringed with curved ribbons that were gilded in gold. He gestured with his long arms, signaling to the crowd to rise from their seats. All of the crowd rose before them and they hailed and called out to the Emperor, to their King, they all hailed the Grand Kirkos. The Ringmaster bowed and turned to the Emperor, awaiting the command from their leader to start the Finale.

Coracis took a moment to respond, he scanned the cheering crowd, the Ringmaster stood frozen, patiently awaiting his command. All of this pleased Coracis as he had rarely been pleased. This small city was but a drop in his grand Empire, this coliseum half the size of his own, but on this day, after the successful reports from his armies, this small city was a great testament to the larger whole. The citizens awaited him, awaited his permission for this entertainment to begin. Coracis took in a deep breath, took in the crowd's attention, drank the thickly spiced wine deeply from his golden cup, then raised the cup to the sky and nodded his head, signaling the Ringmaster to begin the spectacle.

On cue, the Ringmaster turned back to face the arena, swinging his long arms out and up into the air for all to see. The heavy gates from the far side of the arena swung open and bursting from the gates sped a group of one man chariots, light and nimble vehicles strapped behind long limbed race horses. The crowd let out a deafening roar and the Grand Finale of the Kirkos began.

40

———

Eight days had passed since Csoda and Biro stood in front of this gate and were pushed into the arena by the crowd of captives and stampeding bulls. This time, they stood with nobody else, side-by-side at the edge of the heavy door, peering out at its scratched and dented surface from behind the comical masks that had been assigned to them. This time they had been herded by multiple guards, yet had not struggled against returning to the arena. Biro had postured slightly, but it was less an act of rebellion against their inevitable fate and more a release of frustration–a proud warrior revolting at being subjected to wear a costume.

The shame of wearing the foolish attire had angered Biro since he first laid eyes on the grotesque masks, and that anger had only increased over the last few days. Biro's frustration was also fueled by Csoda's calmer demeanor, as he could not grasp why the Shaman was not more disturbed by the mockery they endured or the ultimate danger they faced.

Csoda's costume, the wide eyed dazed looking mask

with simple celestial symbols and references to running horses was, in truth, a caricature of him. The white over-sized tunic was in the same style that he wore as a shaman, the bright green pantaloon pants were covered in symbols that mimicked his people's style of writing, yet held no meaning. The design emanated what the Ringmaster surely thought of as a joke.

Even the requested drum that had been sent to him was an exaggeration, an oversized disc with stretched leather painted bright green and a red, child-like line drawing of a horse in the center. Along with the drum they had provided an oversized mallet, also painted bright green, with tassels of gold that bounced with every hit.

Just as Csoda's costume turned him into a clownish sage, Biro's costume was meant to mock the nomad hunter. His large nosed, red hued mask arched far in front of his face and, as a result of its placement on his head, it made him appear almost hunchbacked. His clothing was a vest of armored leather, with patches of exaggerated fur along his chest and back that looked as if his own body hair was pushing out from underneath the edges. His pants were bright purple, their edges frayed and tinted red.

To match Csoda's childish drum, they gave Biro a giant fake hammer that was painted bright yellow. The hammer was firm, but harmlessly soft to the touch. He nearly threw it away since it was clearly useless, but instead, for reasons unknown to him, he tucked it into the wide black belt that wrapped around his waist.

They could have refused to wear the costumes. But while they were clownish in appearance, they did have a few positive attributes. The farcical masks were protective in their make and materials, and they did function almost the same as helmets and face shields. The two friends had tested the materials and, overall, the costumes fit well on their bodies, protecting them without hindering their movement. They had both determined that it was better to wear them than be exposed to the unknown dangers of the arena naked. This reality helped Biro overlook the insult and he decided that though he may be made to look like a fool, he would fight like a bear. Survival was what mattered.

Csoda was calm because he chose to focus on another thought, one greater than mere survival. In the back of his mind, as he first tapped lightly along the leather of the drum, he heard the Taltos from his vision, "Your enslavement leads you on your path to become the child's keeper. The Shaman disguised as the fool will become his greatest teacher..." This memory of the quoted prophecy calmed him as he dressed in the elaborate costume the Ringmaster had designed for him.

"All is exactly as it is meant to be," he thought to himself, and, though he wished he could express this to Biro, he also recognized that his friend's anger at the insulting costumes would most likely help him in the event ahead of them. So instead of trying to calm Biro, Csoda focused on the task of attending to his inevitable fear and on trying to align himself with the Art of the Pull, to find the connection.

So they stood, wearing their full costumes, waiting for the heavy door to be opened. Behind it they could hear the events unfold, the clashing of armor, the roaring of beasts, the merciless grind of chariot wheels, the pounding sounds of charging horses–and over it all–the cries of the crowd.

41

The ocean-like grasslands spread out before Abelardus, the reeds moving gracefully like waves in a steady and constant wind. Today there was no fog. Instead, the sunlight glinted upon delicate fronds and seed heads, creating a ripple of colors, silver, green and a deep dusty red to wash across the landscape. Here again, he rode into the basin, his armor and rank returned to him, his station secured by the Emperor's decree. But this time his orders were not to lead a small patrol to secure some stolen meat. No, this time he was surrounded by Legions of men and their goal was the land beyond the basin, the desert canyons, the land of the elegant Queen Zenobia.

Their orders were simple even if their task was not.

"Secure the canyon lands and the people that live there. Bring Queen Zenobia, willing or not, to the capital to answer for her crimes."

These were the orders given directly by the Emperor to the top commanders. Abelardus knew this because he had delivered the orders himself. He had knelt before the Emperor and the Senate as the Emperor declared the

Queen a traitor before them all. He had watched the royal scribe write the decree in smooth dark ink upon heavy parchment and witnessed the Emperor sign the decree and then press his personal seal into the dab of hot perfumed golden wax that the scribe ceremoniously placed upon the edge of the folded paper.

Abelardus had carried this same decree with him back to the Legion camps. He had watched his superiors break the wax seal and read the orders with heavy brows and serious, pursed lips. If any of them had concerns about the declaration of war, none of them openly voiced their misgivings. Instead they nodded to him sternly and then relieved him of his duty, sending him back to his sleeping quarters to mull over his private concerns while they planned the invasion.

He had been given a group of soldiers to command, none of them were from the same unit that had accompanied him on the raid. This was a fact he took note of along with the fact that, while his rank was still intact, he was not asked to eat with the generals at their private meetings. Both were signs of the Legion's overall inability to accept failure, even when one was pardoned by the Emperor.

Dressed in uniform, he sat upon an armored horse in the same grasslands of his greatest failure, but he was unable to feel the shame of that event. The landscape was empty of fog, empty of everything but the flowing grass and open blue sky. No hint of life for miles except the hum of the occasional insect or the distant glimpse of a far off soaring bird. Nothing hindered them, and the massive army moved quickly and steadily forward, unhampered, unquestioned, and unmatched.

Abelardus, despite loyalty to his position, fought an internal conflict. He could not help his misgivings for their declared enemy. The Queen, her people, and the nomadic tribes that hovered around the borders of her kingdom, were no longer blank faces to him. He had met Queen Zenobia and studied a painted masterpiece of a master artist from her kingdom. He had been in awe of the nomads, and experienced with them what he could only describe as deep magic. He had found mystery and purpose in his interaction with them all and he, loyal Abelardus, found himself questioning–questioning his rank, his orders and all that he had thought was the right way of the world.

A scout appeared on the horizon and raced back to the Legion, his horse covered in sweat, his findings soon announced to all.

"The bordering villages of Queen Zenobia's lands have been abandoned." Came the message, announced out loud from afar and then repeated back by Legion men whose duty it was to convey the reports, echoing the message until it reached the units at the farthest edges of their ranks. "We march forward into her lands, into the evening. They are on the run. Legions, stay alert, watch your ranks, be prepared for ambushes."

The orders echoed back behind Abelardus, the messages repeating through the units. He turned to look at his men, and asked out loud, "Are you all clear, did you hear the report?"

"Yes, Sir!" They eagerly replied.

He turned back, facing the direction where over 100,000 soldiers moved unhindered. Tonight they would be in the canyon lands. Abelardus took in a deep breath as he urged his horse to quicken its pace. On the far horizon he thought he could see a single falcon soaring.

42

───

The Ringmaster had outdone himself, Coracis had to admit. The games of the day were some of the best he had seen, even in past Grand Events held in the Capital. The chariot races came down to the wire, keeping everyone on edge and betting madly on the sidelines. The winners showed adept skill and ruthlessness, unafraid to attack their closest competitors to keep their position. The hand combat battles were also well orchestrated, the warriors well matched, the winners hard to predict, making for even more fretful betting and animated reactions within the crowd. Brutal events of all kinds between man and beast flowed constantly before them, interspersed with provocative dancers, troops of acrobats and parades of exotic animals from distant lands.

The crowd of Phaedon was entertaining as well. It was filled with rowdy and less polished citizens than Coracis normally observed in his home coliseum. Their antics were similar, though executed with less social grace. The drunkards bellowed and fought in the stands. Well endowed women and men flashed the stands and the Emperor's pavilion. Gamblers hawked their bets to each other along the arena wall, leaning far out over the edge to egg on their chosen winners in all of the games.

While he observed an exceptionally boisterous group of these gamblers, Coracis recognized one of the Senators from Phaedon, a man Coracis did not admire. The fat fool sat unkempt on the lowest levels, his robe half open, his face flush with drink, his hands groping the dancers as they crisscrossed through the crowd offering close up dances to all who paid. Coracis did not look down on the debauchery itself, but on the Senator's puffed up face, his obvious lack of control. The sight ruined his otherwise satisfied mood.

As the sun touched the horizon and the air of the coliseum became notably cooler, there was a pause in the entertainment. The constant flow of activity had slowed and, for a moment, Coracis thought that perhaps there was some mistake, a hitch in the progress of the events. He scanned the quieted arena, the clouds of dust that the last chariots had kicked up settled, and in the far distance he noticed that a single, massive gate now opened wide. Surprisingly, instead of the usual flood of activity that he expected to pour from that vast entrance, out walked two cautious figures. These figures moved into the arena, stopped momentarily to scan the space in front of them, and then steadily made their way towards the center.

The simple act of their walking and the emptiness of the arena was in direct contrast to the entire day of bloodlust, making these two figures stand out above all other men that he had seen that day. They walked in unison, their movements confident, but their heads turning occasionally to observe the emptiness around them as if they too were confused by the lack of activity.

The figures were dressed strangely and as they moved

closer the Emperor found himself leaning forward to focus on them. He could see that they wore large masks with exaggerated expressions. One looked like he was in permanent shock, his eyes wide and round. The other was hunched over, scowling with a large protruding nose, his upper body an exaggerated chest with thick hair. Both wore clothing that mimicked the nomadic clans and when Coracis realized this, he found himself laughing out loud. He was thrilled at the mockery. The crowd began to laugh too, and their laughter only increased when the big nosed figure roared back at them angrily.

When the figures reached the center of the arena they stopped and stood for a moment, waiting, it seemed, for the initial mirth of the crowd to die down. As if on cue, the crowd hushed. The light was dimming with the setting sun and time seemed to pause for a moment, waiting as everyone quietly stared at the comical figures who stood as proud as kings in the center of the arena.

Through the quieted air a deep guttural sound rose. Primal and thick, the sound vibrated from the wide eyed figure, and with it he started to beat a heavy and complicated rhythm that seemed to come from more than a single drum. The sound rose through the arena, growing in volume and thickness, echoing off the walls until it seemed that the entire crowd was swimming in the sound made by this single figure.

Coracis was fascinated, mesmerized to the point that he did not notice that the arena gates along the sides had opened. Out of them walked warriors armed with different weapons, axes, swords and maces. Along with the warriors, two trap doors had opened on either far end of the coliseum, lifting two massive tigers from below, each bound by heavy chains that allowed them to move in a wide radius, pacing and eyeing the men on the ground.

The crowd responded, too. Seeing the threats to the fools in the center, they reacted in a strangely sympathetic way. Their gasps and words of concern were uncharacteristic for a crowd that had entertained itself for the entire day by watching brutality. Still, for some reason, they were noticeably uncomfortable seeing the two fools surrounded by so much danger.

The two clowns with their masked expressions did not immediately react to the warriors who moved towards them. Instead, the large nosed fool remained still while the wide eyed one kept playing his drum. The rumbling guttural hum that vibrated through the air was still captivating, his delicate rhythms upon the drum did not falter, despite the oncoming peril. Even Coracis held his breath, a strange feeling tugging at his heart, making him lean further forward as he clenched his hands tightly together.

The drummer kept drumming, but the large nosed clown took notice of the warriors and began to pace. Despite his comical appearance, his movements were similar to the pacing tigers that shared the arena. He circled around the drummer, eyeing the incoming threats and at first it seemed he would stay in close to protect his companion. Yet, suddenly, unexpectedly, he ran directly towards one of the warriors, a tall warrior with a bronze armored chest plate and a short armored skirt, carrying a large spike mace that he swung above his head menacingly.

The crowd gasped, the large nosed clown threw himself towards the warrior feet first, skidding along the ground. He crashed against the exposed legs of the warrior, making him fall forward even as his swinging mace barely missed the rolling clowns body. Before the warrior righted himself, the clown came out of his roll, leapt surprisingly high behind his armored back and drove both of his feet into the back of the warrior's neck. The warrior skidded face first into the ground, the clown riding upon him, howling an eerie, high pitched wail.

The Emperor stood up, and throughout the stands many of the audience did the same. What they had just seen seemed impossible. The unarmed clown with his gaudy red face, glared at the crowd as he crouched on the back of the unconscious warrior. He pried the mace from the hands of the warrior and then, his face raised upwards towards the sky like some kind of deformed wolf, he began to swing it in the air and howled again. The sound was heart piercing, disturbing, a wail of both anger and sadness.

The Emperor had never felt so much emotion. The drum pounded on and the music felt like it moved through the core of his very soul. While the drummer's sound became part of his own heartbeat, he could not take his eyes off of the large nosed clown who now, with newly acquired weapon in hand, boldly stalked his next opponent as a hunter with no fear stalks his prey.

There were five more opponents on the field along with the two pacing tigers. The red faced clown seemed to dance from one to another, taking them out one at a time with drastic and precise maneuvers. He switched out weapons as he went, using all of them expertly. With the mace he snapped the broadswords of one and then, picking up the broken sword tip, he threw it directly into the throat of another. He twirled and crouched, pounced and danced, the fan of his headdress making him look more and more like a bird of prey as he leapt from one opponent to another. The entire time, the wide faced clown drummed and hummed, and the rhythm eventually became linked to the hunting clown's movements, his actions speeding up and slowing down in harmony with the sound.

None of the opponents made it to the center, none of them came close to the drumming clown. Before they could, the hunting clown had already attacked them, furiously fast, devastating their attempts. At the end a circle of fallen warriors were scattered around the wide eyed clown, whose pale featured mask made him look a ghostly figure in the falling light of dusk.

The warriors were down, but the hunting clown did not stop. Instead he prowled like a wolf, walking in an ever widening circle as he dragged a captured broadsword through the arena sand. The dragging sword drew a spiral out from the center of the arena. He howled at the now ecstatic crowd until he came close to the first snarling tiger.

Instead of killing the beast, the clown held up the sword and with a crashing blow, broke the tigers bonding chains. The beast did not attack. Instead the tiger ran to hide from the aggressive clown and the sound of the cheering crowd, slipping under the alcove of the gated entrance. The clown did the same with the second tiger and that beast hungrily lunged at a fallen warriors body, grabbed snarling and then drug it with it as it also found cover in a shaded alcove.

The red faced clown stood below the edge of the arena wall and the gamblers who perched there leaned over to call down to him. Those who had bet against him threw garbage at his defiant howl, but those who had bet for him cheered and pulled the others away, laughing feverishly, ecstatic with their winnings.

The clown stared menacingly up at the gamblers and then Coracis watched as his neck seemed to stretch out, his nose pointing directly at the drunken Senator. The slovenly man sat on the edge of the wall, his royal robe all that distinguished him from the rest of the gambling rabble. The Senator's senses were distracted by the heavy drinking of the day and he sat oblivious to the fact that he had gained the clown's attention. Instead he fumbled and grabbed at a dark haired dancer who was trying to move on her way, but could not release one captured wrist from his lustful grip. She was swaying like a caught fish, trying to avoid the aggressive touch of his other hand.

The clown stared for a moment at the Senator, but the man was still too distracted to notice. In a sudden movement, the clown flipped the heavy sword in a circle above his head and, with deadly precision, threw the blade into the base of the wood where the Senator was perched, inches away from the man himself.

The crowd screamed. The Senator, shocked, let go of the dancer and stared, dazed, at the sword sticking into the wooden ledge beneath him. He swayed for a moment and slowly shifted his gaze to look directly at the grotesque clown. When their eyes finally met, the clown, with a comical cock of his head, pulled from his belt a large yellow hammer, throwing it with the same exact precision at the Senator's head.

Screams came from the stand. Then the crowd fell into peels of laughter as the hammer, showing its true nature, bounced crazily off of the Senator's forehead, leaving him dazed but unharmed.

Coracis chuckled, highly amused at this attack on the Senator. The man was a true fool, it was fitting that he was being bested by a real man dressed as a clown. Coracis watched the Senator's face contort as he recognized both the potential danger he was in and the obvious insult that had just taken place. Before the Senator knew how to react, the vicious clown in a high pitched wail called up to the man and yelled something.

The first time, Coracis and much of the crowd could not hear what he said. Those standing closest to the Senator stepped to the side, fearing the clown's attention that was now so completely focused on him.

The drummer had stopped playing and sat down, cross-legged in the arena. He paid no attention to the antics of his companion. The noise in the crowd hushed as well, curiosity willing them to try to hear what the red faced clown was saying. When the angry clown repeated his question, his wail, now high and bold, echoed through the arena.

"Whooooo aaaarrreeee yooouuu?" howled the clown and the Senator shook his head at the absurd question.

He answered, his voice weak in the air, "I am Senator Valten of Phaedon."

The clown cocked his head, the mask sneering. The howl came again, this time addressing the crowd and not the Senator with the question, "Whooooo issssss heeeee?"

At first there was no reply. But then, from a mass of men, a voice hidden in the crowd interjected, "He is Senator Drunkard!"

The anonymous reply sent a wave of laughter through the stands. The Senator, shocked, turned to try and see who had called out, but there was no one to see.

Then, from another place in the stands another voice called out, hidden in the crowd, "He is Senator No Pay. Who doesn't stay true to his debts!"

Then another, "He is Senator Cheat, who doesn't go home to his wife!"

"He is Senator All Hands, hide your daughters!"

The calls continued as a flood of accusations and crude jokes ignited throughout the stands. The citizens laughed, booed, and hissed at the fully confused Senator whose rank no longer protected from ridicule.

The red faced clown walked to pick up the soft hammer that had fallen back into the arena. He held his hands up to the ridiculing crowd and they quieted down for him, waiting for his next surprise.

The angry clown, in the same eerie howl announced to them all, "Senator, by decree of the crowd, I declare you a fool!" And he threw the hammer again, lightening fast, hitting the Senator directly between the eyes before it fell and bounced harmlessly on the arena floor below.

The crowd roared, the Senator stumbled towards the exit under a raining barrage of thrown garbage. The gamblers rolled in laughter, leaning against the wall. The crowd called out, praising the exposure of the Senator's ways, crying in great praise of the clowns who now stood undefeated in the arena.

Coracis still stood and quickly signaled to the Ringmaster with a single raised hand for these brilliant performers to be recognized.

The Ringmaster bowed to the Emperor at his signal and then swung back to face the crowd, his long arms swooping. He called out over the stands, "We salute you! The Grand Kirkos Clowns!!! All salute the Great Pagliacci the Drummer of Hearts...and the Great Punchinello the Exposer of Souls!"

The Crowd cheered, and called out, "Great Pagliacci! Great Punchinello!"

The Emperor, standing above all, lifted his cup in the air in salute of the brilliant performers–a true testament to the greatness of his kingdom.

43

———

The courtyard was filled with clay oil lanterns, so many that their flickering lights made the shadows of the night appear to dance with the tabla drums and stretch into the air with the melody of the haunting flutes and the cries of the sitar. The feast was greater than any offered before. Csoda and Biro's prison villa was filled with a harem of dancers, musicians, and a crowd of reveling acrobats. The thick smell of incense and food mingled with the smoke of intoxicating herbs. The space resonated with sound, music and laughter, the chimes of the coins that hung on the belts of the harem dancers, and the clink of goblets filled with thick, sweet wine.

Here were the surviving performers of the first Kirkos of the season. This celebration was their reward, one in which they immersed themselves into completely, escaping their tragedy with intoxication and lust. The entire space over-flowed with people, some still wore their torn and bloodied costumes, painted makeup smeared down their faces, arms and legs. There was barely enough room for the servants to push through to refill drinks or place platters of freshly grilled lamb and pheasant or bowls of olives on the tables.

Every inch of space was filled except for an empty circle in the middle of the courtyard below the star filled sky. A ring of emptiness that contained a singular, brooding figure.

Here sat Biro, his large form slumped upon a simple round stool, his upper body leaning forward, his elbows propping him up on the small hard wooden table that was before him. In one hand he held the mask he had worn in the arena, its face turned toward his own as he stared into the empty holes that were its eyes. His other hand clutched at the neck of a wine jug, his cup long forgotten.

Biro stared hazily at the grotesque mask and contorted his face as if he was trying to match his broad features to its own. He furrowed his brow and curled his lips into a menacing sneer, mimicking the masks expression. The dancers, acrobats and servants had learned to keep their distance, for the warrior clown still bristled with anger, his shoulders tense and his temper short. Even Csoda gave him room, recognizing that his friend's anger and pain had overcome his better senses. Mixed with the limitless wine, Biro's energy created a volatile, almost palpable aura of violence around him.

Biro did not eat. He did not desire women. He simply drank from the large jug of wine and only allowed the servants to approach when they promised to refill its contents.

Deep into the evening, Csoda decided to check on Biro and risk his potential rage. He approached him from the front, slightly on Biro's right side so that his friend could see him. He did not wish to startle a man who could so easily kill him. He came to the edge of the empty space surrounding Biro and took only one more step, separating himself from the rest of the crowd.

There he stopped, waiting to see if his friend would recognize him. Biro continued to sneer at the mask, his eyelids clenched into narrow slits, hardly exposing his eyes. Csoda could hear a low growl coming from behind Biro's clenched teeth that were exposed by his curling lips. Animosity emanated from Biro's being, lingering in the air, creating pressure against Csoda's skin.

"I was in love once..." Biro uttered.

Csoda was caught off guard by both his words and the gentle way they were stated. Biro did not move, his face stayed in its contorted pose, but his eyes widened, exposing the whites all around his pupils as they shifted their menacing stare to look at Csoda.

He locked these manic eyes onto Csoda's and continued, "Today I killed Csoda...." his calm voice cracked, "I killed for entertainment... not war... not to survive... not to protect... I killed to entertain."

Csoda felt a deep pain in his heart at Biro's words. He was at a loss for a way to comfort his friend from the harshness of such truth. He had also felt the energy of the crowd as they fed off of Biro's triumphant kills. Biro's mood not only made sense, but exposed some of Csoda's own shame.

Biro released Csoda from his stare, his eyes rolling back to look at the mask. He continued, his voice now drifting in and out of a slight slur, his focus wavering, "I was in love once..." he continued, "I left my tribe to go see her, to convince her to leave with me. When I returned, they were in battle...and I was caught off guard...captured."

Csoda felt the intensity of his friend's anger subside. Biro's hand that held the mask began to shake, his shoulders slumped, the drink and exhaustion finally overtook him. His sneer shifted into a saddened smile.

"Look at what I have become Csoda…" he said, aiming the mask to face Csoda, "It resembles me doesn't it? They did a good job at making this atrocious thing. This–this is what I've become…"

Biro's voice tapered off at the end, his body slumped forward. He laid his head down on the table, the mask dropping beside his head. Csoda stepped forward and touched his shoulder. The anger was gone. His friend was no longer coherent.

The dancer who often catered to Biro quickly moved in and brought a cup of water to his lips as she placed a small plate of food on the table. Csoda realized that she must have been hovering in the crowd the whole evening, too scared to approach the rage filled warrior. Csoda reached over and took the mask out of Biro's now loosened grip. He nodded at the dancer, approving of her care, and then, with Biro's mask in his possession, he left and let her attend to his friend.

Csoda excused himself from the festivities, even waving of Eir as she offered him food. He found a cloth and wrapped Biro's mask so that its features were hidden by the fabric and went to his private room.

From the window of his room Csoda could hear their new identities being hailed through the streets of Phaedon.

"The Great Pagliacci, the Drummer of Hearts!"

"The Great Punchinello, the Exposer of Souls!"

"The Grand Kirkos Clowns!"

He peered out at the crowds and saw groups of them, reeling in raucous laughter as they reenacted their performance in the arena. Street performers, gangs of loose children and drunken men took on the roles of the Kirkos Clowns and their enemies in the arena. Some even pretended to be the ridiculed Senator, wrapping themselves in disheveled togas and stumbling through the streets as onlookers shrieked in great delight "Senator Drunkard! YOU ARE A FOOL!"

Csoda watched for a while, then turned his back to the window to stare at his own strange costume hanging on his door. Its wide face and ghost color glowed in the moonlight streaming in from his window. Its features intrigued him and he thought of Biro's drunken words.

"This..." he thought to himself. "This is who I have become. This...Pagliacci, this ghost of myself."

The realization both disturbed him and filled him with relief. No longer did he have to be the failed revolutionary. The mask, in all its mockery of who he was, was also a way to leave himself behind.

He walked over to the costume and realized that he still held Biro's mask wrapped up in his hands. He thought of his friend, immersed in drunken anger and pain, and he felt ashamed that a part of him welcomed this caricature of himself, this moon shaped mask, this mockery of all that he used to be.

He took his costume down from the door and wrapped it up with Biro's mask, covering the faces completely. He left them in a bundle upon the floor against the wall farthest from where he slept. Then he laid down on his bed, still listening to the chants and cries drifting through the window from the streets of Phaedon.

"The Great Pagliacci, the Drummer of Hearts!"

"The Great Punchinello, the Exposer of Souls"

"The Grand Kirkos Clowns!"

He listened for a while, wondering if he would be able to sleep at all on this strange night. His mind wandered to other thoughts, thoughts of the bodies of his people burning, of the dark evil smoke that had filled his lungs and stolen his connection to the magic. Magic he had not been able to find again until he had stepped into the deadly arena.

He listened to the voices chanting outside and remembered how the people in the crowd had become ecstatic, their energy resonating into his very core, as they watched Biro kill their opponents in the arena. He thought of the Emperor looking down on them, cheering them on and saluting them at the end. Emperor Coracis, the same man who had ordered his soldiers to cut Csoda's tongue from his mouth in front of a similarly sadistic crowd.

Despite his exhaustion, this flood of thoughts threatened to keep him from sleep, even more than the braying crowds outside. Rage filled him from within his chest, a violent anger similar, he imagined, to that which engulfed Biro.

Then another memory drifted in over the others and covered his rage. The image of the small boy he had seen in the crowd before they took his tongue. The image of the man that had appeared in this very room. His future son. He thought of that man, his son, and the words he had spoken to him.

"I am standing in the ruins of Phaedon," his son had said.

Csoda, in his sleepy rage, thought of those words. He let the words repeat in his mind. The ruins of Phaedon.

Csoda found peace in that idea, that the world which so encompassed him now, the world which enslaved his body and stripped both him and Biro of their culture, of their very names, would at some point in time be rubble, a scattering of bones in the desert sands.

"My son," he thought as he slipped into sleep, "will walk in your ruins."

And this thought made him smile.

THE END

ABOUT THE AUTHOR

TBalogh is a filmmaker, author, and artist with a highly diverse creative background and an art repertoire that includes everything from sculpture to computer animation and film. An accomplished horseback rider since childhood she uses her life experiences and her fascination with folktales and mythology as inspirations for her work. The entire Kirkos series comes from her rich imagination and her unique ability to tap into the reader's soul.

For more books in this series and other great titles, go to knowheremedia.com/publishing

www.ingramcontent.com/pod-product-compliance
Lightning Source LLC
Chambersburg PA
CBHW030806200726

48285CB00015B/1537